going

going

kevin oderman

VANDALIA PRESS

MORGANTOWN 2006

This novel is a work of fiction. The places are real, but all characters and events are the product of the author's imagination. Any resemblance to actual people is entirely coincidental.

Vandalia Press, Morgantown 26506

13 12 11 10 09 08 07 06   10 9 8 7 6 5 4 3 2 1

ISBN 1-933202-13-0

Library of Congress Cataloguing-in-Publication Data

Kevin Oderman 1950–
Going/Kevin Oderman
viii, 264 p. 22cm.

Library of Congress Control Number: 2006927243

Vandalia Press is an imprint of West Virginia University Press

Front cover image: "Devil and Fireworks" © 2005 Eva Serrabassa
Back cover image: "Pomegranate (half)" © 2006 Peeter Viisimaa

Book design by Than Saffel
Cover concept by Andrea Ware

for Sara Pritchard

I am lost
in the gold
light on this salt and sleepless
sea I haunt an old
ship

George Oppen
Primitive

Granada, 1999

I

The boy stopped. He listened to the night sounds in the alley. He wanted to look over the low wall he was hiding behind, but he didn't look. He wanted to run, but where? He pulled the hem of the skirt he was wearing over his mouth to muffle his breathing. He heard cars, motorcycles down on the street along the Río Darro, drunks singing in Plaza Nueva, but what he'd heard before had been closer, footfalls. Maybe lovers, or a tourist out for a night walk, but more likely one of the street punks of the Albayzín, one of the addicts who often roughed him up for the few coins that could be shook from his pockets. Then Asur heard it again: someone trying to walk quietly. He sat down on his heels in the night shade of the low wall on the second-storey terrace where he was hiding.

"Eh, *guapita*, where are you? You know I'm going to find you. If not now, *mañana*. Then I'm gonna have a look at just what you're hiding under that dress. *¿Me oíste?* A little one, I think. You don't seem too proud of it. But I hear it's a big mystery how a girl could grow one at all, even a little one."

The voice passed, was going on up the alley. The child relaxed, his fear going. The addicts, they never chased him for long, it wasn't worth it. But just to be sure Asur sat quietly for another five minutes, looking at the moonshine on the roofs and the yellower light of the few bare bulbs he could see on up the hill. Then he stood, loosening the belt that held his skirt up. The skirt was soiled and too big, white, with small red polka dots that looked like they might itch. He reached into the plastic bag at his feet and pulled out a dusty, but neatly folded, pair of pants; a green, frayed shirt; a light jacket with bulging pockets; and a Red Sox ball cap. He changed out of the skirt, the frilly blouse, and the pair of scuffed white shoes. When he had dressed again he corralled the black hair that fell in ringlets down his neck in a rubber band and jammed it up into the Sox cap. He picked up the red purse he'd stolen from a rack of Moroccan leather on Calderería Nueva and carefully removed the handful of coins he'd begged that evening. He put the coins in a pocket and the purse in the sack. He hid the sack behind a large pot of bougainvillea and stood staring through the barred windows into the dark interior of the house. No one home. No one was ever home during the week. Sometimes he slept on the terrace tiles but tonight the place felt unfriendly.

Asur was a small boy but older than he looked, strong and agile for all his slimness and the girlishness of his face. He peered down into the alley, then swung over the wall, dropping quietly onto the cobbles below.

A few minutes later he was washing his face in the stream, where the Río Darro runs between high stone walls, the Alhambra hill on one side, the Albayzín on the other. But even here the Darro runs like a real stream, rippling, in bends, shining with moonlight over smooth river stones. There are trees, and the echoing traffic on Carrera del Darro is not so loud down by the water. The child walked downstream, wading, his shoes' laces looped over his belt. Up ahead, he could see the great mouth, where Granada swallowed the Darro; from there the stream ran below ground, under the city. He found the place he wanted. A thick vine ran up the wall, on up over a worn brick foundation, a few thin vines finally finding their way into the ironwork of a railing that protected a small veranda.

Asur started to climb; his bare hands and feet shone in the foliage as he lifted himself up, feet catching hold, then reaching again. At the level of the street he looked around, hoping there was no one to shout *thief*, then climbed on up, until he could see into the house behind the iron railing. A candle burned close to the window, but the boy looked past that, into a room full of winking reflections.

He knew the back wall was hung with dozens of mirrors, that the mirrors reflected the candle, that they cast the yellow shapes that swam on the walls and ceiling. But, even knowing, the lights were magical, helped him forget his loneliness. He'd first seen them weeks ago, from across the Darro, and he'd come to look, first for them, and then for the woman who lived in the house, an American woman. And he'd found her friendly. On the plaza, she had given him a coin without being asked. She had smiled, seeing a girl in a dress, and when she'd asked his name he'd said Luz, the beautiful name of a girl he'd known when he lived on the *vega*.

Now, holding on with one hand, he reached the other through the iron railing, between the potted flowers, and set a large and perfect orange on the terra-cotta tiles of the veranda. When he reached through again his hand held a small, clay figure, cruciform. He set it next to the orange. They were for her. Then he climbed back down into the riverbed.

The boy slept under a tree near the stream. He tore the staples from a cardboard box and spread the cardboard under a snarl of roots and debris where the Darro had washed the dirt away in a sudden flood. It made a rocky bed but hidden, and Asur fell asleep without difficulty. In the night, the cold came and he woke, wishing he had his polka-dot skirt with him so he could curl under it like a blanket. He thought dawn was close and he didn't try to sleep again. He watched as the world took shape out of darkness, waiting. When it was light enough he got up, shook himself, rubbed a little warmth into his arms and legs and started walking. By the time he climbed out of the riverbed it was light enough to see clearly. When he walked into Plaza Nueva the high clouds that ribbed the sky had turned a chalky pink, the sky behind a powder blue. The façades of the four and five-storey buildings that rimmed the plaza had turned each their own color, and the railings on the balconies and the grates on the windows shone a shiny black. Here a man wheeled a stack of chairs out on a handcart. A couple, tourists, rolled their luggage out to the taxi stand. Asur walked across the checked paving stones of the plaza, feeling safe now, purposeful. He glanced over his shoulder at the façade of the Church of Santa Ana, looking at the three statues high in their niches over the great, arched doorway, confident up there. The plaza was waking up, not hurrying yet, but getting ready. Asur knew that soon there would be a press in the cafés for espresso and *café con leche*, for something quick. And if it wasn't silent now, if the noise had already begun, soon there would be clamor. The paving stones, cool in shadow, would get bright and hot in the sun. The fears that dogged him in the dark would leave him, already had. He turned out of the plaza toward a *panadería*, a little bakery that sometimes set out day-old bread in a box at dawn. Asur hoped to get some.

The sound of a guitar echoed up from the *placeta*, but it was nothing like the polished playing of Granada's strolling buskers. No, this was a rough strumming that sometimes rose into a fever before dying back down. And there was a hand drum, more beaten than coaxed. When the music was loud and a racket, it made Cy's head hurt, worse. He stood back from an open balcony door and looked down on them, the street people of his own small square. A rough bunch, most of them young and none too clean. They always had a bottle going round, or a joint, or among the saddest of the lot, a needle. The agent who had arranged the rental hadn't mentioned them. Apparently, they were not counted among the most charming features of the neighborhood. The ads had stressed the low white buildings of the Albayzín, the weathered tile roofs, the cobbled alleys of the city's old Muslim quarter. Cy pulled the shutters in and pressed the slender doors shut. He had time. There was no need to hurry.

It was dark in the room now and he walked to the table uncertainly. He put a match to the longest candle in the candelabra then pulled the others from their sockets, one by one, dropping them into a wastebasket that was already full of discarded paper. He lifted new candles, long white tapers, from a box on the table and lit them, one by one, from the candle that was already burning. With the candelabra fully lit there was light enough to read by. He scraped at the drops of wax on the tabletop with a fingernail, but halfheartedly, and soon he stopped. Eccentricity hadn't put the candles on the table. The lights in the little house were too bright; they glared against the whitewashed walls and that brightness hurt him, aggravated his headache and nausea until he spit bile. The candles were better, dim maybe, but the light soft, a gauzy yellow. Even the candles were not without risk. Sometimes when he shut his eyes hoping to sleep, they floated up again, on the inside of his eyelids, licks of flame shifting fore and aft in the murk.

When Cy turned from the table he saw the crowd of shadows he cast on the wall. "How thin you've grown," he said, mournfully, fingering the bunched-up material of the waistband under his belt, "how very thin." He now carried a walking stick with a silver handle, which he'd bought in an antique store on Elvira. He liked the sound of it, the metallic click of it on cobblestones in narrow alleys, and the way he could lean on it standing on a busy corner, waiting for the light. He liked to point with it, to flourish it. But sometimes he felt woozy and he needed it just to keep from falling down. Then he lurched along like a drunk, nauseous, near blind with headache. Recently, he hadn't done much walking.

He ate little. He'd been a man of appetites but that was over. He woke up to morning sickness most days now, and he kept a pan by his bed. For a while, morning sickness had been the great joke, a man giving birth to his own death. Like most jokes it had gotten old, less, and then not, funny. The first joke of his sickness had been its name, *astrocytoma*. He'd tried to get a laugh out of it with friends, the stars in his head, but they couldn't forget for a minute that *astrocytoma* was the name of his kind of brain tumor.

Cy set the candelabra on the night table and rolled onto the great bed, with its smoke-blackened headboard and thick mattress. The light seemed to travel the room in waves, washing around him where he lay alert on the bed. He had always felt that there was something boat-like about a bed, that he sailed, on good nights anyway, into new and liquid realms when he slept. In a lifetime, he had never gotten tired of sleep. It did not bore him even now. He thought the phrase *falling asleep* was all wrong. No, a puff of wind, just enough on land to lift the leaves, and the bed shifted and began to move off, crossing over. Always it had seemed to him a fair wind.

He rolled over on his side and looked down the room toward his writing desk, where the light lapped fitfully. His sacred shelf, his favorite books from a lifetime of reading, hung from the wall, the spines more familiar to him than the faces of friends. He'd not only shipped the books over from Pittsburgh, he'd shipped the shelf itself, painted years ago by a long-gone lover. He loved the shelf still, the archness of it, the outsize gallery covered as it was in what looked like Byzantine icons, with faces not of saints but of poets, each surrounded by a faux frame worked in gold paint. The gilt picked up the candlelight, but the faces of the poets were lost in darkness from Cy's end of the room. His lover had wanted to paint Cy's own likeness in one of the frames, and had, so sure she was of his coming fame, but Cy had felt superstitious seeing his face there and asked her to paint it out. She had done what he asked. He'd watched as his own features disappeared under the brush, and within an hour, another face, Lorca's, had appeared in "his" place.

Now, here he was, a dying man in Lorca's town. He'd had some fame, but not fame like Lorca's, and, he knew, he had not written poetry to compare with Lorca's either, or to any of the other poets on his sacred shelf, for all his acknowledged facility and technical brilliance. Maybe he hadn't had greatness in him, he'd never know; he'd shied from the deep water, he hadn't dared. It galled him now. He had thought maybe in Granada he'd get a last chance. As if the world was a different place, as if he would be forgiven his trespasses. Still, he'd come, and he'd been working, and although the wastebaskets all through the house were full of his failures he'd had a few successes, too, small poems maybe but poems in which the whole man lived. He'd wanted more.

Cy sat up and looked at the book on his night table. It was not poetry. It was the Hemlock Society's guide to last things, *No Exit*, and it contained a how-to chapter on unassisted suicide under the title "Self-Deliverance Vía the Plastic Bag." "Cha cha cha," Cy murmured. He'd read it several times; he'd been to the pharmacy for sleeping pills and Corte Inglés for a Steel Sac and a roll of duct tape. Rubber bands were recommended, so the duct tape, he thought, looked like overkill. He laughed, just the kind of joke his friends stateside had refused to find funny.

Cy had never read directions in his whole life, never tried to do anything with the help of a how-to guide. He hadn't been able to. He hadn't been able to abide the English. The irony of working through the directions in *No Exit* hadn't been lost on him. But he'd done it; he wouldn't need to consult the little book again. He put it down.

He roused himself, "No hurry," he said again, and he worked his way back over to his writing desk, to his sacred shelf, and stood there, looking at the portrait of Lorca. Lorca hadn't been self-delivered but dragged out of Granada and shot by the Falangists in the hills above the Albayzín, near a spring known as the Big Fountain, common human ugliness licensed by the Spanish Civil War. Cy leaned forward. The likeness of Lorca was good, caught the look of the face in the photographs, formal and mercurial at once. The wide and prominent cheekbones, the big, clear brow, the lively mouth. Cy picked Lorca's selected poems from the shelf, and opening it at random, read, *y el que teme la muerte la llevará sobre los hombros*, and he who fears death will carry it on his shoulders. Cy looked at the penciled check in the margin, his, he realized; he'd liked the line when he'd read it a healthy man. He liked it still. But healthy he had probably imagined himself among those who did not fear death, who did not carry it. Then, he hadn't felt the weight of it. He'd carried it lightly, but he'd been carrying it all along, and now it felt heavy.

He fished the sleeping pills out of his pocket. The recommended dosage was two, so the prescribed dose, just to lull anxiety, would be four. He pressed six out of the plastic-and-foil packet, looked at them skeptically, and set them on his desk. He screwed the lid off the water bottle he'd picked up from the floor and swallowed the pills one at a time, a little water to chase each pill. Minutes to go. He surveyed the litter on his desk, the half-written letters and aborted death poems. He hadn't been able to write one he thought good enough to keep. He crumpled the lot and stuffed the wad into the wastebasket. He thought about Irene, his colleague and friend back in Pittsburgh, who had wired from Madrid announcing her arrival in Granada tomorrow. He was touched that she'd come so far, but he knew she'd come to take him back for what his friends called The Treatment. Cy hated to disappoint her, but he just couldn't face her, couldn't bear even to think about the energy it would take to resist her. Poor Irene. He hoped she wouldn't guess her good intentions were just the nudge he'd needed to be going tonight.

Cy replaced the Lorca on his sacred shelf. Enough of reading. His eyes felt heavy, hard to focus. Almost time. He opened the desk drawer and took out a Steel Sac and a roll of silver duct tape. He stood up, wobbled, and started for the bed. His head had begun to reel again, and outside, the drum had grown loud. Someone was singing, screeching, and the house seemed like nothing so much as the body of a wildly strummed guitar. He sat down on the bed, head in hands, then kicked off his shoes. He was able to sort out the plastic bag only with difficulty. He shook it open and looked inside. Time to set sail. Cy took a deep breath—he couldn't suppress the impulse—then pulled the thing down over his face until he felt the bottom of the bag snug against the crown of his head. He sat there, the bag loose around his shoulders, and tried to be still, to let the drugs lull him to sleep. He felt around on the bed and found the duct tape. The sack was loose enough, he thought, to let him breathe once he taped it around his neck, but not so loose that dying would take very long. He knew he'd go on breathing, that the nitrogen would allow him to go on breathing for a while, even after there was no oxygen left in the

11

sack. He felt for the end of the tape and when he found it pulled off about two feet. He wondered if it was really him with his head in a sack. Holding one end of the tape to his throat with his left hand, he just managed to circle his neck with his right. Snug. Then he rolled over, his head on a pillow. His eyes hurt, as if he was very tired or about to cry. And the thrum of the music. The smoky, plastic smell of the bag repelled him, and the air in it soon felt hot and wet. Somewhere, as if off in the distance, he felt a wave of panic begin. Then he understood that he was going to be sick, and he was. By the time he'd torn the front of the sack open his face was painted with clotted vomit.

3

She felt good, and for Madeleine James good meant more alive. Apparently there had been no reason to worry. But she had regretted saying yes to Sam's invitation, worried that having him in mind would preoccupy her morning, because in the morning she worked. To her surprise she had painted well. That is, she had gotten into the trance of painting. She had entered the paint, made sense, found the order of things. She knew from long experience this didn't mean she'd necessarily like the work tomorrow, though probably she would. But today her brushes had felt friendly in her hand, responsive, intelligent. Today when she'd mixed colors, the colors she'd wanted had appeared without her worrying the mix. The smell of paint and spirits, the drag of her brush across something not so good she'd painted yesterday (because yesterday she hadn't painted well at all) had all felt right, just so.

She had made a great many choices in her life—choices not always obviously related to the time she stood in front of a canvas—to be able, some days, to paint well. So she hadn't liked to compromise her chances for catching up on old times. But she'd known Sam quite well at the Rhode Island School of Design, which is not to say she'd always liked him. There had been something a little self-righteous about him, a little cocksure. While she had been feeling her way forward, and feeling buffeted about by the storm of opinions that raged over College Hill day after day, Sam had only smirked.

She'd been seeing him around Granada for weeks now. They'd spoken, but only to say hello. He radiated superiority. He carried himself in a way few American men ever did. He had, she thought, a distinguished carriage, a touch of satisfied self-regard. He dressed well and conservatively, and he had acquired, it seemed, urbane and deliberate good manners. Perhaps it was the manners that had led to the invitation. Would she like to visit? See the wonderful old place, a real *cármene*, where he was overseeing a renovation? Drinks, tapas? She'd agreed, he'd written an address in the Albayzín on a card.

Her day had started oddly. When she'd pulled up the bamboo blind on the porch by her bed she'd been surprised to see, on the veranda below, a dab of brilliant orange. It *was* an orange. When she'd gone down to investigate, she'd found not only the orange but a strange clay figure, archaic and disturbingly powerful. Her veranda was private; she couldn't see how these things had gotten there. If it had been the orange alone, she'd have assumed it was thrown. There was a tall stone wall with broken glass ragged in the coping on one side of the veranda, and the sheer side of a three-storey brick house on the other. The third side was guarded by an ironwork grille, not to keep intruders out, but to keep people from the straight drop into the riverbed of the Darro.

Perhaps she would have been frightened at the intrusion if the orange and the clay figure hadn't felt so much like gifts. She'd accepted them that way, taken them inside to her studio, and soon enough found herself lost in her work.

The streets were dark when she stepped out her door onto Santa Ana and turned right toward the plaza. A pedestrian alley, Santa Ana was little frequented and after dark it sometimes seemed forbidding. She walked quickly, past the ancient *hammam*, the *Baños Árabes*, and on out into the plaza. At night, from where she was walking to the far end of Plaza Nueva, a party atmosphere often reigned. There were several restaurants with tables outside and most nights crowds of drinkers traipsed from tapas bar to tapas bar down on Elvira. She had seen guitarists perform on the plaza, of course, but also jugglers and mimes, even a fire-eater. Anybody might turn up, panhandlers or pickpockets, street people with dogs or drums and perhaps a magic routine or a little business in tarot cards or hashish. Streetwise Gypsies. She'd watched more than once as an old lady in a blue sweater navigated the sidewalk cafés stealing tips. If it was a little seedy, Plaza Nueva seemed to welcome the whole human circus. James loved the way the place buzzed with life, the way she could feel it on her pulse.

She would have liked to linger, but she crossed quickly, weaving up into the warren of streets that was the old Islamic quarter, the Albayzín, a bottle of Rioja in her right hand like a club. She doglegged on San Juan de los Reyes and took a flight of narrow stairs on up to San Gregorio and then walked on up the Albayzín hill. She heard a woman shouting up ahead, pleading and angry. It took her a moment to register that the woman was shouting in English, that she could understand her. She walked out into a *placeta*, where four alleys met at odd angles, and stopped. She was going to have to consult her map.

Across the way, a yellow-haired woman stood before a low door, gesturing, "You're not doing anything! Are you just going to give up?" A man's voice answered from inside, pitched low, grave. "That's right. I have given up."

"Just like that?"

And again the man's voice, he had come outside now, stood looking down at the woman standing there, crying, "Go home, Irene. Tell them whatever you like, but make them understand I'm not coming back, not ever."

The man ducked inside but emerged again immediately, a suitcase in his hand. "You're a good person, Irene," he said, "Now go be good somewhere else. I don't want it." And with that he stepped back inside, closing the door quietly behind him.

James, having found Sam's street on the map, walked by, on up the hill. She could hear the woman, Irene, beating on the door behind her, sobbing, "You're a coward, Cy. Open the goddamned door! Please! You can't just give up . . ."

Sam pulled open a small, iron-studded door cut from a much larger door set in the rammed-clay wall of a medieval house, a true *cármene*, just as Sam had promised.

"Look at you," Sam said, stepping aside for her. "Don't object, my taste is renowned. I know beauty when I see it." The sally seemed overdone, delivered with verve but to a woman without illusions about her looks. They would do. "Watch the threshold," he added.

She held out the Rioja and stepped through. She realized then that there was a woman standing behind Sam, and that she had the real thing in beauty. Sam did know; he was a collector, even when it came to people.

Sam turned to perform the introduction. "Paula," he said, "this is Mad James. I believe you admire her work. James, Paula, my assistant here." Paula stepped forward and they shook hands.

They ate in the garden, on a worktable with a red Moroccan blanket spread over it for a tablecloth. Paula ate with them but was often up for the next round of tapas, a small salad of wild greens, cheeses, olives, and the inevitable *jamón*. Several bottles joined James's Rioja on the table, mostly sherries, of which it seemed Sam had made a great study. Soon they had a small forest of tall, stemmed glassware on the table in front of them.

When Paula was in the kitchen cleaning up, James asked about her.

"She had a perfectly respectable position at a museum in Boston when I met her. Backroom stuff. But she knows a great deal about the history of decorative arts in Moorish Spain and in North Africa, in Morocco, Algeria, Tunis. I'm afraid I've compromised her reputation, plucked her right out of the realms of disinterested knowledge and dropped her into the sordid world of commerce." Sam smiled brightly.

"But Sam, your kind of commerce doesn't count as sordid, does it? Last I heard you were quite respectable, a well-known restorer in Boston. Isn't that what you're doing here?"

"Well, that's what my German patron is paying us for, and, really, we are doing some of that. But we're also doing a little buying and selling. Some of it for the German," he added dryly.

"Doesn't he pay well?"

"Oh, yes, very well. But I have ambitions, I'm afraid. I'd like to own this place, or something like it. Why should the industrialists own it, while we just squat here? And for that matter, I'm not so sure our Herr Schmidt would approve of our living on the premises. So I charge him, for security." Sam laughed melodiously. "Still, I make a little extra on the gray market, and, just occasionally, somewhat larger sums on the black market. Much larger, if you want to know. Just now it's a deal in Qu'rans of let's say suspicious provenance."

James pushed her chair back and cocked her head. "Sam?" she asked.

"Yes? I know what you're thinking. Once upon a time, darling, it would have bothered me, too. I was such a moralist, such a prim little man. I'm less prim now."

"What happened?"

"Something did happen; that's the odd thing. But it's a bit of a story, and it's getting late. Are you sure you want to hear it?"

James nodded. People, she was thinking, are so surprising.

"Well, then, let me check what Herr Schmidt has in the way of brandy."

James looked around at the villa's garden while Sam was inside. Even cluttered with cones of sand, a cement mixer, ladders, and a wheelbarrow, all the signs of a renovation in progress, the beauty of the enclosed space, its proportions, were evident. She understood how Sam might want it all for his own, but for herself, she preferred to want less. She could hear the murmur of Sam and Paula talking inside and thought she heard Paula say goodnight. James glanced at her watch, almost eleven.

Sam came back grinning with two snifters and a bottle. "Quite acceptable," he chortled, pouring liberally. "Where to begin? I had been doing rather well at work, as you said, and I had a long list of clients begging me to take on private commissions. So I decided it was time to buy a house, and I had it in mind that it should be out of the city, in the woods if possible. James, what can I say, back then life in the woods seemed more wholesome to me!"

James settled in, nodding him on. She could see that Sam was warming to the story. She'd heard him before, at school. He had the storyteller's gift.

"It was winter. Cold, had been cold for weeks. When I bought the place I inherited two or three cords of firewood, rough cut, and every day or two I'd spend half an hour splitting rounds with a sledge and mauls. I liked the work. So manly!" Sam turned an elegant gold ring in his fingers, smiling ruefully. "The clang of the hammer on the maul, that sound skating across the ice on the lake. There was snow, but the wind had swept the lake clean. I felt like I was the only man in the world, the sound of my hammer the only sound. After I got into the rhythm of the thing, I warmed right up, and I stopped to take off the loose coat I was wearing over a sweater. I hung the coat up on a nail and set another maul. The world so still."

Sam paused for effect.

"I had the hammer in the air when I heard the cry, plaintive. I brought the sledge down anyway, the round splitting wide at the first stroke. Then I stood there, head down, listening, wondering if I'd imagined it, a frightened and drawn-out call, 'Help!' Nothing more. Just that pitiful little cry. A boy's voice, coming from somewhere down the lake."

James raised an eyebrow.

"I straightened up slowly, leaned the yellow handle of the sledgehammer against the house, listening. The air itself felt thin, menacing. I retrieved my coat from its nail and put it on, looking toward where the call had come from, down the lake, from behind a stand of trees. A Boy Scout, at the ready.

"I felt for my keys in my pants pocket, found them, and jogged down to my car at the end of the driveway. Before I knew it I had the car in reverse and backed out onto the lake road. Then I shot forward. I remember how the car felt, the steering stiff from the cold, the tires running muffled in the snow and shifting side to side in the ruts. Over the hood, a great emptiness seemed to rush toward me, bright, banded with sunlight where the sun was streaming through the trees. Then the trees along the lakeshore thinned, and I could see out onto the frozen lake.

"I could see the hole in the ice, the ragged broken pieces churned by the floundering boy. A small black dog, a terrier, was running over the ice from the other side of the lake, toward the boy. When I got even with the kid I ran my car onto a spur and got out. Immediately, I heard the yapping of the dog and the boy's pleading, 'Help me, help me mister, please!' He was swinging a ski pole around over his head and then I saw the tracks: he'd been skiing on the thin ice."

Sam shook his head, glancing at James's expression.

"My head hurt. I felt, more than anything, just irritated. My head was throbbing, the air itself seemed to pulse. I shut the door of the car, slammed it. I was angry. I thought something like, so fucking stupid, then I started down the slope to the lake.

"The dog had made it out to the hole in the ice and was dancing crazily on the ragged edge, twirling around in mad circles, yapping it up. I recognized the dog and remembered the fat boy I'd seen playing with him in summer.

"The hole in the ice wasn't far out, maybe thirty yards from my side of the lake. As I ran down toward the ice I heard shouts, adult voices. Across the lake I could see four men turning over a boat left upside down at the end of summer. The lake was long and thin; they weren't so far away, maybe a couple hundred yards. I noticed they were not dressed for the weather, only one or two of them had on coats and they weren't wearing gloves or hats. I stopped at the lake edge. I looked out at the boy. I saw his head go under and then come back up. He, anyway, had on a hat, a ridiculous stocking cap with a tassel at the end of a long tail. He was beyond pleading now, bobbing, terrified. He just howled."

Sam paused, again glancing over at James, who sat quietly, listening, the snifter of brandy forgotten in her hands.

"Even so, I didn't do a thing. My little adrenaline rush was over. My head had cleared and I'd decided: that kid wasn't worth the risk. I put my hands in my pockets.

"Across the lake the four fellows with the boat ran out onto the ice, two on each side, the boat between them. I was impressed. Smart, I thought, safe. But they didn't make it far out onto the ice before they crashed through. First one guy, then his pal on the same side of the boat, broke through and hung chest-deep in water, the boat tipped half over their way. The four of them over there were doing a lot of shouting. And the dog, he was running circles around the now empty hole in the ice. The kid had stopped coming up.

"Over there—it all seemed over there—there was a great commotion. Where I stood it was quiet and I just said softly, 'Sorry, no way.' You know, James, standing there, I had no idea that there would be consequences for not acting. I only thought about what the consequences were likely to be if I tried to save the kid. I wasn't going to drown for that kid.

"The guys in the boat weren't getting anywhere. One of them tried to run ahead of the boat and broke through and had to be saved himself. The dog was looking nervously into the water, picking up his cold feet one at a time. It looked bad for the boy.

"Then a jeep ran off the road above me, ran right down to the water's edge. A guy named Joe, one of my redneck neighbors, jumped out of the driver's side of the jeep and his son out of the other. They ignored me standing there. Joe tied a rope to the end of the line on his winch, grabbed at the line, and started out onto the frozen lake. His son manned the winch, playing out the line as Joe worked his way across the ice. I expected him to break through, too, but he didn't. When he got to the hole in the ice he just plunged in. He didn't hesitate at all.

"Going across the ice Joe looked huge, outsize, a shapeless buffalo-plaid coat over loose gray pants, big rubber boots. A big man, and not dressed for swimming. But when he got to the hole in the ice he put his arms out and just leapt in. Then he was gone."

Sam paused, sipped at his brandy.

"There must have been a splash but I can't remember hearing it. I remember it as quiet, suddenly still. All eyes turned toward the hole in the ice. Even the dog had shut up. Then Joe's voice, just one word, 'Pull.'

"His son winched them out of the water. Joe had his arms wrapped around the boy, and they came out of the water all wadded up together. When they were up on the ice, Joe's son turned the winch off, and Joe knelt next to the boy's body, taking a loop around it, under the arms. Again, he yelled, 'Pull,' and the winch went into action, dragging the boy, head first, toward shore. He still had on the stocking cap; his skis trailed behind him at the end of their straps.

"Joe had hold of the rope, too, and they all came across the ice together, the boy down and Joe kneeling next to them, the winch pulling them toward shore. The dog leapt up on the boy's chest, hitching a ride, licking at his face. Heartwarming, you can't imagine.

"When they had the boy on shore a great shout went up. I wasn't sure where all the people had come from, but there was a crowd of them. They called the boy back. I was still standing there, hands in my pockets, when they got him to his feet. He caught my eye. He remembered, it was plain, that I was the guy who had just stood there while he sank. James, I almost stuck my tongue out! I wanted to.

"I walked back to my car alone. I started it and sat there, the fan blowing air onto my face, while the road cleared behind me. Then I drove back home, went the long way, on around the lake loop.

"I'd thought I was someone else. I'd thought I was the kind of guy who saved the kid or died trying. But that guy was Joe. I was surprised. I remembered then, I still remember, having seen such things on the evening news. Some dope who ran into a burning house to save the child he saw dancing in the flames. Some kid who dove into muddy water, into a flooded river, to pull a woman and her baby daughter from their bobbing car. The reporter sticking a mike in his face asking how it felt to be a hero. And the hero just not getting the question, denying he'd done anything heroic at all, insisting he'd done what anyone would have done in his place. I'd thought those guys were right and the reporters just fools. What else could you do? Nothing, apparently.

"Back at the house I blew the fire up out of the ashes and sat down in the old steamer chair I kept close to the hearth. I sank into it, into the soft leather and the warmth of the fire. I slept. When I woke it was dark and the fire was out. I had come through.

"It wasn't even painful. I simply got up out of that chair free. I had been carrying around a big shining image of me; I had imagined I was a good man, and imagining it, I had been. But I didn't get up mourning lost innocence, nothing like that. I got up light, alive, pulsing with desire."

Sam fell silent, peeked over at James coyly, and laughed, a sort of delighted whinny. "Perhaps I should have told you all that down at the cathedral, in a confessional box?"

James roused herself. "So you're hoping for absolution?"

Sam shrugged, at ease.

"But, you aren't much in need of it, are you?"

He shook his head.

James laughed in spite of herself. "Well, you're appalling, of course, but maybe lucky, too. It's possible to live for a long time without anything clear-cut ever happening, to just drift along. Something happened to you. Not the best thing, but something."

Sam nodded. "Talk about appalling," he said, "I asked you up to see the house and I haven't shown it to you." He glanced up at a second-floor window. "And Paula's gone to bed . . ."

James looked around at the faïence mosaics and carved stucco she could see from the courtyard and said appreciatively, "Looks like the real old stuff."

"Oh it is real, everything's real. Just not as old as it looks. I'll explain how it's done, next time, if you're interested."

4

The morning after he'd shut Irene out, Cy woke up and was not sick. He opened the doors and the windows, the shutters, and let a cool, moist breeze blow through. Except for the tiny bathroom at the top of the stairs, the third floor of the house was just a single room, longer than it was wide, with a terrace on two sides, and he much preferred this room to the others. All the rooms were small, and a bit shabby, but on the roof he felt a little removed, at a desirable distance from the world. When it wasn't too hot or bright out, he spent a good deal of time up there during the day, but no matter what the weather, it was his night room, where he went to write and to read, to gaze on the stars of his own private heaven, trying to navigate still.

There was a much larger terrace on the second floor, over a storage room too dirty to count as habitable. The rest of the first floor was hardly better, but the entrance was there and a stair up to the livable floors of the house. The terraces were lined with pots full of flowers in bloom, and Cy enjoyed going round with a watering can, bringing the rains.

From the terraces, Cy had a plain view of the Alhambra occupying the heights on the facing hill. Red and massive, it showed its military aspect to Granada and very little of the pleasing grace, the heart-thumping beauty on view inside. That beauty called to him still. The designs in the faïence tiles; the elaborate, carved stucco; the delicate columns. And the way light and shadow talked to each other there. He thought he'd go again, soon, to wander through the cool rooms of the Nasrid Palaces. They were often crowded with tour groups, of course, but he'd found by walking clear through, to the exit, and then coming back, against the grain, he could always have the rooms to himself for a while. Part of the attraction, he thought, was the murmur of voices in other rooms. And he enjoyed seeing the faces of the tourists as he passed them going the other way. Few places, he thought, registered as forcefully as the Alhambra. He could see it in the tourists' faces, many of which looked awestruck or simply stunned—mute testimony that beauty was still a power.

But in his months in Granada, Cy hadn't tired of his view over the Albayzín either. It didn't have beauty on the order of the Alhambra, of course, but it was a neighborhood deeply grounded in a vernacular tradition he loved. Everywhere he looked there were low, whitewashed houses, stucco over stone, thick walls under tile roofs without much in the way of eaves. Some were freestanding, but most accommodated themselves to the walls of the houses next door and curved with the bend in the streets and pedestrian alleys. Because the buildings were white, the paint on the doors and the shutters stood out boldly, and trees and flowers grew green or flowered with what seemed a startling vividness. From the air, Cy knew, the Albayzín looked honeycombed with enclosed gardens and courtyards; from above, the privacy of the place—guarded from the street—was broached. Al-

27

though the guidebooks insisted on the rewards of wandering about on the neighborhood's twisty streets, Cy had met few tourists there, which, he thought, was another of the place's many attractions.

Even when he didn't feel strong enough to walk there, it made Cy happy to watch the light shift over the Albayzín; the volumes of the buildings seemed to change hour by hour. Sometimes the little houses looked baked like loaves in the sun, and then a few clouds would cover the neighborhood in shadows, and it was as if boats were sailing over a city long submerged by the sea.

When Cy had finished watering the flowers he went inside. He looked in the bathroom mirror, remembering the face he'd seen there two nights before, gaunt and filthy, framed by a halo of silver plastic. That face had shocked him. Somehow the reflection in the mirror had made him believe in his coming death as nothing else had, not his doctor's prognosis, not his friends' worried expressions, not even the morning sickness or the Steel Sac over his head. He wasn't the denying kind; he'd tried to believe in his approaching end, but it was difficult. Death, he'd gotten friendly with the idea a long time ago. But that wasn't the death he'd die. Of course, he understood that short of dying there could be no real knowing, and maybe not then. But he wanted his death to feel real before he got there, he wanted its judgment on how he'd lived, that reckoning. So he found he was not unhappy to be back for a while. He smiled at his face in the mirror. He still could; the smile looked genuine.

He went out late in the afternoon, walking down San Gregorio to a tea shop in Little Morocco, Tetería Alfaguara. There were several *teterías* to choose from in the neighborhood, most of them on Caldereria Nueva, and Cy patronized more than one of them, but he liked best to sit in the hallway in front of the door at the Alfaguara. It was private enough that he could write there, but when he didn't feel like writing he could watch the traffic in the street, an endless parade of pedestrians, running the gamut from Moroccan women observing *purdah* to streetwalkers barely dressed, from tourists to old *granadinos* who had lived in the Albayzín their whole lives, from svelte students fresh from checking their e-mail to ragged Rastafarians. An unlikely mix, but here people talked to each other. Cy liked to listen. Sometimes he joined in.

He was on his second pot of Pakistani chai when a woman walked in and sat down at the table behind him. Cy recognized her immediately, an earnest, determined face, a clear forehead, soft, brown eyes. Hair the color of an old penny. She'd been the one who'd stared when he'd shown Irene the door. She'd looked quite shocked.

Cy swiveled around in his chair and called the waiter. "They don't come unless you call," he said. He smiled, to set the woman at ease if he could. "I'm sorry," he said, "about the little drama the other night."

James recognized him all at once. "Oh, no, I'm the one who should be sorry. Here everything we say seems so private and then another American walks by . . . I've seen you around, other times, I mean. I didn't mean to eavesdrop."

"I'm a little embarrassed. I'm not usually the one making a scene."

"That's okay," James said. "Sometimes you've just got to break it off."

"It's not what you're thinking. We weren't lovers. Colleagues, actually, professors in Pittsburgh." Cy glanced into James's face. "Don't hold it against me! I've quit, anyway, taken a terminal leave."

"A what?"

"I'm not going back."

"And she wanted you to go back?"

"Yes."

The waiter stood at the table. James ordered a pot of Assam. Then she held out her hand to Cy. "Madeleine James," she said, "but please, just James."

"Cy Jacobs," he said, adding ironically, "poet-at-large."

James knew she could seem stupid, that her attention came into conversations irregularly. Often her interest drifted, to tricks of light falling through old glass, to patterns of flaked paint. Her friends understood she couldn't help herself. They forgave her or gave her up. Those who stayed found themselves happily surprised that for all her straying attention she often came back to them with a look that had nothing conventional about it, was frank, even intimate in its directness.

Cy shifted in his chair uneasily.

"Your face," she said.

He looked bemused.

"It's interesting," James said and fell silent.

Cy thanked her, a little facetiously, thinking she would qualify her judgment, but she didn't.

"It's a new face," Cy added, as a prompt. "Used to be rounder."

And she came back to him, asked him, "Is it serious?"

"Serious enough," he said gravely.

She let the subject go. Instead, James told him, without his asking, that she was a painter, had a studio on Santa Ana, behind the *iglesia*. She asked him if he'd like to stop by, have a look at the paintings. "I'm out of it, here, of course, I *want* to be, but sometimes it helps me to have someone, someone with an intelligent eye, just stand in front of my work. I see it differently. You'd be doing me a favor. You needn't say anything at all."

"How about now," Cy said, "when you've finished up?"

They kept to the quiet, cobbled streets in the Albayzín, walking most of the way on Los Reyes, then down Santa Ines to the Darro and across on Puente de Cabrera, an old stone bridge built on an incline up, supported by a single, outsize arch. From the bridge James pointed downstream and across to her place, a two-storey white stucco building with a roof terrace and a veranda on the ground floor built right up to the rock wall that here channeled the Darro. It looked, Cy thought, newer and cleaner than his own place.

Up above, a corner of the castellated walls of the Alcazaba on the Alhambra hill hung menacingly over the neighborhood, graceless, acknowledging the role of brute force in the order of things. James's windows opened on the more urban and urbane prospect of the white village that was the Albayzín, though terrible things had happened there, too, Cy knew.

"I live upstairs," James said, "but I paint down here. Sorry about the smell; it's an occupational hazard." She had stepped aside for him, and he walked by her slowly. Four paintings were tacked on

31

the wall on the right, apparently in progress. There was a large tea cart standing in front of one, covered with tubes of paint and what looked liked outsize crayons, tin cans stuffed with brushes, lidded jars, and a neat stack of rags. On the floor, cans of oils and solvents lined the wall, sitting on a yard-wide strip of canvas, clearly there to keep paint off the terra-cotta floor. On the left, there were perhaps twenty stretched canvases turned face to the wall. Two raffia chairs with leather seats stood in front of the paintings there, a small tile-topped end table between them. There was a worktable in the corner by the window with a bucket of water under it and, lined up on the canvas-covered tabletop, a row of small heads modeled in clay.

"I love the feel of a studio," Cy said. "All the stuff a painter needs. A really attractive mess."

"Mess!"

Cy turned toward her then and saw that the back wall of the room was covered almost entirely in small mirrors. "What's this?" He asked, curious, but immediately taken by the effect.

"Well, a collection, I guess. I like mirrors, and one day I bought one at a garage sale—this was back in California—and suddenly I was collecting them. I rummaged most of them, but I've bought them everywhere I've been. And then the gifts started. It's an epidemic by now."

"You lugged them all the way to Granada?"

"Some of them. There's a flea market that starts in Puerta Real and some days runs almost all the way down to the Río Genil. Maybe you've been? I bought a few there. I can't help myself! But I make this wall wherever I go."

"It's quite wonderful."

"I hang them with fish line. They're always moving. Every one reflects a different view of the room. I like that. Every one whole and shining with confidence."

Cy walked over and peeked into a few. He looked a slightly different man in every one of them.

"And at night," James said, "if I light a candle, they're like fireflies, my private starry night."

James sat at her table, watching, as Cy worked his way through the finished paintings, mostly square canvases or nearly so, two or three feet on a side. She felt at ease, and perhaps because of that, Cy said little, his exclamations limited to the occasional muted, "Huh." He turned them around to face the room two at a time then backed off until he found what seemed to him the best distance.

Usually, Cy agreed to look at paintings, or to read poems, with fear and trembling. Most often the work was bad, the painter or poet a pretender, someone attracted to the life more than to art. He had never found that much more than a glance was required to know if the work was bad. Usually a couple of lines would tell him if a poem was going to embarrass him. To separate out what was wonderful from what was merely good, that was a more difficult task, and never as certain.

Just how good James's work was, Cy wasn't sure. But she was a painter; he knew immediately that there was nothing of trends or schools in what she did. The work was hers, her problems, her solutions. He liked it; it had beauty and also gravity. Weight, however lightly carried, had come to seem a requirement to Cy long before his illness, and it seemed more pressing now. When he despaired of his own work, it was because it seemed to him to float off, wonderful, maybe, but weightless.

The paintings were figural and markedly dense. There was a consistent ambiguity in them between figure and ground. The people seemed half absorbed in where they were, yet there was something that struck Cy as distinctly individual in every one of them. It seemed a world full of dappled shadows and bright reflections, full of broken light. The shadows seemed to sink in, the reflections to shine through.

"As if the world had been laid on an anvil and struck," he said at last, "hammered into something brighter and yet more full of shadows."

James laughed. "Flatterer," she teased.

"I do like them."

"The world is brighter and more shadowed than what we see," she said.

Cy told her which of the paintings he liked best; he pointed to figures, gestures, particularly felicitous feats of composition, contrasts in color, at everything that worked especially well for him. He stressed the *for him*, but that wasn't necessary. If James was defensive, it didn't show. She seemed, more often than not, to agree with his judgments, and when she disagreed, she did so lightly. She liked the way Cy considered the work, how animated his face became when he noticed the way a girl's dress seemed to merge with a wall or how a woman's hauteur was conveyed by a few broad strokes.

He was decidedly unselfconscious, not at all bashful to admit it when he didn't have the words to describe what he saw. "But this bit," he'd say, gesturing helplessly, "well, yes. That lovely green, look at that green! And, here, here I'm entirely lost, but happily lost, I mean, I don't care. But right here," he was pointing again, "yes."

Quite suddenly he sat down and pressed on his forehead at the hairline with his fingers. When he looked up James saw fear in his face, and her heart seemed to dilate in her chest. But soon he had composed himself; he asked for water, and she brought him a bottle from the kitchen.

"Just a little spell," he said, cracking a crooked smile. "But perhaps it's time I was going." He looked out the windows over the Darro, to the sky black now over the Albayzín hill. "My kind are notorious after dark," he added. "You really shouldn't take such chances."

"Your kind?"

He let her question pass and was picking up his walking stick before James was quite ready for him to leave.

"And do I get to see some of your poetry?"

He grinned sheepishly, "Sure."

When he'd gone James went back to her worktable. She reached into the bucket under the table, feeling around for a suitable lump of clay, which she fashioned quickly into roughly the shape of a head. She worked at the clay with her thumbs, finding with extraordinary speed the basic planes of Cy's face. Soon she was modeling the clay with a variety of small tools she kept in a can for just this purpose, dental tools, a wire hook, a waxed Popsicle stick, whatever she'd found that worked in the years since she'd begun modeling heads, as a kind of discipline, but also as a way to let go of painting at the end of the day. If she had easy access to a kiln she sometimes fired them, first blowing a thin coat of iron oxide over the faces with a pipette. In Granada, she'd just been letting them dry on her windowsill. Sometimes, but rarely, she shrouded one of the heads with a damp cloth and closed it in a cardboard box to keep it soft so she could work at the clay again another day.

She didn't attach any value to the finished heads, often giving them away to the first person who admired them. She just liked the feel of the clay; when paint seemed refractory or simply stubborn, she found the clay utterly responsive, "like an affable penis," she'd once said to a friend.

When she'd finished up, wiped her hands, she looked into the face she'd modeled, remembering the look of fear she'd seen in Cy's eyes. She could see his skull rising up under the flesh; so much of what was interesting, expressive in his face was dependent on just that. Our expressions, she thought, must be muffled by our very flesh. She raised her hands to her own face, ran her dry fingers over her cheek bones, her forehead, her lips. All so smooth. And yet she could feel the flesh under the skin, the bone under the flesh. Her fingers found her skull easily.

She looked a last time at the paintings tacked on the wall, where she would struggle again in the morning. She didn't try to see ahead to what she'd do tomorrow. Often, she'd found if she saw too clearly in the evening that very clarity got in the way the next day, when the first brush stroke changed the whole and there were entirely new problems to face. She solved the problems slowly, worked through them stroke by stroke.

She poured herself a glass of Rioja and turned off the light. In the dark she fumbled with the matches but soon had a small utility candle burning, stuck to the lid from a jar of olives she'd finished the week before. She sat back down, twisting her chair toward the wall of mirrors. But the wall had dissolved, it always dissolved, and in the dark room all she could see was a curtain of small, yellow lights.

She wondered if the evening with Cy was the beginning of something, or if now they'd wave when they passed in the plaza and keep on. She thought again about her painting, about the uninterrupted hours she required in front of the canvas. She knew that what started with the planes of Cy's face, a fascination with how his face was put together and how light showed it now handsome in the manner of Greco's painted saints, and now more suggestive of the damned in the black Goyas, that what started there had little to do with Cy and whatever claims he might make on her. She looked again at the paintings. She felt like painting right now. She wondered if that was a good sign. She came close to turning on the light.

Cy sat on a bench in the Plaza Nueva, his walking stick between his knees. He said no to a shoeshine boy and tried to relax. His head felt better now, the cool air outside felt better. But he wished he was already home, on his bed, asleep or trying. The headache had surprised him. It had come on so suddenly; usually if he had headaches at night they were lingering, something leftover from a bad morning. He was reminded again how fast his world could tilt toward disaster.

He watched a Gypsy woman working the tables set out in front of the plaza's many restaurants. First the free flower, then the begging, sometimes very insistent. What you paid for wasn't the flower but getting the woman to leave. He remembered once watching a couple of scruffy Gypsy boys work a restaurant in Greece, one with a drum, one with a loud and reedy pipe. The boy with the pipe just bellowed, aiming its flared end right at whoever looked richest at the table. Cy had laughed, admired them, and paid up when they came to his table before the playing had even gotten started. The kids had grinned, a complicit expression in their shining eyes. Cy had smiled back, thinking he had the better of the bargain. And he had, he'd gotten a poem out of it, and a tidy check from the glossy magazine that had published it.

It occurred to him only when he'd stood up that the headache might be just that, a headache, and not some terrible harbinger about his cancer, about things to come, if he let them. He thought maybe he should try aspirin. He walked by the kiosk where he bought an English-language newspaper some days, past the Lisboa, a favorite coffee stop. On Elvira, he passed the shuttered antique shops and, turning right at the corner of Calderería Nueva, he began the slow climb up toward his house on Placeta de la Cruz Verde. The cobbled street was rough, with a gutter in the middle, and he walked carefully, picking his footing and tapping along with his walking stick. The teterías were all closed now, in fact almost every storefront was shuttered. Granada was like that, a town where streets came alive at different hours and closed at different hours. The tapas bars would be open for a long time yet, and after that the nightclubs. Cy knew he'd be asleep before some of those places even opened their doors, or dead, he thought grimly. Still, he'd had a day he was glad to have lived. He hadn't had many lately.

And he'd met someone new, Madeleine James. James. Of course, he'd seen her around Plaza Nueva and in Little Morocco, too. Almost always alone. She had struck him as quite amazingly distracted, as the kind of person who must often walk into a lamppost or tumble off the edge of a curb. He'd noticed she never walked a straight line, but meandered along in a distinctive, loose-jointed way, lost in what she was thinking or perhaps in what she was seeing. She seemed, at least when she was walking alone, entirely free of self-consciousness. She looked vulnerable in ways that Cy now thought, having talked to her, she probably was not. How glad he was to have liked her paintings!

Walking the empty alleys up to his house, Cy thought about how the roads seemed less peopled the closer he got to the end, how soon enough he'd be turning into ever narrower alleys until there was only room for two abreast, and then only room for himself, and then, if there was still any walking to be done, no room for a self at all. But the image was all wrong, he realized that; the streets he was leaving teemed with life and, after he was gone, would still.

5

Asur begged at the door of the cathedral, the door where tourists were directed back out into the city. *"Por Dios."* He heard a couple speaking English and said, "I am alone, help me," holding out his palm. That was worth a coin, from the woman, who dropped it from well above his small hand, not wanting to touch him. "God bless you," he said. The child thought he should be able to tell who would give him a coin but he couldn't. The pious were often thrifty. Or perhaps they had left their change in the locked boxes to pay for the candles they had lit. His own mother was one like that. His own mother, who had damned him when she caught him in his sister's dress. Not the first time, not even the second, but when she realized that the boy was never going to be like the other boys, she had cursed him. He had not understood what was happening to him. He hadn't had anyone he could tell. So he had run away from the little village he was born in out on the *vega*, run to Granada. He had run away when it got warm enough to sleep outside. He did not know what he would do when it got very cold again.

He straightened his Red Sox cap. He didn't try to look worse off than he was when he begged; he just asked. But he knew he was looking worse off all the time. He sometimes rinsed his clothes out in the Darro but they were wearing out, both the pants and his sister's dress, and he'd have to get something new soon.

"Help me," he said without much conviction to two teenagers who looked to be runaways themselves, wild and pierced, but the boy gave him a coin. Two in a row. This was rare. He felt the coins in his pocket and decided he had enough for breakfast, and he headed down to Plaza Pescaderia. It was Saturday and there would be stalls set out on the sidewalks, fruits. He loved fruit, pears, and oranges, so sweet. He would buy milk and a roll and a piece of fruit, and maybe if he was lucky he'd see a box of very ripe things meant for the garbage, and he would ask if he could have some.

He ate in Plaza de la Trinidad, happy in the sun, no one around to bother him. The milk came in a small plastic bottle and he twisted off the cap and drank greedily. It was cold. The roll was fresh. The small oranges were sweet though difficult to peel. And he had two overripe bananas. The bananas for free.

He walked back up toward the cathedral on Capuchinas, by a storefront window full of polka-dot skirts where the street bent right. He noticed his reflection in the window and frowned, a grubby boy in too-short pants and a baseball cap. Red Sox? He'd found the cap on a bench, and when he'd tightened up the strap at the back it had fit. When his hair had grown out he'd used the hat to hide his curls under. Wearing the hat had also helped with the American college students doing a semester in Spain. Some of them were softhearted and good for a coin, and some of them wanted to ask about the cap, ask if he was a Sox fan. He didn't understand the question, but he said, "Yes," and learned a little English in the bargain. Once in the plaza, one with a Chinese face, orange hair and an earring, had saved him from a street punk who was dragging him toward the shadows to shake him down.

He's with me, the orange hair had yelled, and stepped between the man and Asur. That American was called Thomas, and he knew Asur was sometimes a girl. He had recognized the same face under a cap and surrounded by curls. He'd looked into the child's face, at the skirt and the hair, and just said, "Hey, kid, how you doin'?"

"Okay?" Thomas knew, and he thought it was okay.

Asur arrived in Plaza Nueva quite late. It had been a difficult night, little pity for a girl in a dirty dress. He'd had to run from the police and had stepped on his skirt and taken a tumble. The fall had hurt and the laughter had hurt, but he had gotten up with only a skinned elbow and run some more. He had hardly arrived when he saw the juggler, carrying her satchel, walk out of Elvira into the plaza. She walked like a toreador, a tautness in her, as if borne by extreme confidence. The child loved the way she walked; he wanted to be like her, straight and unafraid.

Once before, the juggler had allowed Asur to pass the hat when she performed. Though it wasn't a hat; it was an old and chipped crockery bowl, a beautiful yellow with a blue design in the bottom. The juggler had paid well, smiled at the child when she took the money from the bowl, giving him more than he had expected.

So Asur asked, "May I help you? ¿Te puedo ayudar?" And the juggler said, "Sí." Out in the plaza, in view of dozens of tables crowded with diners, the juggler set down the satchel. She took out five torches and a red plastic squeeze bottle full of kerosene. She lined up the torches on the cobbles and doused the wicks. She handed the child the bowl and nodded toward the tables, where a few heads had turned curiously toward them.

The juggler lit the torches, which sent up tall flames and roiling black smoke. She walked toward the tables but said nothing. Soon the torches were flying, turning end over end in the black air over the plaza. The juggler seemed to reach up and grab them from the sky, a look of intense concentration on her face, which shone brightly whenever a flame passed in front of her. The child roamed through the tables and through the crowd that soon gathered around the juggler. "*Para la señora,*" he said. "For the beautiful lady. For the brave lady." And the bowl began to fill with money.

On the second pass through the crowd Asur saw the American woman, smiling, standing next to a tall, skinny man. She pushed a bill into his pocket, said, "For you," and touched his shoulder. The man dropped a handful of coins into the bowl, but he was watching the torches. The juggler was very good. When she extinguished the torches there was sustained applause, and she bowed deeply from the waist, formally. Then she packed the torches in the satchel and said, "Come on." Together the child and the juggler walked away, up along the Darro toward Passeo del Padre Manjon, where the juggler would perform again. Her arms and shoulders were sweaty and streaked with black soot. Her face looked smoky but intent. A hawk's face.

"What is your name?" she asked at last.

Asur hesitated, then said, "Luz."

43

"Marcela," the juggler nodded. She held out her hand, with money in it, saying, "For you."

6

Sam worked the mastic onto the wall with a trowel, displaying the unrushed competence that made him so good at his work. Even as a child he had loved to watch skilled craftsmen at work. He'd watched masons, men good with bricks and mortar, finish carpenters, even a man at the local body shop who was a magician with a paint gun, spraying perfect coats of cherry red over a coat of flat gray primer. Later, he'd watched potters, iron workers, glass blowers, restorers of paintings and posters; he'd known a man who made a good living making new "antiques," to the layman, at least, indistinguishable from the originals. To talk to them, they were very different people, but whatever their culture, their race, or class, they shared, or at least it seemed to Sam that they shared, a similar relationship to their materials. A deliberateness, knowing hands that did not rush. As far back as he could remember, Sam had wanted to be that good at something, anything. As it turned out, he had become that good at many things.

For years he'd thought of the deliberation he'd acquired in his mastery of sundry arts as a virtue, as related to goodness. Then he'd stopped thinking that. He had come to believe that mastery was morally neutral, a discipline and a pleasure, yes, but only that. Recently, he'd found himself going further, thinking that there was something dark in all mastery. The impulse that made for mastery always put the how ahead of the what, technique before content.

He had begun to place the faïence tiles now, his head full of the intricate patterns that the tiles would take, but he realized as he pressed a mustard-yellow rhomboid into place that there was something oddly puritanical about his train of thought, and he laughed. Concentration broken, he tipped his weight back onto his stool. If the ideas were puritanical, he thought, he was seeing their attractiveness from the other side. God's armies, maybe, saw good and evil and felt righteous in cleaving to the light, but for us, he thought, scandalous civilians, the pleasure is all in the lurid glow of knowing how the judgments would fall if we were ever found out.

Paula's bare feet slapped at the doorway of the room where Sam was working.

"How are the tiles?"

Sam held out a green, rectangular tile that would find a place in the border. The glaze was dull and noticeably uneven. The tile, chipped a little on one side, bore a spiderweb of minute crazing and scratches and looked a little dirty.

"You are good," she said, "no doubt about that. It looks like you stole it right out of the Alhambra."

"Now, if I can get just the right amount of slop into the design," he murmured. "One of the first rules of the job—don't be too good at it!" Sam chuckled, "To be great one must not be too good." As an afterthought, he whispered, "In any sense."

"I heard that." Sam glanced up. "Don't worry," she said derisively.

46

"I haven't noticed you're in any danger."

They'd cleared the room out for restoration, so Paula lowered herself onto the floor, pulling one foot after the other into her lap. She had her dark hair tied back in a square of cheap silk. She had oriental eyes and a dusting of red freckles, a lively mouth, too lively. Her opinions were often read there, but her expression was rarely pouty or inward. Not everyone liked her looks, but most people did.

"So how are your plots going against Mad James? Are you going to make a campaign of it?"

"I'm considering." Sam was working again. He had made himself a small map of the design, but he didn't refer to it often. He picked up the tile he needed from one of the neat stacks he'd prepared before he had begun.

"What is it with you? I don't get the attraction."

"Did I say I was attracted? I'm provoked. She's so damned serious. Painter with a capital P. And what's worse, she's modest. Really unconscious." Sam moved his stool a few inches to the right. "Saint James."

"But why bother with her? I just don't see the point. There's no money in it."

Sam leaned back, to get a little distance on what he was doing, then hunched forward again.

"Are we invited to see her new paintings?" Paula asked at last.

"I have a suspicion you like her work."

Paula pulled her feet out of her lap and stood up. "Was that an answer?"

"Superior wallpaper. That's what I'd call it." Sam didn't look up. "We're invited, of course, open invitation. Anytime after noon. She won't expect us to take her up on it, but we will. We're interested, right?"

"I haven't seen her work, not really. Just postcards for exhibitions. But I think I might like it, actually."

"You know how long it would take me to paint one of her canvases?" Sam had stood up and was looking flustered. He had his hands out in front of him and they were shaking.

Paula turned away from him, allowed her body to flow in a way that rarely failed to get Sam's attention. She looked back over her shoulder, said as sweetly as she could, "But it would still be *her* work you were copying, wouldn't it?"

Paula crossed the courtyard of the *cármene* and climbed up the stairs to her workroom. She'd chosen it because of an oddity; the room was only accessible from outside. She knew there had once been a connecting door to the rest of the house; she'd found it with her hands, running them over the face of the wall where she thought the door would've been. In some lights, she noticed, you could see a slight concavity in the wall there. Probably a watchman had been lodged in the room, or perhaps a son who insisted on his privacy. Not a daughter, of course, her privacy would never have been respected so far.

Paula slept in the room when it suited her. She kept a narrow bed against the back wall. She'd found an antique chamber pot in the house and had appropriated it, used it, too. Most nights she slept in the house with Sam, but she thought a woman needed a retreat. It was invaluable for winning arguments, or at least for getting her way. She'd known women to forswear the power of their beauty; political animals, she'd thought, and fools. She believed in playing her trumps.

On her table there were several pottery shards she'd bought from dealers in Granada and Cordoba, from the kind of men who kept a very respectable shop in town but who, if you showed the right kind of interest, would take you to a small locked room somewhere else in the city, where they kept things for discriminating buyers without scruples. She had disappointed them, with her interest in shards. One had looked so disappointed that she'd bought a couple of archaic figures, cruciform and rudely made. These were old, from before the Roman occupation. They hadn't been expensive, a hundred dollars each. It was just that she had little use for them. But she needed the shards. She had a library of books on the decorative arts of Moorish Spain, things to guide her in her work, but to make the crockery believable she needed to have a close look at the shards, to gauge the clay, the thickness of the walls, the handling of applied designs. Their client wanted a glass case of Islamic pottery for the villa, and Sam thought they should salt whatever they bought with a few choice pieces, pieces so good they "rarely came on the market." Perhaps Sam would apply a museum identification number to these pieces, to suggest they had a pedigree a little too illustrious to examine closely. And work so exquisite, of course, commanded a very high price. He'd make a phone call late some night, asking if he should buy those pieces he'd gotten wind of?

Desire would make them real, or seem real. Desire conferred reality on many things that were not what they seemed. Paula knew this, knew it in the rustle of silk across her hips, knew it in the cupidity of a collector's gaze. Sam's idea, she had to admit it, to add a museum or collector's identification number, was a happy stroke. How, having purchased such a piece, could the German then inquire about its provenance?

Paula looked critically at the small, wide-mouthed jar on the table in front of her, comparing it to a larger piece in a reference book that was open on the table. She'd taken the jar, and a few other pieces, out of the kiln only an hour before. Close, she thought. She broke the piece by striking it lightly with a hammer, and then looked at the texture and color of the clay. She'd dug the clay out of the riverbank of the Darro up in Sacromonte, only a few minutes by car from where she was sitting. Both the color and the consistency were remarkably similar to one of the shards she'd bought in Granada. She'd make a few pieces from this clay, but one, and one only, would go to the German. The rest would have to find other homes. She felt a small thrill, a shiver of pleasure. She'd made a beginning.

7

Cy didn't think it was going to be possible to make his rooms look good. He hadn't been thinking about visitors when he'd rented the place; he'd thought of it as the last in a long line of rentals, rooms, apartments, even a house or two, before the long stay in the infamous carriage house in Shadyside back in Pittsburgh. He'd never owned his own place. He could look back on that, anyway, with perfect equanimity. Still, now he wished he'd had the painters in, had the floors scrubbed and waxed. The place had the feel of a lair or an animal's den, even though it was sparsely furnished. Like an old man's house, he realized with a start. He wanted to object, But I'm not an old man! I'm only forty-five! Which was true, but maybe the smell of the lair didn't come so much from years lived as from death sidling up.

He decided to mop, anyway, and filled a bucket in the bathtub, poured in a couple of jiggers of the all-purpose cleaning fluid he'd bought at the market. While he mopped he tried to remember what had possessed him to ask James over. She'd shown him her paintings. That was it, the polite thing to reciprocate. He'd been slow to, actually.

As he mopped the stairs, Cy forgot the evening in front of him. He'd had a bad morning, a prolonged nausea that was not relieved when he vomited into the waiting pan. He'd sat back down at his desk, his whole mind woozy. When he'd looked at the opening of a poem on a notepad, the word *nausea* had floated up in his consciousness, looking suspicious. He'd lately been under the influence of images of boats, and now he saw the boat in *nausea*. *Naus.* He had only studied Shakespeare's "less Greek," but it was enough for him to recognize the Greek word for *ship*. He'd looked it up, of course. Nausea must have been what sailors felt on days when the sea was rough. Boat sickness. Then the word had gotten associated with the feeling and the sea had been lost. Cy had remembered it, it seemed, in his own sickness. He'd put aside the poem he'd been writing in favor of a new poem, a poem about remembering the sea in his illness.

When he finished working, the day had run. Cy stepped into the bathtub, which he'd left to fill while he mopped. The water was warm and if he wasn't careful would leave him drowsy. Even in a tub he could feel himself beginning to float. Like a boat, but capsized. The sternum, he knew, must be the body's keel. The ribs of that ship his ribs, running up around his clean lungs and good heart. The structure of his boat was showing more than ever, he thought ruefully, looking at his thin chest. It would be a ragged boat he sailed over the bar.

He dressed carefully. He could be a clean man, anyway. Black slacks, a dark green shirt, and a black linen sport coat. After he cinched his belt he pulled the extra pleats in the waistband around to the back. In the mirror, he still looked good. A full head of black hair, prominent bones. He collected his walking stick at the door and headed out into the night. Cool, blue shadows, a starry sky. For a moment, he felt a future scrolling out in front of him, that feeling of long sea roads yet to sail. Although he knew it was an illusion, he did not try to push it away. To be again, just for an hour, a man going out to meet a woman, and nothing more.

James appeared at her door in a straight, deep purple shift and a black Pashmina shawl. They strolled down into the plaza where they'd watched the juggler a few nights before. They crossed Elvira and wandered into the short streets that ran between Elvira and Silleria. These three streets were lined with old-fashioned tapas bars, not so ephemeral as those haunted by students and budget travelers closer to the plaza. They cast a welcoming yellow light into the dark alleys; Cy invited James to choose one and they walked in. A bar in blackened mahogany ran the length of the premises. The room was trimmed out in dark wood, a few stand-up tables away from the bar, and tall doors thrown open on two sides. A thin cloud of blue smoke drifted between the doors on a breeze and kept the place fresh and cool. The principal decoration was edible, a display of *jamón* hanging in front of the mirrors behind the bar and over the bottled liquor. They ordered wine and olives, ignoring the hams hung on hooks and the casks of sherry. At another bar, they had wine and a hard, Spanish cheese.

Cy was struck yet again by the elegant yet assertive stance of Andalusian women, their refusal to unwind into a slouch. Out for the evening, they wore clothes that fit. Cy thought he could see something of North Africa in the faces of many of them, a vivid high color. He noticed that James was looking, too.

She glanced into Cy's eyes and said, "They make me feel quite pale. Not just how they look. They're so sultry. That one," James said, gesturing with her chin.

Cy looked. He ached. Not for love but perhaps for lost life. The woman had a ferocious quality, seemed furiously alive. Her glance shone now with a hard glitter and then, at the bat of an eye, went soft, out of focus, that look a man might drown in.

Cy turned back to James, "Nevermore," he said. He laughed. "Jesus, Jesus . . . Thank God!"

Outside the moodiness of the half-lit streets crept into them. They began walking the Albayzín hill up to Cy's place. Cy leaned on his stick. He was subject to fits of cold lassitude. It was as if a tide of seawater suddenly washed through him. He felt that now. He stopped for a minute, wiping his clammy brow, hoping the moment would pass, as it usually did, and not prove a prelude to something worse.

"You okay?"

"It's nothing," Cy said, and he started to walk again, to the click of his walking stick.

They were nearing Cy's small house, moving slowly over the rough cobbles. James had taken his elbow, and Cy had let her; he wasn't sure why. Something in him had tipped over, beyond pretense.

Cy opened the door and didn't apologize. He let James pass by him. "Just on up the stairs," he said. "There's a switch at the top." As he was shutting the door, Cy glanced out at the small crowd of street people sitting opposite on a flight of stone steps. So far, it looked like a night for wine. He could see a glint of green glass from a large bottle parked between two of them, a couple with quite similar Rastafarian hair.

"I have a pleasant terrace on the third floor," he said, following James up the stairs. "We can sit outside."

"But I want to snoop!"

Cy smiled, "Well, okay, while you snoop I'll polish the stemware."

He sent James up to the third floor alone, while he gathered together a split of expensive Rioja, a bottle of sparkling water, and four glasses. He arranged them on a tray, but before he carried them up he rinsed his face off in the sink. When he lifted his face from the towel it glowed, felt as if it might peel off and leave him no more than a naked soul. He took a deep breath, steadied himself, then he too climbed the stairs up to the third floor.

James had wandered down to the other end of the room and was looking at his sacred shelf. When she heard him, she swiveled around, said, "I like it," in a dusky voice Cy hadn't heard before.

"They're poets," Cy said.

"I recognize a couple." She pointed to a woman's face and said, "Akhmatova, isn't it?" And to a thin-faced man in wire rims, "William Carlos Williams?"

"Very good! One more and you win a stuffed animal."

She pointed again, "Pessoa?"

Cy sat the tray down on the bed and began to applaud. "What'll it be, lady, want the panda or the sock monkey?"

"I'll take the monkey."

She bent closer to the painted gallery, pulling out a volume or two, then peered under it to where the backsplash was visible beneath the shelf. "Looks like feet," she said. "Kinda gray?"

Cy grinned. "That's right," he said, "feet of clay, to be exact."

James looked quizzically in Cy's direction. "Oh?"

"The shelf was painted by a lover, and, well, once she knew me better, right before she left in fact, she added the feet."

James laughed, "I see. But what are these?" She had picked up copies of two of Cy's books from his desk. "*What She Said*, I believe I've heard of this one." She flipped the book over and read. "My, my," James murmured, "the blurbs make it sound a bit scandalous. 'The most acid tongue on the subject of love since Catullus.' Since who?"

"That would mean in a long time, I think. He was a Roman bad boy. But I think that guy must have forgotten Rochester."

"Isn't 'acid tongue' rather odd praise?"

"Yes. If it's praise," Cy added.

"Will you read me one?"

"I'd rather not, not now, anyway. Maybe I could read you a poem I didn't write, but love?" He walked across the room, stopping at the sacred shelf. As he reached out, he glanced across his shoulder, to look at James, as if he were taking her measure. The books on the shelf were all worn. Many of the dust jackets had gone soft with handling; they were the kind of loved books that just fall open when picked up. His hand hesitated in front of the shelf, in the act of reaching, then settled on the spine of a Rilke.

"Perhaps you know this one," Cy said softly, "from the *Sonnets to Orpheus*, #13 in the second part." For a moment Cy seemed scholarly, almost officious. He read the first phrase in German, "*Sei allem Abschied voran*," then started again, in English:

Be in advance of all parting, as though it were
Behind you like the winter that is just going.

His voice, as he read, submitted to the poem, to its trance-like measures. James realized that in reading to her, he was reading to himself. And it seemed to her that his voice might break but it never did, though she heard in it, deep down, a muted quaver.

When he finished he let the silence stretch a bit.

"I'd forgotten how good it is," Cy said. "He called to the darkness."

"Yes."

Then Cy said, "But really, isn't the advice to be dead while you're still living?" Cy's eyes teared up, but he was laughing. "It's strange, James, but often that's seemed like good advice to me."

"And often not?"

"Often not. Still, there is something so lovely, so fetching, about the implied green of the first two lines. What is ahead of the winter just going? The coming green. But that's not the green of earthly spring for Rilke, though that's the green I want, still want, that first green. No, for Rilke, green is the color of his abnegation, the springtime of saying no to the world. Some reversal," Cy concluded, looking a little embarrassed.

"That's a blunt summary."

"Yes, but I'll stand by it." After a moment, he said, "Why don't we take the wine outside? I get carried away, I'm sorry. You understand, don't you, that I love the poem?"

"Of course."

The terrace shone dimly in the light from Cy's windows. Cy uncorked the split while James poured out the water. They settled into their chairs, faces in shadow. James pulled her shawl up onto her shoulders and looked out over the scattered city lights to the Alhambra on the hill across.

"Can I borrow *What She Said?*" When Cy didn't answer, she added, "If you like, I'll loan you a painting. We can make it a trade."

"Ah," Cy whispered, "bribery." He laughed again. "Sure, James, that's a deal, and a good deal for me. It will give me a chance to look at your work in different lights, different moods, in sickness and in health . . ."

"Very funny."

"I only hesitate because I'm not very fond of the poems." He looked away, into the darkness over the Sierra Nevada.

"Why not?"

"I imagine when you're painting you sometimes have lucky accidents. You just stumble on something that works, that answers. Well, I had those kinds of lucky accidents writing, too. And then I had an accident so lucky that it overwhelmed me. Look," he said, his head swinging back to face James in the darkness, then away again, "one night I brought a girl home, a girl too young, too beautiful, but not too sweet. There was nothing innocent about her. I'd known her by sight for perhaps a year. I bumped into her often; it seemed as if we lived in the same world. She was interested, that was obvious, had been interested for a good long time. But I thought I had to draw the line somewhere, and however old she was, she was on the other side of that line. I knew it. Nevertheless ..." For a second, Cy saw her again, the soft mouth, her lipstick a little smeared.

"One night I went to a movie at this very funky theater called the Beehive not so far from where I lived in Shadyside. This place had tables and chairs inside the theater, even couches, and that's where I sat down, on one of the couches."

"What was showing?"

"*The Conformist.*" Cy hooted, "How appropriate! They must have been doing a Bertolucci retrospective, I don't remember."

"I liked it."

"The movie?"

"Yes."

"Oh, me too. Anyway, this girl follows me down the aisle and sits down next to me on the couch. 'Mind?' she said. 'No,' I said. Then the lights went down and more or less out for me. So we ended up at my place on the bed and we did the expected thing. Not well."

"Are you telling this story with that famous Catullan acid tongue?"

"I don't think so."

"But you are talking about the so-lucky accident?"

"Well, no. But after we were done, we were—I don't know—staring at the ceiling and she said, very quietly and in a curiously detached voice, she said, 'At your age, is that as hard as it gets? Doughy?'"

"'Doughy?'" James had covered her mouth with her hand but even in the dark Cy could tell she was giggling.

"Exactly. That was the so-lucky accident. She said, 'doughy.'"

"How old were you?" James was laughing audibly now, a beautiful musical laugh.

"About thirty-five."

James gasped and pulled her shawl over her head. "I'm sorry, really, so sorry."

"I didn't argue with her. She had testified. But later that night I wrote the first poem in *What She Said*. I sent it off to a slick, the kind of place that doesn't publish much poetry but pays handsomely for the privilege. Well, they took it, and in record time. When that poem appeared my life changed. I started getting a whole new kind of attention. Editors started badgering *me*. This was novel but good. So I wrote a couple of other things in the same vein. Then some odd stuff started happening. Occasionally some guy I hardly knew, standing at a urinal in a public bathroom or just anywhere, would start telling me about the worst thing he'd ever heard in bed. And odder still, women started propositioning me—for bad sex—I'm not kidding, just to have the chance to whisper something really terrible in my ear afterwards, that might, just might, appear in print someday. 'I usually get paid for this,' one woman said, winking large, then sticking out her lascivious tongue."

"So I wrote a series of such poems, then a whole book: that one." Cy gestured toward his desk inside. "By then I was on the circuit, getting big money for readings and invited to teach at workshops in places like Aspen and Taos. I said yes to pretty much all of it. Things got so out of hand I agreed to a photo essay in *Metro Living*, featuring my carriage house in Pittsburgh, with closeups of the iron bed where it was presumed all those terrible things got said."

"I like to listen to a story told in the dark," James said.

"Told with *brio*?"

"Yes."

"But a sad story. I had a case. Of course, people tired of my poems. Long after I tired of them, but in the end they came around to my view that the poems were puerile. And repetitive. All the same poem, really."

"And then?"

"I remained notorious. Sought out for many dubious things. It was like I had a hangover that went on for years."

"And?"

"And I lost the thread in my own writing. I soldiered on, poem after poem. But they weren't, finally, mine." James reached over and pressed Cy's hand. Cy said, "So you can see why I hesitate to loan you the book?"

"Sure, but still, I'm curious." And then she said, "And it's all true?"

"You're lucky you're a painter, you have no idea . . ."

"Just kidding!" James said, "I'm kidding, I can imagine."

When James clicked off the reading light next to her bed, the clock on her night table had already ticked past 1:00 AM. By Spanish standards, it was not late. She could hear the life of the city pulsing at her windows. She did not mind the noise, liked the energy of the streets in Granada, which, she thought, for her, kept loneliness at bay. It was enough, most times, just to have people around. But she wanted to sleep now, to be up by seven and ready to paint by eight, and she knew that wasn't going to happen. When Cy had said goodnight he'd reached up and caressed her cheek, a gesture wistful and resigned. James didn't think she'd been touched that way since she was a girl, and then only by old men. She had thought there might be a spark, a sudden current of understanding in the merest show of tenderness. She did like him.

Back home, she'd sat with a sketchpad, thinking about his face, the odd angles at which he held himself. She'd drawn, just let a black crayon find its way across a sheet of soft paper. Later, in bed, she'd read a few of the poems in *What She Said*. They were better than Cy had suggested, much better, hard and glittering, and funny, and giving no quarter to anyone in the games of Venus. As good as the poems were on the page, she could easily imagine that they would be better out loud, that reading them Cy would have created quite a stir in the audience, an excited, audible buzz. For all that, she understood Cy's apprehension about being known by the poems. She thought it would be easy to mistake him starting with the poems. Then she felt uneasy, wondering, in spite of herself, which Cy was Cy? The man she thought she was beginning to know or the poet who wrote, "I Shoulda Told You," a litany of suppressed truths getting said too late, after. The poem, she thought, was only superficially funny. Under that it felt uncanny, and in the end, terrifying. How in love we are exposed.

Finally, she had gotten up, stepping into the sandals she kept by her bed. She'd pulled the red doors inward, and stepped up to the iron grate, listening for the Darro in its bed down below. It was then that she'd seen the design on the veranda in front of her studio, a cross described by seven small oranges. Blood oranges, as it turned out. She'd carried them in and put them in a bowl in the kitchen. Beautiful, mottled oranges. For a moment, she'd wondered if Cy had arranged the oranges on her veranda, but then rejected the idea as ridiculous.

Now, back in bed with the light off, the thought that someone had been on her veranda made her uneasy. There were iron grilles over the window and the door that opened on the veranda, but she didn't like the idea of a stranger out there in the night. And why oranges, why a cross?

❖

8

Asur had been shopping in Granada with his mother when they'd lived in the village out on the *vega*. Then, he'd spent most of his time trying not to lose his mother in the jostling crowds. He hadn't paid much attention to how clothes were bought or where they were sold cheaply. He wished he had. He'd been distracted by fast cars and tall buildings, by the kinds of people. Impossibly elegant women, young and aloof. Old dandies sitting over their small cups of sweet coffee or glasses of Jerez at outdoor cafés. The hot eyes of Gypsy children. The quiet faces of African women, sitting patiently beside stacks of leather goods for sale. Clusters of American tourists in bright shorts and funny hats. Once he'd watched a mime performing on a sidewalk. Another time he'd wanted to follow a man walking a monkey down a side street. He had returned to his village from those trips very little wiser about the ways of the city, about how buying and selling was done.

When he'd pulled the bill the American lady had given him from the little pocket on his blouse, he'd blushed. Two thousand pesetas. With the money still new in his hand he had decided to buy a real dress. He thought the money would be enough, but if it wasn't he could spend what the juggler had paid him for passing the hat as well. But he was scared. To buy a dress he thought he should arrive at the shop as a girl. He thought they might know, that he might be exposed. He remembered the window full of polka dots near the cathedral and he knew that's where he would go for the dress. He thought he would like a shawl, too, an orange shawl, maybe. He remembered that the street vendors near Puerta Real sold shawls, shiny, silky shawls with fringes. He wanted one.

At the shop door Asur quailed. He'd been looking in the window. He wanted the green dress with small white polka dots. He wanted it enough that he pushed the door open and entered. The shopkeeper looked up from her newspaper and smiled. She pushed her chair back from the counter and stood up awkwardly. She was old and gray but she liked children, liked their bright faces. Asur could tell; his fear stepped away.

"*Hola*. Can I help you?"

"Yes, please, the green one," and he pointed.

"*¿Qué talla, muñequita?*"

Asur didn't know what size, so he shrugged.

"Try this one."

In the dressing room, he pulled the dress over his head and unwashed chest, over his dirty underpants. With his head through and the buttons done up, he dared to look at the image in the mirror. His eyes went wide; the dress was beautiful, so beautiful. Even Asur saw a pretty girl when he looked in the mirror. "*Muñequita*," he murmured, "*muñequita*." He imagined a voice calling his girl name, Luz, and her answer, "*Mamá, aquí estoy.* I am here." Tears pressed at his eyes.

Then he heard the shopkeeper trying the doorknob, and his heart pounded and he backed up against the door. "*Momento,*" he said, before he realized he had the dress on; he opened the door a crack. "*¿Sí?*"

"Do you like it?"

"*Sí. Mucho.*"

When he looked at the price tag he almost sobbed. It was too much. He didn't have enough. When he came out of the dressing room his face looked stricken, and the old woman asked what was the matter.

He held out his hand, all his money in it, 2,600 pesetas, but the dress was 3,500.

"Your mother?" The shopkeeper said doubtfully.

"My mother doesn't know me."

"*¿No te conoce?*"

"No. I am alone."

"*Ya veo.*" The old lady reached down and took the two-thousand-peseta note from Asur's hand. She looked into the child's eyes, saw both the bravado and the fear there. She sat down the money and lifted the dress, slipping it into one of the shop's polka-dot bags. "Next week the dress will be on sale," she said. "Why not start the sale today?"

The child beamed, said like the old woman, "Why not?"

The sound of a piano rose out of the trees to where Cy stood with James, listening. Dusk was coming on and the house under the bridge was in deep shadow. Light shown from a back window out into the woods that bordered the stream here where it ran out of the hills. On the bridge, they seemed to be standing right in the trees' leafy branches where they grew into the last of the sunlight. There was no traffic on the narrow road. The music broke unencumbered from open windows into the open air. Whoever was playing down below had a feel for the music, made it live. A bird trilled.

Cy turned to James and shook his head; he wanted to just moan he felt so happy. He wanted to explain, to say, Nothing can come of this, I am dying. He wanted to say, Even so, this is enough. God sings in the birdsong.

"What?"

"It must have been you," he said, "who deserved this." He gestured at the light, the music. "It wasn't me."

"Deserved? No," she said. "I don't think so, but I like it."

"Me, too," he whispered, still listening to the music, to the rustle of the stream under the bridge. "Me, too."

They had walked a long way, from the far edge of the Albayzín into Sacromonte, taking the road that parallels the Darro upstream. But they hadn't seen the Darro for some time and Cy wondered if that might be it under the bridge. There was no one to ask.

The piano fell silent and when it didn't start back up again James said, "That must be our cue," and they turned back toward town. They walked the twisting road through farmland, over small rises, the Darro thick in willows on their left. They passed by orchards, almonds and lemons. Soon the whitewashed buildings of Sacromonte shone palely along the road and up the hillside ahead. Many of the houses were nothing more than a façade on a cave, the old cave dwellings of Sacromonte, set amid prickly pear and cypresses that looked at this hour like immense black candles. The neighborhood was poor, a ghetto for Granada's Gypsies, but a far more interesting place to look at than the concrete high-rises of Granada's newer neighborhoods built out on the *vega*. Here, the hills were inhabited. There, the *vega* was dominated.

It was dark before they'd walked all the way back to the Albayzín. But Cy found the darkness more welcoming than he had the fiery sun. He'd worn a soft straw cap and dark glasses to ward it off when they'd hiked out of the plaza in the afternoon, and he stopped for a moment now to take the glasses off. "Better," he offered, looking around. "I can see you."

"Well, I'm glad that counts as better."

"Much better." But he'd agreed to the long walk out through Sacromonte thinking it was foolish, that he might well collapse. He'd decided to go anyway, deciding that it was only vanity—still vanity—that said don't go. So what if there was a scene, if someone had to toss him in the backseat to get him back to Granada? So what if he died on the road? He wanted to be beyond that, not to feel the need to comb his hair and straighten his collar to be ready to die. "Sure," he'd said to James. "What time?"

When they got back to the foot of the bridge over the Darro by James's place they crossed without discussion. They turned right into the alley on Santa Ana and stopped at James's door. While she was working the key into the lock, Sam and Paula strolled up the alley from the direction of the plaza.

"Is this a good time?" Sam said, glancing with open curiosity at Cy.

"To see the paintings?" Paula added. "We're not interrupting?"

James looked over at Cy, and he held out his hand, first to Sam, then to Paula, introducing himself. "We met here, in Granada," he answered, when Sam asked how he knew James.

They passed directly into the studio, Sam and Paula stopping in front of the paintings in progress on the wall. Cy opened the door and walked out onto the veranda for a couple more chairs, the wrought-iron café chairs that James kept outside. Looking back in, Cy saw what seemed to him a charmed world, muted conversation, quiet, easy laughter. Lively faces. The wall of mirrors unstill in the quickened air. The chairs were heavy and he carried them in one at a time. They were turning the canvases around now, looking at finished things.

Cy sat down at James's worktable and inspected the clay heads lined up against the wall. The one on the far right, he noticed with a sudden rush, was his own, modeled, it must have been, from memory. He felt confused and wondered if he might be blushing. He wasn't flattered in the clay, but intensely seen, and he thought there was a kind of regard in that. When he looked at the row of heads a second time, he realized that the honor of James's attention might not be all that personal.

He heard Sam say, "Well, these mirrors suggest a preening self-regard I never imagined in you, James. Really, at RISD you looked the kind of girl who never gave her face a second glance."

James hesitated, then said flatly, "Is that so?"

"Even that unkempt look is a look, wouldn't you say?" Paula put in, seemingly to no one in particular.

"I like mirrors," James said simply. "I guess that's obvious," and she smiled wanly. "I'm not sure why you ever would have thought otherwise, Sam. Though to look in a mirror and be pleased seems to me not interesting enough to do very often. Look, these mirrors are things, reflection has been fashioned—given a handle—in all these ways. It's true many of these mirrors were made for women, and girls, to gaze into, to find their faces there. Mirrors are such an everyday magic, we hardly notice them, but for all that a big mystery. I think so, anyway."

"Are we going to be so serious?" Sam interjected archly, as if aggrieved. "We came to see your paintings, after all, what could be more flattering than that? And we like them, don't we Paula?"

"We do," Paula said. "I do, especially."

Paula had come over to stand by James's worktable; she'd picked up *What She Said*, which was sitting on a short stack of books on the table. "Why Cy," she exclaimed, "it looks like you're the author of this book!" She turned a few pages. "But it's poetry . . ."

"I know it's a disappointment," Cy said.

"Do you mind if I have a look?"

Sam picked up a tube of paint off James's tea cart, dropped it back, then began to rummage through a tray of oil sticks. "You favor Sennelier, I see."

"Do you mind, Sam? I try to keep my stuff in order. When I'm painting, I don't like to have to search for what I need." But it was more than that; she wasn't sure she wanted Sam's fingerprints on her brushes and paint sticks. His fingers struck her as intrusive. His hand didn't look like it should be straying among her things.

He ran a finger over the piece of glass she used as a palette and lifted his hand to his nose and sniffed. "You do clean up," he observed. "I believe you not only scraped this but washed it off with turpentine. So neat, my God, your paintings must be made by immaculate conception."

James started to object but Sam wasn't finished.

"Latex gloves!" He had picked a paint-streaked pair out of the garbage can. "A sterile workplace, for sure. You operate like a surgeon."

"You know full well, Sam, that if you choose oils you're agreeing to poison yourself. No need, really, to rush into that. I'm—"

"Trying to keep my exposure low," Sam finished for her. "I'm sure that's best. But don't you ever want to just roll in it? Eat it?"

Their conversation was interrupted by Paula's laughter. "Sam," she said, "you should read this," she held the book up, "really instructive. I'm taking notes." And she looked up at Cy with a small, conspiratorial grin.

"What's it about?"

"Bad sex, Sam, some really bad sex."

Cy looked across at Sam and nodded. "That's fair," he said.

"Then I'm glad you think I need instruction, Paula," Sam responded.

"Cy, can I borrow this?"

"I'm not quite finished with it," James interjected, quietly.

Then the doorbell buzzed and all four of them jumped.

James laughed and walked down the passage to the door in back. When she opened it, she saw the little beggar from the plaza standing in front of her, beaming.

"Thank you," Asur said in English, gesturing at his new green dress. "You buy."

Cy had come up behind James and smiled, said, "*Bonita*. That's a very pretty dress."

"*Muchas gracias*," Asur said again, trying something like a curtsey, hair falling in curly profusion about his face.

James heard Sam's voice behind her, saying, "Isn't that the kid we hired for odd jobs up at the house?"

Paula had come to the door, too. "That was a boy," she said, "or seemed to be."

When Asur saw Paula he backed away from the door, looking wild, then bolted down the alley. James stepped outside and called after the fleeing figure, "Come back! Hey, it's okay!"

But Asur either didn't hear or he didn't think so. He kept running.

Cy didn't sit back down after the excitement. The constraints of being four together were, momentarily at least, broken. Cy shook hands with Sam and Paula, who pressed his hand a little more warmly than he expected, then he leaned close and kissed James lightly on the cheek. "I won't forget that piano," he said.

"No. Not anytime soon."

They agreed to meet at the Lisboa on the plaza the following afternoon, and Cy stepped out onto the cobbles, walked past the lit entrance to the *Baños Árabes* and on down the alley. James hadn't mentioned Sam and Paula, so their turning up—inopportunely, he thought—had come as an unwelcome surprise. Still, they were interesting, unusual types, clearly willing to reach out and shake you. Cy knew few people with their kind of worldly, glittering charm. He envied them their sheer confidence, how they'd managed to respond to James's work articulately even as they talked wittily about other things. Then there was Paula's beauty, the incongruous smattering of large freckles on her startlingly modeled face, the odd slant of her sleepy eyes.

Sam and Paula stayed on for a drink after Cy left. Having inspected the wine, Sam asked for a whiskey. Paula and James each had half a glass of a Spanish white. They stood outside, at the railing over the Darro. The houses high in the Albayzín looked blue at night. The city walls were just barely visible on the hills beyond. A sliver of moon sailed high overhead.

Sam said they were thinking about a trip to Morocco, to Fez, probably.

James had never been. Although it was close by, she hadn't yet begun to desire more Islam than Al-Andalus. Yet, she knew she would, that the day would come when she'd want to hear the muezzin's call from the minaret. Much of what she liked about Granada, she knew full well, was what was left of Islam, and of course there would be more of that in Morocco. She would want to go, but not yet.

"What will you be doing there?"

"Looking," Sam said slyly. "Perhaps buying. It's a little dangerous, but not too. Just enough to make things interesting. I love old Fez. It hasn't got an Alhambra, but the place is intact. If you want to know what's been lost here, go there. Or to Marrakech. Fez all white in a bowl, you just walk down from the rim until you're lost in the heart of the city. Marrakech is the red city, built on a plain inside castellated city walls. You'd have to go a long ways to find a place more alive than the Assembly of the Dead, odd as that sounds."

"So I've heard."

Sam paused, stared in at James's mirrors for a moment. "The French in North Africa left the old towns alone, built their own towns a few kilometers away, not surprisingly Frenchified places like what you might find in Provençe."

"Have you been?" James addressed the question to Paula.

"Me? No. But I hear a woman gets a lot of attention down there, and I like attention." She laughed. "Of course, not all attention is equally gratifying, and I imagine a lot of what a girl gets in Morocco is of the not-so-gratifying kind."

"No doubt."

"But everyone insists on the beauty. Why don't you come along?"

"Not just now," James said firmly. She gestured toward the wall where her in-progress canvases were pinned. "I'm in the thick of it, as you can see. But maybe another time."

"Do you think Cy might want to go?" Paula asked, watching James coolly.

James glanced over at Sam and saw he had not expected the question, was perhaps even alarmed by it. Then she said, "You'd have to ask him."

James was almost asleep when it occurred to her to be surprised that the beggar girl knew where she lived. Somehow she'd failed to notice the oddity of the girl's ringing at her door in the hubbub of the moment, but it *was* odd. The girl must have followed her home at least once. And James thought she knew now who had left the gifts on her veranda. She couldn't see how, but still, she thought she knew who.

9

The Lisboa proved hot and bright. Cy felt sick waiting for James, and when she arrived he suggested they find a darker place. By chance, the Tetería Tuareg was open low down in the Albayzín. Cy had never seen the door anything but shut, and he'd walked by often. Although the building had a modern façade the Tetería Tuareg occupied basement premises with serious age. Stone pillars that looked very old, perhaps even Roman, were doing the work of holding the building up. The floor seemed to be live stone and the tiny rooms were separated by low stone arches that required ducking to get under. They sat down at a small table in a niche lit only by candles. On the way to their table, they had walked by a narrow passage leading to what was presumably the kitchen, down which electric light poured, and music, Tuareg maybe, certainly North African.

The *tetería* occupied the premises ever so lightly. The walls had been whitewashed but not too recently, a few plastic milk crates leaned against a pillar, dubious tables and chairs had been dropped wherever there was room enough. Occasionally a waitress with a tray or a rag wandered by, looking bored. The tea, when it came, was weak and no hotter than warm. For all that, Cy had settled into his chair with relief. He'd needed the dark and the cool and didn't mind the transient feel of the present establishment.

James sat across from him, her eyes roaming. "Do you think it was a bathhouse? A modest little *hammam* for the neighborhood?"

"Maybe, likely I guess."

"How are you?" James asked, suddenly attentive. "I've never known anyone to look so different day to day."

"I have bad days, and days a little better. I haven't had one as good as yesterday for a long time."

Then James said, "Ah," just *ah*, but throaty and held, a single vowel drawn out that joined her compassion to his. It was not pity, not as distant as that; she said, I know, to his suffering, not to what was particular in it, but to what was common, hers as well as his. She reached across the table and took his hand.

"Can you tell me why you're here?"

"I don't know, I don't know if I should."

"You should," she said.

"Still, I don't know if I can. The short answer is I'm dying."

"I guessed as much."

"Well, it's a brain tumor, an astrocytoma, and a big one. These things, they don't make a neat, removable lump; there's a mass but it's like crabgrass all around the edges; it's infiltrated my brain. The news is not cheery. It's not the kind of thing that can be fixed. But from the very first the doctors just assumed I'd want to fight, that they would operate, radiate, and that there would be a course of chemo. I said no. Do you understand that?"

"Yes."

"My friends didn't. My family didn't. They thought my best chance was with the doctors. So I visited the wards. I sat in on support groups. Everything was about the tumor, the treatment, test results, a whole world of false hopes and bucking up and doing the best you can, getting the best medicine has to offer. Just appalling. I agreed to one last consultation. Then I went home. I was dying. I am dying. Maybe the doctors could give me a few extra months, maybe not; they weren't promising. Either way, the rest of my life, all of it, I would be a patient. When they asked me if I'd rather be dead, I didn't hesitate, I said, 'Yes.'"

James squeezed his hand. "That was your decision to make, Cy." She felt an old anger rising in him.

"So few people thought so," he complained bitterly. "But who had chosen my friends if not me? I began to think the world I'd called into being was the world I deserved. My Prospero's island. I decided quite suddenly to leave, to live while I could. I wrote a will, I packed, and I flew over. It took me less than a week to get here. I set my life down and just walked away from it. Nothing to it. The gravitational field of my life in Pittsburgh proved almost wholly imaginary."

James nodded, her eyes dark, sympathetic. "I understand about the going," she said, "but why here, why Granada?"

"That's the harder part to explain. Harder for me to understand. Maybe I don't."

"It doesn't matter." James lifted her hand up and brushed Cy's hair off his forehead. The gesture seemed a mother's or perhaps a lover's, and for a moment she felt confused. "I can be awfully intrusive. I forget myself, forget that there are such things as decorum and privacy."

"Decorum!" Cy echoed, shaking his head. "It's not that, I'm touched that you asked. I'd like to understand myself. I know a little. I know some things that happened in Pakistan years ago are part of it."

James leaned back, surprised at this turn.

"I taught for a year in Lahore, American literature. A Fulbright, back in the days when I still had academic credentials good enough to trade on."

"What happened?"

"They got old."

"I mean in Lahore," she said, shaking her head at Cy's attempt at a joke.

"How can I talk about it? You see, whenever I try to say anything about life in Lahore I find . . . I find I grind to a halt. Every little thing seems to require explanation, context, and then the context requires context, too. One morning I woke up and I was in Pakistan, there were hoopoos strutting on the lawn. There was a river, the Ravi, but it ran red, though it was said that blind, freshwater dolphins still finned its murky currents. When I first arrived at the university, to teach, all the students stood in welcome, and one came forward to lay dozens of roses in my arms. They called me *sahib*, which they pronounced like *sob*. James, I was lost, I . . ." Cy stopped, surprised at how much he wanted to tell the story right, fully. For James, he realized, for her. "I am trying to talk about a student," he said at last, "Nasreen, and, you see, to do that I need to tell you about the school. The high, cool walls. The thick air stirred by a pair of dusty paddle fans. The cool, filtered quality of the light standing in the tall windows, and behind the unwashed panes at the back of the room, indistinct, the pale glow of a small white mosque in the courtyard of the university. The call to prayer began, suddenly, and the women in the classroom who didn't already have their hair covered reached for their *dupatas*, six feet of silk, and pulled them over their shining black hair. Except for Nasreen, who made no move. I had fallen silent at the front of the room, I was looking at Nasreen. The woman next to her turned her head to look at Nasreen, too, and her profile was all compassion, and she plucked at the *dupata* she had over her own hair, lifted it, and pulled it over Nasreen's head as well as her own. I was at the front of the room, looking, waiting for the call to prayer to end, when I would begin to teach again. And Shabina, Nasreen's friend, leaned her head onto Nasreen's shoulder. She joined her under a makeshift tent, that there should be community still, that Nasreen should not offend."

Cy paused again, remembering. "That moment, so still, the yearning voice of the muezzin, yes, but under it, everything unmoving, occupies my memory like a small blue lake, unruffled, in which the world shines, a world so crazed and fallen, so incomprehensible, that when I look directly at it I despair of speech. It's easy to say that Nasreen sat in the dignity of her grieving, to say even that Nasreen had a grievance with God, and that Shabina knew somehow how to give whatever comfort it was possible to give. My heart broke, but what cracked it was not so much the disaster as my admiration for them, for how steady they were in the face of it. They knew how to face it as surely as my friends did not when disaster came for me, too."

"What disaster?"

"Nasreen's? Well. One day I arrived on campus; my driver pulled the car off the Mall into the lot at Punjab University, and before I had a chance to get out I saw Seeta at my window, her pure sad face in the morning light. 'The class is gone,' she said, in her high, reedy voice. 'Gone?' I was expecting more. 'They have gone to Nasreen's village.' 'Nasreen?' I asked. 'Nasreen Farouqi. Her sister has been murdered. The class has taken a university bus, gone all together to offer condolences.'

"I was shaken. Nasreen was my favorite, I admit it. And beautiful, I admit that too. But that's not it at all. She had a kind of sweet deference. She spoke often. Her voice had a high drone in it. I had to listen closely, to lift the words a little, to separate them from that resonant drone, as if she were her own squeezebox, playing in company, a drone and words.

"What she had to say was her own, not out of the crib sheets used by so many of her fellows. She spoke out of a deep equilibrium, as if it could not matter how her ideas were received. Sometimes they were well received, and she was pleased, or they were not, and she was pleased to hear a better idea. Either way, her serenity filtered into everything. Serenity, I have not met it very often."

"Who killed Nasreen's sister?"

"I didn't find out for some time. The class returned from Nasreen's village and we resumed. For a few days the weather turned cold. The students huddled in clumps as they bent over their books. Even standing up front, I could feel the heat radiating off their bodies. I was teaching a set syllabus and having a big success with Robert Frost, whom my students called the Punjabi poet, failing to register

81

his particular localism. The Frost of thick green and snow pulverized into the dramatic dust of the Punjab."

"But who?"

"I told you it was a long story! I'm sorry." Cy smiled sadly. "I didn't expect Nasreen to return. I simply didn't see how she'd be able to. By then I had heard the story, nothing like the whole story, but enough. Nasreen's sister had been murdered by her father-in-law. He'd been picked up almost immediately.

"The killing hadn't been random, or a crime of passion, but punishment. Nasreen's sister and her husband had married out of med school; she'd been the gold-medal winner in her graduating class. They'd seemed a charmed couple. Internships or fellowships, I'm not sure which, in America. But in Ann Arbor there must have been trouble. Nasreen's sister filed spousal abuse charges with the authorities there. Probably that day, handling the difficulties in the American way, she crossed over. Surely she must have understood that to go back to Pakistan would be dangerous, that her American act would not be understood in an American way when she returned home. Perhaps that was it, home. With a new child, she wanted to go back.

"She lived with her husband and the baby in Lahore's old town, in that great tangle of streets, but not for long. Her husband returned to the States for a conference, and while he was away her father-in-law and a cousin opened the street door with a key, crept quietly up the stairs to where Nasreen's sister lay sleeping, the baby sleeping next to her, and then her father-in-law put a pistol to her head and fired."

"Her cousin?"

"Yes. James, I can still see the stricken faces of Thalat and Shabina telling me the story. It's hard to characterize their expressions, a mix of resignation and horror, I guess. 'And you know,' Thalat said, 'Nasreen's sister, she married her cousin.'

"So I didn't expect to see Nasreen again, but she did return, only a week or a week and a half after the murder. When I entered the classroom the students sat down, all at once, as they did every day, and there she was, erect as ever, if a little drawn, looking washed out, dull, as if someone had thrown dust or chalk onto her glowing skin. I nodded. There was nothing hidden in her face. The grief was simply there. And allowed to be there, acknowledged by everyone. If my heart was broken, if Nasreen's classmates felt the burden of her suffering, she didn't lean on us. She was grave, but as poised as ever. Perhaps because no one pulled back from her, pulled away from her pain, she was able to sustain it."

James nodded. She too was there, in the hearing, simply and fully there.

"Then something unexpected began to happen, untoward even. Nasreen began to speak in class in a way that brought her grief into the discussion, brought grief itself, mortal seriousness, into talk about literature. Had I made the world in my classroom so thin a place? I don't know, but quite suddenly our discussions had more dimension, a greater sense of depth and feeling. I remember one day she said, to introduce an observation on a Frost poem, 'As the one who has suffered most recently . . .' She spoke with such authority! It was only that night, in bed, staring at the ceiling, that I saw the ambiguity in her words. She had suffered the most, or most recently suffered? I

83

decided that she meant most recently suffered, that she wasn't claiming extraordinary suffering for herself. No, I think she meant that we take turns suffering, that it was her turn, and by implication, that the rest of us would likely get a turn later. But for a time, she claimed a deeper understanding about how suffering transfigures the world. She could witness."

"And eloquently, it seems."

"Yes, eloquently."

"Did you feel, in Pittsburgh, that your turn was going unacknowledged? Cy?"

"I didn't feel singled out."

"No?"

"Denial is general. In America there aren't any turns, not public turns, anyway. James, it was a common occurrence, in my neighborhood in Lahore, to see the dead wrapped in sheets and carried down the streets on their beds, a man at every bedpost, a crowd of mourners trailing behind. I'm not criticizing, quite the opposite. It's honest. I'm trying to explain why I'm here in Granada, talking to you. And not making much progress . . ."

"There's no hurry," James got up from the table, said, "Wait," and ducked under a low arch and into a passage. When she came back she said, "More tea on the way, Pakistani chai," and she laughed lightly. "Please, go on."

"I was just thinking about Lahore. Remembering, I guess, rather than thinking. Remembering the feel of the place. Some days, after class, I walked past the little mosque in the courtyard, past the Anglo-Mogul architecture of the university, and out the back gate of the campus, to plunge directly into the silk shops of the Old Anarkaly markets. Shop after shop of brilliant silk in bolts stacked to the ceilings, or shopkeepers shaking out a bolt here or there for the crowds of women at their counters. Bicycles careening through the crowded market streets, two or three cages of brilliant green parrots lashed to a rack over the rear tire. The birds only caught to be ransomed out of bondage, for luck. Set free in the air, an arc of green over the chaotic streets."

"You miss it."

"Yes, but I never went back, never wanted to." Cy paused. "Then we started Hemingway's *The Sun Also Rises*, the next thing on the syllabus. I remember, when I disclosed the nature of Jake's infamous injury, his impotence, the more conservative students stood up and walked out, scandalized. Walked out in their dark *shalwar kamis* and headscarves, eyes averted. After class my office was besieged, the girls, the other girls, come to tell me I had no choice, there was nothing else to be done. Scandal was easy." Cy laughed. "One day I set aside my regular khakis for jeans and when I entered class to teach there was an audible, collective gasp."

Cy paused again. "When we'd finished up with Hemingway I agreed to a day of debate. I stood at the front of the room, introducing the topic. 'Is *The Sun Also Rises* a misogynist book?'"

"What?" James was wagging her head.

"Why not? Anyway, a few hands went up as a prelude to questions; some of the students didn't know the word *misogynist*. 'Woman-hating,' I said, explaining the etymology. The murmuring in the high room got loud, a buzz. I called for teams to debate the question and the students began to call back and forth, making alliances. The class was verging on chaos. Amid all the commotion I saw a long, slim arm raised aloft and heard Nasreen's voice speaking quietly in the roar. And then everyone noticed her hand and a hush fell over the room.

"'Is there a word like *misogyny*,' Nasreen asked, 'that means man-hating?'

"No one made a sound. And how many hearts besides mine broke in that silence?

"'*Misanthropy*,' I spoke the word at last, 'but it means human-hating.'

"'I mean a word for hating men.'

"'No,' I said, 'perhaps there should be. We say *man-hating*. There are occasions for hating men, surely. Better for our own hearts, though, don't you think,' I was struggling, 'not to hate all men?'"

"Who won the debate?" James asked, disingenuously.

"Ah, the debate. A raucous affair, conducted in near dark under stilled fans: the electricity failed us. After the shouting stopped, I asked for a show of hands to see who had carried the day. By a narrow margin, they voted to convict: *The Sun Also Rises* was judged a misogynous book. In the dusky light their raised hands burnt like flames. You know, there, it seemed we were all burning, our lives combusting at our fingertips, in our hot, moist breath."

Cy sipped at his chai. It had been a long time since he'd done so much talking all at once, and his throat was dry.

"My students didn't see anything of Islam in Hemingway's Spain, and perhaps in truth there is little enough to see. But one day I visited a gallery across the Mall, at the National College of Art. The show on was photographs, black-and-white shots of Andalusian Spain. The Pakistanis at that exhibit remembered Al-Andalus, remembered it as Islam's great, lost, golden place. Walking through those rooms full of photos, I decided for Spain, for the south. And it seems I have finally got round to why I'm here. That sense of the lost place, of Islam's occupation and retreat. The way that rhymes with our occupation of this earthly clay. The beautiful remains. My own heightened sense of transience . . ."

"And here we sit in an old *hammam*," James said, "in a *tetería*, in little Morocco, drinking Pakistani chai. Islam must be creeping back. I think there is even talk of a mosque here in Granada."

"That would be good. I'd love to hear the muezzin's call again, a human voice, passionate, over the city. It speaks to a poet's sense of values."

"Morocco is just there."

"Would you want to come along?"

"Yes, I would." James reached across the table and pressed Cy's hand again. "Let's go, you and me." She beamed. Then her face darkened. "But it's a little awkward."

"What is?"

"Sam and Paula asked me to go with them just last night."

"And?"

"I told them no."

"Well, good! It's a large country. If we zigzag we should be able to avoid them."

"Paula seemed to be thinking of asking you to go, too, Cy."

"Really?" Cy feigned interest. Then he smiled. "Let her. I'll find a way to wiggle out of it."

10

Asur wandered down the first block of Elvira out of the plaza, picking pizza crusts off the paper plates abandoned on the curbside. He
walked toward a table where four college girls, Americans, were just
getting up, and when they did he made off with all they hadn't wanted, enough for dinner. For such work, it was necessary to be lucky, to
arrive at the table at just the right moment, before someone else sat
down or a waiter arrived to clean up. Loitering wasn't tolerated. More
than once he'd been chased down the greasy cobbles. And when he
ran the waiter laughed, and sometimes the patrons laughed, and Asur
didn't like that. He didn't steal leftover tapas often, but he'd said "excuse me" and "please" for hours down in the pedestrian mall behind
the cathedral without much luck. The shop windows had flooded
the night streets with golden light, the bright fashions of the coming
summer had mesmerized the strolling crowds, and few of the shop-
pers had admitted to a coin to spare for a girl in a green dress. The
green dress was a problem, Asur understood that. It was too new,
looked too good on him. Who would believe he was hungry?

He leaned against the barred window of an antique shop, eating
his salty crusts, looking back toward the plaza where the crowds had
begun to gather around the tapas bars. He loved the sound of their

chatter, the smiling low whispers and laughter, the way the sound
of it all mixed became nothing more than a warm rustle, a little like
a breeze in the green of a leafy tree. In his village, the light sound
of human happiness had been a rare thing. Quite suddenly, he felt
lonely, wondered if he would ever find a way into that sound, find his
voice mixed in the whole, and not be outside, a boy in a dress listening at a safe distance.

At night, the Albayzín scared him. He walked quickly upward,
heading for the terrace where he had stashed his boy clothes in a sack
behind a pot of bougainvillea. Tonight, he thought, there was little
to fear. He had almost no money to steal in his little red purse. But
the blue shadows that hugged the walls worried him. He tried not to
look at the bright, bare bulbs where they hung here and there over
a doorway, but walked by them shielding his eyes. Still, they made
seeing into shadows difficult. He walked on, quickly, as far from the
shadows as he could get.

The alley bent right and the house with the low wall, the one he
was heading for, came into view. His head jerked up and he trailed to
a stop. The terrace, which had always been dark on weekdays in the
past, shone with electric light; whoever owned the house was home.
He ticked off the days of the week on his fingers. Thursday. He
swore, "¡La gran puta!" Suddenly he was crying, silently; he couldn't
even risk a sob.

Wiping his eyes on the sleeve of his dress, Asur marched toward
the house. He stood in the alley, listening. Pulling the dress up nearly to his waist and knotting it, he prepared to jump. Then he leapt,
just took off, catching the top of the wall around the terrace with his
hands; he pulled his body on up in a single fluid motion, his head

rising up over the wall, only to find himself face to face with a bald man in a chair, drinking a glass of wine. Asur mumbled, "*Perdón*," and pushed off, awkwardly, and he landed hard back down on the alley cobbles. He howled.

The bald man, standing now, shouted down at him over the wall. "Get out! *¡Gitana puta!* Come back and I'll see you get a beating! Thief!"

Asur struggled up; three faces showed over the wall now: the bald man; a hard-edged, henna-haired woman's; and a pudding-faced girl's, looking interested. "*Hola*," the girl said. Asur wondered if he should ask for his sack and decided he shouldn't. When the bald man disappeared from the wall, Asur limped down the alley, expecting to be chased, but he wasn't. He glanced back at the bend and the little girl waved, smiling. He waved back, continuing on down. Perhaps very late, when the family slept, he'd be able to retrieve his sack. In the meantime, he thought, he'd need a place to hide.

Asur listened for a minute to the low laughter and the strummed guitar before deciding it was safe to enter Placeta de la Cruz Verde. He knew the vagrants of the Albayzín often gathered on the steps in the *placeta*, and he tried to avoid them after dark, but it was a long way around and his knee ached. Besides, they seemed to have arrived at a state of drunkenness or drug-induced lethargy that made their making a fuss over him unlikely. He edged around the corner. Immediately he heard a shout, "That's the one, my sweet *guapita*." A man staggered to his feet, pointing. He was bearded and dirty, and called out, "Help me catch her! I promised I'd have a peek between her legs, and I'm going to!"

Asur started to run, heart pounding, down the side of the square. Another night he would have made it, but his knee shifted under his weight and he tumbled against a wall. When he looked up he saw no one had moved to help the man but that the man was on him, had a hold of his arm. Asur screamed, and a greasy hand clapped over his mouth and nose. He got his mouth open and bit the heel of the man's hand. For a second, the hand pulled back and Asur started to screech again; then the man cuffed him hard and the boy's head spun down into the paving stones. The hand slammed tight over his mouth and a voice shouted "¡Cállate!" in his face. Then he felt himself lifted into the air and carried out of the little square. In a vacant lot the man tossed him face down onto a pile of debris and Asur, though dazed, leapt up. The man faced him, arms spread wide. Asur's head swiveled around helplessly.

"Try me," the man said, grinning. And Asur did try, dodging the man's outstretched arms, but not successfully.

With his sweaty face close to the boy's, the man said hoarsely, "Now, let's see which thing you got."

Asur started to keen and the man's hand clapped over his mouth. He pulled up the boy's torn green dress and stuck his other hand into Asur's underwear. "So it's a prick, is it? But you wanna be a girl, don't you?"

He pinned Asur face down and pulled his shorts down around his knees. "Wanna be a girl?" he said again.

Then the boy heard a sharp cry and felt the man's hands let go. He rolled over. The man was writhing on the ground, a thin man with a walking stick bent over him. "Run," the skinny man shouted at Asur.

"*¡Corre!*" Then he lifted his stick and slashed the drunk man's face again.

James had gone to bed early, but sleep had not come. Her memory, a gift to her as a painter, haunted her now. When she closed her eyes Cy was there, the brave face he'd put on to tell her he was dying. But the fear had peeked out, a widening of the eyes, a staggered deep breath, a slight catch in his voice. He had the haggard look of knowing too much. A look that said help me then disappeared again, to leave Cy there, just a man talking. She imagined it must have taken a hot dose of bitterness to send him out wandering alone. She thought the refusal to accept death made death a poison, and made dying poison, even grieving. Fear just rippled out until it got far enough away from the dying that it was lost in the general clamor.

James got up, went to stand at her window over the Darro. Even as she watched, a figure climbed up the vines and over the railing, dropping onto the terra-cotta tiles and rolling onto its side, knees tucked into its chest. She recognized the dress, the white polka dots just visible in the low light. She heard the child weeping. She looked down at the receding perspective, at the figure on the tiles, at the stream in its bed, its skin glistening in the moonlight. Then she turned away from the window, slipped on a long black kimono, and walked quietly down the stairs. When she opened the door Asur recoiled, and James said, "It's okay. It's just me. *Solo yo.*"

Before she could walk across the veranda Asur pulled himself up on his knees and began to bow. Spreading his arms wide he bowed forward until his forehead banged against the tile.

"*Por favor,*" he whispered, his speech slurred, "let me sleep here, please."

James recognized the pose. She'd seen it before in the most abject of Granada's beggars. A stark request for mercy.

"Please," James stammered, "get up. *¿Qué pasó?*"

But Asur only slid forward, his forehead scraping toward her across the tiles, his arms still spread wide, until he lay stretched facedown at her feet, looking crucified. James bent down and touched the child's shoulder, the long sleeve of her kimono covering him like a wing. "Get up," she said again. "What happened? *¿Qué pasó?*"

Asur shook his head, too ashamed to say anything.

Even outside, James could see the child was bleeding. "Come in," she said. And she led the way inside, up the stairs to the bathroom. She nodded toward the shower. "Wash yourself," she said, handing over a washcloth and a towel. "I'll be outside," and she pointed, "*afuera.*"

Cy locked the door and leaned his walking stick in the corner. He felt jittery, a nervousness that made his hands shake. Now what? he wondered. When he'd heard the scream he'd simply stood up, a word half written in his notebook. He couldn't remember how he'd gotten across the room or down the two flights of stairs, but he did remember the gleam off the silver handle of his stick. Like a bulb sweating in the dark. It shone dully, and one hand took it as the other opened the door. Outside, stray rays of porch light streaked the *placeta*. Across the way, the vagrants had fallen to singing. But Cy had heard a screech from the alley across and lunged forward. When he got there, he'd recognized the dress immediately. He hadn't hesitated.

He'd given no warning. The stick was in his hand and he used it. He heard a high-pitched whir and then the man had cried out and gone down, thrashing in the trash strewn about the lot. The girl ran, and when the man looked up, Cy had hit him again, with all the strength he could muster, and left him there. When he'd marched back out into the *placeta* he was expecting a confrontation, but no one got up, no one had noticed a thing, the singing had gone on unabated.

Cy opened the refrigerator and took out a bottle of gin. He poured an inch in a water glass and sniffed it. He hadn't been drinking spirits; he thought they made his morning sickness worse, but he wanted a stiff drink now. He tilted the glass back and tasted the thick gin. He went back upstairs and outside, where he had a clear view from the terrace of Placeta de la Cruz Verde. He sat down quietly in a chair, listening. The party on the steps seemed in danger of dying out. A dog trotted into the square, sniffed, then trotted on out, down the alley that led most directly to the plaza. A couple rolled onto the ground, in what looked to be listless sex. A bottle went round. An hour later the last of the vagrants wandered off and the *placeta* stood empty. Cy wondered about the man he'd struck. He was a regular in Cruz Verde and likely to be back.

Inside, at his desk, Cy stared at the poem he'd broken off, then closed his notebook. Half the candles in his candelabra had burnt out and the remaining few cast distinct shadows around the room. Cy thought he'd let the last of them burn out on their own. He undressed, draping his clothes over the footboard, and got in. The muscles across his chest tightened, and Cy took a few slow, deep breaths, until the fear washed out of him. "Nothing to do about it," he whispered.

On his back, he looked over at the painting James had loaned him. A purple wall, green trees, the heat of summer baked through it all. Two girls in summer dresses ran in circles under the trees in front of the wall. Someone was reading a blue newspaper on a wrought-iron bench. The light, the beautiful light. Everything itself and accidental but suggesting somehow that the accident was divine.

"What's it called?" he'd asked James when she leaned it against his wall.

"*The Blue Newspaper.*"

"Oh," he'd said. As in all of James's work that he'd seen, there was an abstract element that allowed for a shrewd balance between figure and ground. Different things came forward in different lights, in different moods. At first he'd thought the painting was about the girls, then the newspaper and the man unseen behind its blue pages. Lately, he'd been thinking that finally what mattered was the purple wall, that what stood in the background was foremost. But tonight, in the candlelight, again it was the girls, more particularly their dresses, summer dresses luminous in the candlelight. This fragile human world.

He eased onto his side. There, on the floor next to the bed, he'd rolled out a mid-nineteenth-century Yomut *engsi*, a yurt "door rug." Of the whole oriental-rug-shop décor that had made his carriage house infamous, especially after the "Thousand and One Bad Nights" feature in *Metro Life*, this rug and the sacred shelf were the only decorations he'd brought with him from Pittsburgh to Granada. The *engsi* was a design known as *hatchlu*, which Cy had read somewhere meant cruciform, though he'd never done the research to determine whether or not this was true. The field, a deep, purplish brown, was barred into four separate quarters, which made the gloss on *hatchlu* plausible. He had come to know a great deal about rugs. He knew the sources of the dyes; he knew many of the names for the designs. The extended ends of this rug, the *elems*, were decorated with Yomut firs at the top and Yomut eagles at the bottom. Small geometric motifs, *guls*, seemed to float in diagonal bands across the four quarters of the field. They looked winged, and each one had a tiny blue cross at its center. It was the way *guls* were handled in Turkoman weavings that drew Cy to their work; he knew that. Although there were often, in old tribal pieces especially, irregularities in the colors of the *guls*, the design itself was repeating; indeed, the suggestion was that it was eternally repeating, that the borders of the rug arbitrarily framed a design that went on forever. Once Cy had seen this, he'd loved them.

When he'd left Pittsburgh he'd attached a name to each of his many carpets, and in an addendum to his will he'd asked that the carpets be dispersed according to those tags. Some of the people getting them, he suspected, would be very surprised to be remembered.

When the last candle went out Cy rolled onto his back. He understood he wasn't going to worry about the consequences of using the stick. He was the one there with a stick in his hand, the one who had heard the child's cry. Using it had fallen to him. He had done the only thing possible, submitted.

James rinsed Asur's cuts and abrasions with hydrogen peroxide and applied antibiotic salve and then Band-Aids. The child had tried to hide the evidence but was clearly a boy. When he realized James had seen he cupped his hand over his groin and squeezed his eyes shut, whispering, "*Un error.* God made a mistake between my legs."

"I won't tell," James said. "It's your secret." But her heart ached. "Poor boy," she whispered; she thought the world would make the child pay for God's error.

In her bedroom, James searched her closet for a calf-length cotton tunic in a figured print. She found it and a black, ribbed sweater that had shrunk in the wash. They were not girl's clothes, but would do. The green dress was ruined.

The child accepted the clothes meekly but would not sleep inside. He insisted on sleeping on the veranda, close to the Darro. So James prepared a bed with a couple of loose cushions and a blanket, set out a bottle of juice, some bread and a few olives, and, without comment, two blood oranges.

"Can you tell me what happened?" she asked.

But he couldn't, couldn't begin to tell her. It was only after she'd left him to sleep that he connected the tall man with the stick with James's friend. So James would find out. His humiliation would be complete. He didn't think to be thankful that Cy had been there to save him.

II

Cy stood at the counter in Nujaila, the Moroccan bakery on Calderería Nueva. When he'd first come to Granada he'd been tempted by the shop's sweets, each one a surprise for being unfamiliar, sweets of the Maghreb. Now he came for the bread, very dense and chewy, and sometimes a bottle of sour, cultured milk, which reminded him of buttermilk. It sat well with him. Now he left the sweets alone. He liked the brisk manner of the shopkeeper, the big, comprehending eyes behind round glasses.

Both the shopkeeper and his wife kept to traditional clothes, and looking at them Cy expected to hear the muezzin's call over the Albayzín at any moment, and he wished he would. This shop, more than any other place he knew in Granada, recalled North Africa, peopled the Islamic buildings of Al-Andalus.

The wife was counting out Cy's change when he heard his name called. He swiveled round, saw a woman's silhouette in the doorway. He smiled, but it took him a minute to place her. Paula. He lifted his package, two small loaves wrapped neatly in waxed paper and a small bottle of the cultured milk carefully arranged in a plastic sack. "Thank you," he said, waving to the shopkeeper, who nodded quietly in return. Cy wasn't making much progress with being friendly, though he worked at it every time he was in, three or four times a week.

"Do you shop at Nujaila?" Cy asked, outside, walking on down toward the plaza in Paula's company.

"Never tried it. Should I?"

"Well, yes, I think so, the only real bread in the city, as far as I've been able to tell. If you like bread, of course." He lifted out a loaf. "Feel the weight of this," he said, handing it over.

She lurched into Cy when he let go, as if the weight were too much for her. "A regular brick," she laughed.

"But it's good!"

"I'll take your word for it."

"Maybe you shouldn't. Shall we have a cup of coffee in the plaza? I'll cut you a piece of bread, and you can taste it for yourself." Cy listened to his own chatter as if it were a conversation overheard. And surprising to him. He sounded flirtatious. No doubt Paula heard that note, too; he suspected it was something she heard regularly, with her fey good looks. She didn't seem to take it amiss, in any case, agreeing at once to his suggestion.

"How about Mardini's?" she said. "I like that guy."

Cy liked that guy, Imad, too. A real adventurer in languages. Although he spoke little enough English or German or French, he spoke them all with charming conviction. Loudly, with gestures. A delightful guy, the show of service he put on was worth the price of a coffee every time.

They settled in under a large canvas umbrella. When Imad came to the table, Paula had no trouble whatever convincing him to bring two plates and butter for the bread. She asked him if he'd like to sit and join them. Of course he said no, pleading work, but he produced the plates and the butter and two cups of steaming *café con leche* with a flourish. Paula was clearly a favorite of his as well.

"So when do *I* get to read your book," she pouted histrionically.

"James has it, sorry." Cy cocked his head, wondering why she was asking. "I only brought the one copy."

"And James has it . . . I liked what I read. Funny stuff. And you seem to know something about women."

"A flattering conclusion," Cy said carefully.

"I had a favorite, just of the ones I read."

"Really." Paula was acting shy, Cy thought, her head down, looking half through her dark hair in his direction, but she wasn't shy, he was sure of that. She was just enjoying the fetching act.

"Well?"

"Okay, which one?"

"'Twenty-three is Flesh.'"

"Oh, that one," Cy said, actually embarrassed.

"A suggestive ambiguity in that title."

"Thank you."

"But what you said is so true."

"Which thing?"

"Well, *What She Said*." Paula laughed. "So many men do have a paint-by-numbers understanding of a woman's body. Erogenous zones and all that." Cy waited for her to continue.

"How-to books. Diagrams. A lot like paint-by-numbers, really, and nothing at all like painting."

Cy raised his eyebrows sympathetically, wondering where Paula would take this.

"You're not the guy in the poem, are you?"

"Of course not!"

"What was her name?"

"Karen," Cy said, without hesitation, laughing roguishly, "and no end of trouble."

"Still, the poem catches perfectly what it feels like to find yourself in bed with a man with a diagram in his head."

"Oh?"

"Sam, for instance."

"Sam?" Cy asked, somewhat taken aback.

"Yes, and look, there he is!" Paula pointed over the tabletops toward the kiosk where Sam stood buying a newspaper. "Should I call him over?" She looked over at Cy, a question, if not the one she'd asked, on her beautiful face.

"Sure," Cy said, "why not?"

"Well, I can think of at least one reason, but . . ." and she turned and waved, catching Sam's attention so easily that Cy thought he must already have seen them.

Sam sat down, smiling. "I wondered where you'd gotten off to, my dear, and here I find you deep in conversation with another man." Sam nodded toward Cy. "A perfectly nice man, I'm sure," he added, a hint of sarcasm in his voice.

"We were sampling the bread from Nujaila. Paula said you hadn't tried it, so . . ."

"But we have tried it," Sam said, waving to Imad, who was already carrying out an espresso for him. "Paula, I thought you found it a little grainy, too healthy, or some such? Preferred bread a little more refined, I think you said?"

"Yes. But that was over a month ago. A girl gets tired of the same old thing all the time, however refined."

"I should imagine. Anyway, Cy, thank you, but I admit to having had the experience before."

"We were talking about poetry, Sam. Cy's quite a well-known poet."

"He does have the look. Wispy!" Sam smiled wryly, tasting his espresso. "How long are you staying in Granada, Cy?"

"Oh, the duration," Cy said simply, "though I may be taking a little trip to Morocco. I haven't been in years."

"But we're going!" Paula said. "After you left the other night I asked James if she thought you might be interested in coming along."

"She mentioned it."

"She said she didn't know. Would you like to? Travel with us? If it's okay with you, Sam? I mean, since we're all going, we'd have strength in numbers; we'd be able to overpower the touts."

"I doubt that," Cy laughed. "We'd need tear gas . . . Anyway, no thank you. Probably I won't go. And I prefer not to travel in a party. No offense?"

"None taken," Sam rapped out, as if there was nothing more to be said on the subject. He jingled the change in the pocket of his loose white ducks. "I'm heading back up to the *cármene*," he added, having counted out change enough and then some. He centered his straw hat, said goodbye, and strode off purposively.

"He means I should get back to work, too," Paula said.

"James said you're overseeing a restoration?"

"You're welcome to visit, or just inspect," she said, giving him the address. "Where do you live?"

Cy gave her his number on Placeta de la Cruz Verde.

"And am I welcome?"

"I imagine you find yourself welcome just about wherever you go."

When James woke up Asur was gone. The cushions had been arranged in a neat stack, the bedding folded. Looking over the railing down into the Darro, James felt a momentary dismay at how responsibility crept up, if this was responsibility. She felt quite sure the boy would be back. She went inside to paint. Again, she was surprised at how easily she solved the problems she found on the canvases, moving from one to another and back again. Even as she was painting, she was aware that the size of the problems, their felt magnitude, seemed reduced. She felt that she was working in a world amenable to her interventions.

Around noon she realized with a start that she'd been painting for almost four hours, a day's work done. She cleaned up carefully, scraping the last of the paint residue off the glass she used to mix paints on with a hard spatula. She sat outside while she cleaned the brushes, the bristles blue from use, letting the fumes disperse in the light breeze that cooled her veranda. It was a warm day, the sky a hard blue and close. She wondered if the defended space she'd made for her painting might not be too hermetically sealed, if there might be some final difficulty in the distance she'd made between herself and the world of entanglements.

While she was setting out lunch Asur returned, carrying a black plastic sack stuffed with boy's clothes. He came to the back door and

James let him in. He was limping and his face was bruised, but he seemed not to notice. He sat on the floor in her studio looking at the wall of mirrors while she finished making lunch, putting together another plate and filling a second glass full of juice. They ate on the veranda. James asked the boy his name.

"Asur," he said, simply.

James said, "I'll leave the cushions out at night; if you need a place to sleep, Asur, you can sleep there. It's okay."

He said, "Thank you. When it gets late I'm scared to be a girl."

After lunch, she left him on the veranda, quietly locking the door into the house. He sat outside on a chair, in her clothes, trying to juggle the balled-up socks he had fished out of his sack. He must have practiced before. He had no trouble juggling three socks at once and could keep four going for a while. James watched his face, smiled at his look of gleeful concentration. A gamin, no doubt. But she found the face interesting, and the way he moved unusual. She thought that soon she would sketch him. She thought he would find a way into her paintings.

She went out. She walked into the plaza, then further afield, down into the new town with its tightly packed low-rise apartment blocks. At Corte Inglés she went in, bought groceries in the basement and lifted the bags for the long walk back home. She stopped for an ice cream cone, watching the flow of people on the sidewalks. She let her eyes wander, the pattern of a dress carrying over onto a wall, a man in a suit in front of a shop window. Leaf shadows teeming like small fish. She loved the look of reflections, the plaques of light made by windshields, the shininess of glass and paint and the matte texture of stone and stucco. The world so rich in color and shadow, all of it revealed by light, made of light. Light was the great solvent, and James often felt dissolved in it, ravished by it. She knew this experience was related to her desire to paint, but that painting held back from it. She held back from it. For order. She wanted dissolution *and* order.

The ice cream was wonderful, *arroz con leche*. Sweet and chewy. Her mind turned to the boy, Asur. Afraid to be a girl late at night. But not afraid to be a girl sometimes, not afraid to be Luz. She thought she counted that brave rather than not. Of those who found themselves in the wrong body, how many admitted it even to themselves when they were children?

She knew it would be a sad story that had led Asur to climb the vines up onto her veranda in the night, a boy alone already at what, ten maybe? Nine? How he must have clung to his own truths, however he understood them. She thought he deserved a break, a break he was not likely to get. She could think of ways to help him get by, day to day, but long-term she couldn't even imagine what real help might be. She could let him sleep on the veranda, see he had something to eat. Buy him some clothes. She would. But it didn't seem like much more than putting out a bowl of scraps for a stray cat.

12

Although the morning was mostly spent, Cy still wore a bathrobe, a beautiful old thing worn soft, with a silk rope for a tie. The robe had been a gift, yet another gift from a lover. A Beacon robe, a thirties design. Its blue ground suggested a night sky, the figure a pattern of tawny diamonds hung in a grid. How it had found its way into his luggage, he couldn't remember. But it had proven useful in Granada, where the nights and mornings could be cold, even in late spring. The snow on the Sierra Nevada visible just over the low hills said so. The morning sky had not yet cleared, though it promised to. Soon it would be time to dress.

Cy tilted the spout of his watering can over a pot of geraniums, then moved on to the next, leaning with his off hand against the wrought-iron railing on the terrace edge, head averted a little from the *placeta* below. The morning had been difficult. But the nausea seemed to be going. He had come to recognize the signs of relief as surely as the signs of onset. *Naus*, he thought again, and this must be the boatman's feeling when he sails into the smooth water of a safe harbor. The sickness abates.

Cy leaned down to break off a dead flower. When he straightened back up, the geranium smell was strong on his hand. He liked the smell of it now, astringent and clean, though back in Pittsburgh he'd thought the smell too loud, almost unbearable.

"Cy?" Sam stood on the cobbles down below, dapper as ever. "I think a girl would know better than to wear a dress so near the railing."

"Probably she would. But another girl might stand at the rail just for that reason. Don't you think?"

"Likely."

"I'm the second kind of girl."

"So I've heard. Some kind of reverse braggart?"

"Perhaps perverse," Cy said, "but I'm glad to hear you suggest there might be art in it." Sam burlesqued a bow. "Want to come up?"

Sitting in the sun, they did not make a pair. Sam sleek, groomed, an expensive Panama shading his alert blue eyes. Cy in his robe, hatless and unshaved, his feet stuffed sockless into scuffed Doc Martens. Cy felt suddenly seedy, but thought compared to Sam he'd probably always been a bit seedy. He liked to dress, for occasions, but didn't require it for himself. Sam, he thought, probably did.

"When are you going to Morocco?" Cy asked.

"Soon. Waiting on a couple of phone calls. People to meet, and no use going if they're not going to be there. Besides, we have a car—a Ford Ka—so we can be on our way in a matter of minutes."

"So it's a business trip?"

"Yes. Shopping, more or less. How about you, are you going?"

"Perhaps. But it would be strictly sightseeing of the lowest order. Just walking around, looking."

"I wouldn't call that the lowest order," Sam allowed. "Most people are led around, and if they're looking, they're not doing much seeing. Especially in Morocco, where, as you know, the street touts in the cities pretty much pester most folks right back onto their tour busses if not clear out of the country. It's interesting to see just how poorly most people protect themselves from the assault."

"Yes."

"But you are? Protected, I mean."

"Protected? I can be."

"Well then," Sam said, "it's a magical country. Good place for vice, too, if your taste runs that way."

"I've never found vice to require a particular country." Sam looked at him approvingly, but Cy shook his head. "I'm afraid my vices are tamer than what you seem to be imagining."

"One of the timid of the earth?"

"Wouldn't that depend on what I desire?"

"Perhaps," Sam said, considering, "but perhaps it depends on how fully you act on your desires. Desire, indulged to surfeit, and then on to something new and perhaps unexpected . . ."

"Is that your experience?"

"Yes, it is."

"But you and Paula? Aren't the two of you, what, a couple?"

Sam laughed at the question. "Careful now, effrontery is my game."

"Surely two can play?"

"Exactly. And two can play at vice. We have. We're partners, mostly it's business, but not always. Pleasure is allowed." Sam seemed altogether at ease, if prickly.

"Oh," Cy said simply.

"Don't lose your nerve so easily! Cy, surely you want the lowdown? I mean, your profession, those poems must be an open invitation, how would you say it, for folks to 'unload'?"

Cy's *oh* hadn't been in response to what Sam had said. He'd seen "his" vagrant walking across the *placeta*, his face striped with two angry welts, one, a scabby line across the forehead, and the other running at an angle down from his eyebrow, across his mouth, and onto his chin. That eye was swollen shut and both lips had been split. He hadn't looked up toward Cy, and Cy began to hope that the man had been so drunk, or the lot so dark, that he didn't know who had struck him.

Cy said, "Many have, unloaded, I mean." The man had sat down on the steps across the way and seemed to be intent on screwing the top off a bottle wrapped in a paper sack.

"Paula widened my horizons, at first, anyway," Sam said. "Beautiful, I'm sure you noticed, but my thought was, useful. Tremendously talented at restoration. But I didn't have much of a job to offer her, at least not money up front. So, I thought, seduce her. Aren't most women led around by the short rope of their affections?"

"I thought that was whoever cared most," Cy said. The man had hardly raised his bottle once when two more regulars walked into the *placeta*, one carrying a drum, the other a guitar. Impressive nose for a free drink, Cy thought.

"Isn't that generally the woman? At least that's what I've found," Sam observed. "You wouldn't think it, but Paula was inexperienced, very. As if she'd been waiting to be touched a long time. When I put my hand on her arm, just lightly—we were in a gallery—her hips came up, her breasts; her head rolled back; and her eyes went wide and blurred. I swear, just standing there, I could smell her."

The guy with the guitar started to strum. Cy said nothing.

"She was up for anything and skittish at the same time. Wanted it, and wanted to run. I don't know; I thought I saw the root of the thing in her."

"What thing?"

"Sex. Desire. Oh. I approved, mind you. But we hadn't been together a week when she said she thought she liked things a shade darker than I did. Several shades, as it turned out, but it was a moving target. I mean, I soon learned to like what she liked. Still, the one of me was not enough. Pretty soon she was bringing home the neighborhood."

The drummer was working on a syncopated rhythm that had nothing to do with what the guitar player was committing on the strings. Cy thought it looked like a good day to get out of the house. Finally, he turned to Sam. "Real trouble, eh?"

"Real trouble. But useful at the same time. I began to worry she would disappear on me. So I widened my net. Lust isn't the only desire."

"Do you mean this as a warning, Sam?"

"Exactly."

"You have very little to worry about from me, really. I'm surprised you'd think I look like competition." Cy's attention wandered. He wanted a shower. He wanted to be alone or with someone he liked better. "You needn't have been so oblique, you know," he added.

"Nothing at all surprising about a lover issuing warnings."

"A lover? I thought you were the one pledged to Eros?"

"Perhaps I am."

Later, standing at the mirror shaving, Cy remembered Sam's phrase, *pledged to Eros*, and he thought it said a good deal about him, more, no doubt, than Sam could imagine. He wondered if love was a habit, that it still occupied him now? Or had he somehow written his name in love's book, pledged his mortal self? He wondered if it was love that kept death, most of the time, at a distance. Sometimes fear came for him, for a moment, or a minute, or even a bad night of cold shakes. But most of the time this world still seemed the more real place. He loved. He loved James's uncoordinated walk, her abstraction and her absorption. Her uprightness. And he wasn't proof against Paula's charms, either. *Charms!* Her bedroom eyes and outspoken readiness. The constellation of freckles that somehow seemed to stand in front of her face. He shook his head. His eyes had not grown tired of women, nor of much else. He longed for the world. He wasn't ready to give it up, not yet.

The sky had cleared low down in the west and a late-afternoon sun slanted over the city, thick and yellow. Asur had led the way down into the riverbed of the Darro and the three of them, Asur, James, and Cy, were walking downstream in the shadows of the tall stone walls that contained the river where it ran along the shoulder of the Albayzín. On the Alhambra side, the stone walls were continuous with the foundations of buildings that seemed to tower over them.

They walked under a bridge, a single stone arch, and Asur pointed to the vines that grew out of the riverbed up to James's veranda. He had gathered together a few table scraps at lunch, and he now began feeding a family of cats that lived among the exposed roots of a scraggly tree. James smiled. Traffic rumbled along Carrera del Darro, but down in the riverbed it sounded muted, distant. They seemed to have dropped down out of Granada, to be invisible where they walked along the Darro toward the great arch where the river flowed out of this world into the underworld of the city. Above, the familiar spectacle of the Plaza Nueva must have been in full swing, but here there was nothing but a great brick arch with a dated keystone, the river running under it into darkness.

Cy sat on a rock and tore a piece of paper from his notebook, a piece of paper on which he'd begun to write a poem. He folded it expertly into a tidy boat; he found his hands had forgotten nothing of his childhood passion for paper boats. Asur watched keenly, waiting. Cy folded a second boat, then a third. He gave one to James and one to Asur, and nodded toward the water. The Darro ran in a riffle then opened into a pool just before it disappeared into deep shadow.

The boy asked for a pen and wrote his name, Asur rather than Luz, on the side of his boat, then set it in the water. Immediately, it raced from his hand, bobbing and turning wildly on the small riffles before sailing out, suddenly almost dignified, into the smooth water of the pool. Even before Asur's boat was out of the riffles, James set hers on the water; if it did not keep its prow forward very well, it did not capsize either. Then there were two boats, steady, in the pool. Cy held his boat out toward James, gesturing, and said, "Now *this* is a sonnet for Orpheus." Then he set his boat into the water, too. Perhaps he reached a little further out than James or Asur had, because his boat moved swiftly in a fast, central current, and riding high, sailed past the other two out into the center of the pool, and on, into a subterranean world.

"Have you been thinking about Rilke's *Sonnets*," James asked, "the one you read me?"

Cy smiled at her, watching Asur, looking so childlike, transfixed by the boats, but of course he *was* a child.

"'Be in advance of all parting,'" she quoted effortlessly.

"It's hard advice," Cy said, "to be 'ever dead in Eurydice.' Not the advice, if I had any, that I'd be giving to Asur, to a child, setting out on life, however fraught it's likely to be."

James stepped up beside Cy, who was sitting again with his tablet on his knees, putting her hand on his shoulder. "No," she said. "And Eurydice must have wanted more life, trying to walk out of hell that way, climbing to the sound of the lyre."

Cy nodded, then said, "But I wasn't thinking about that poem."

James laughed. "Okay then," she said.

The last of the boats had disappeared into the mouth of the tunnel, and Asur ran back upstream, asking for another. Cy folded one from a clean sheet of paper. James knelt down beside him, and using the tablet on Cy's knee for a table, quickly decorated the tiny boat's hull with "magic" signs; "*Mágico*," she said to the boy. Under the bill of his cap, Asur's face wore a lopsided grin, the terrors of the night for a while forgotten. At first the boy had been shy when Cy had turned up at James's door, remembering, no doubt, that it had been Cy who had brandished the stick, who had seen his shaming.

Asur carried the boat on upstream, to the pool above, to give it a longer run. James sat down on the rocks next to Cy, crossing her legs, suddenly quiet. Cy sat quietly, too, while Asur ran down the Darro, in the water, in the wake of his boat.

"I meant it as a joke, my poem sailing into Hades, the underworld, just over there."

"Yes."

"But I have been thinking about Rilke. Do you know the *Sonnets to Orpheus* were dedicated to a girl, to Wera Ouckama Knoop?"

She didn't know.

"Back in Pittsburgh I had a picture of her. Sometimes I'd take it out, just to look at her. Just a face, to me. And for Rilke she was no more than an acquaintance, or less, the daughter of acquaintances. A peculiar beauty, an Oriental cast to her eyes; Rilke himself remarked it. But diseased. A glandular disorder. The girl, a dancer, suffered a sudden and growing heaviness in her limbs, until she could not dance, and didn't want to. So she made music, until she had to give that up, too. Then she began to draw. And then she died, at nineteen. I guess Rilke thought of her as Eurydice to his Orpheus."

"But aren't the sonnets to Orpheus?"

"Yes. But he celebrates the girl in one of them, in #25. Her dying he calls entering '*das trostlos offene Tor*; the hopeless, open door.'"

"Ah, just so."

"His mom dressed him like a girl, of course."

"What?"

"Rilke's mom. Georg Trakl's too. Apparently a good beginning for a poet."

"I hadn't realized."

"Maybe Asur has the makings," Cy joked uneasily, "our Luz," he said, looking at the child framed downstream by the mouth of the great culvert.

"Not quite the same case, I think."

"No, not the same case," he agreed. "Their mothers dressed them up like dolls. Asur's mother disowned him for a dress."

"That's what he says."

"I can believe it."

"Oh, I can believe it, too."

While Asur tried on the skirt and blouse James had bought for him, James showed Cy two new mirrors. One was quite attractive, old, with a green, Bakelite handle. "Gifts from Asur," she said. "I imagine he steals them."

Cy looked into her worried face. "No doubt," he said at last.

"I wish he wouldn't! What if he were arrested? And look at this." James had walked over to her worktable and picked up a raw, clay figure, cruciform, and oddly compelling. "He left this as a gift before I ever met him. When Paula was here, she recognized it. She didn't seem distressed, but she'd seen the thing before, I'm sure of it."

"So tell the kid no more gifts."

"I was thinking maybe I'd hire him. To run errands, and maybe to sit. I have an idea for a painting . . ."

Asur walked in wearing a polka-dot skirt, light yellow with small green spots, and a white blouse, gathered around his shoulders with elastic. They clapped and he jumped, smiling, hair free now around his face.

"Cy, there's something I've been wanting to play for you." She was flipping through a stack of CDs. "This one," she said, opening the jewel case and putting the CD into her changer. "Your talking about Lahore, about Pakistan, reminded me of Nusrat Fateh Ali Khan."

"Oh yes, Nusrat."

"Those songs he did with Eddie Vedder for *Dead Man Walking*."

Cy nodded.

"Have you heard the version of 'Long Road' from the movie's score?"

Cy hadn't, so she played it. "'Long Road,'" he said. "'We all walk the long road, cannot stay.'"

Cy's eyes had teared up.

"Dance with me," she said. And while they were dancing, James like a gift in his arms, she whispered, "All our dance partners, Cy, all our lovers, walk the long road. Everyone we've ever laid down with someday will lie down with death."

"'Cannot stay,'" he said.

"'Cannot stay.' That doesn't make it a *danse macabre*."

They looked across the room at Asur, Luz, spinning in the new skirt in front of James's wall of mirrors. The skirt pinwheeled out and they laughed and the child was suddenly self-conscious, but pleased, they could see that, with the new clothes.

❧

13

Sam clicked his cell phone shut and slipped it into his pocket. "*Inshallah*," he murmured.

"So it's that kind of deal?" Paula spoke quietly, setting down her fork. They'd been in the middle of dinner when the call came but Paula had gone on eating, not one to let her food get cold when the call was for Sam. He sometimes kept secrets about the business; she never knew why. For all his bravado there was a core of caution in how he went about things. Perhaps he felt secrets were safer, but Paula thought if she was going to share the risks, she should know what they were. Under that, she just didn't like the caution; it was an itch she had to scratch.

"What kind of deal?" Sam said abstractedly, looking uncharacteristically weary.

"The *inshallah* kind."

"For Muslims everything depends on God's will."

"Yes," Paula said, "but God's part is insisted on more when the odds are long, wouldn't you say?" She picked up her wine glass off the worktable, gazing around the courtyard, looking fetching, she imagined. She had pulled her hair back and worn an off-the-shoulder blouse, just to get Sam's attention, but she noticed she wasn't getting it. She went back to eating, pulling at a stale baguette with her teeth. "How much do we stand to make on this deal, anyway?"

"That's the good news, a great deal."

"If?"

"If the Qur'ans are good enough. I'll be counting on you to know, and that's part of the problem." Paula looked blank, so he added, "Your being a woman."

"Come on!"

"They're very conservative."

"The sellers?"

"Yes, if we actually meet the sellers. But even their representatives, in Morocco, would be very conservative, fundamentalists." Again, a fugitive look crossed Sam's features, weariness or wariness.

"Who are the sellers?" Paula found herself interested; she hadn't intended to be.

"I don't know."

"What?"

Slowly, unwillingly, Sam began to explain. The sellers were in the resistance in Algeria, or were terrorists, depending on how you looked at it. Terrorism, apparently, is expensive, and sometimes there are shortfalls. Payments from abroad gone astray, robberies at home not producing the expected cash. "What do I care?" Sam threw up his hands. "It's an opportunity for us. They have two very old Qur'ans, thirteenth or fourteenth century, out of Spain—illuminated, quite wonderful." He pulled a stack of Polaroids out of his pocket and pushed them across the table. "Herr Schmidt, in Munich, he wants them. The Algerians will deal but for cash only. Still, Herr Schmidt is willing to assume the financial risk; he'll front the money. He's very excited about the pictures he's seen of the Qur'ans. It's a mania with him. He said he'll drop everything and meet us in Seville with the money on two day's notice. And come back as soon as we have the Qur'ans in Spain."

"So what's that leave for us?"

"Authenticating them, judging the condition, handling the negotiations, and bringing them back across the channel into Spain."

"The expertise and the risk?"

"I guess so. But Herr Schmidt is free with his money, and if we can drive a bargain there should be plenty to skim." With that, Sam returned to his cold dinner, a steak he had grilled himself. "I'd be happier," he said, setting his knife back down, "if we were in direct contact with the sellers. Instead, we have the American, Alan Williams, who is in contact with the sellers' representatives, who in turn are in contact with the sellers. Too many links. Not to mention our Herr Schmidt, who is a bit of a thug under his bespoke suits."

Paula looked up from the photos. "Masterwork," she said, "or seems to be. I'll want to do a little research, just to be ready to know what I'm seeing."

Sam nodded. He liked Paula, he did, when she showed her useful side. "You're the expert," he said warmly, winking at her, "really," he added.

"Sam, I've been meaning to tell you," Paula paused until she had his attention, "you remember those figurines we bought when we were gathering up pottery shards? Just to keep that fat guy happy?

Well, it's the oddest thing, but I saw one of them over at James's little house."

"What were you doing over there?"

"I wanted to borrow Cy's book, *What She Said*, but James wouldn't let me. I think she means to keep Cy for herself," she paused, "or try."

Sam shot her a sardonic smile. "The same figurine, not just something similar?"

"The very one. Of course, I wondered what it was doing at her house. I almost asked her, but I didn't. When I got back here I looked for it in my workroom, just to double-check. One of them was there. The other one is at her place."

"She never went near your workroom when she was here for dinner," Sam said emphatically. "We never got as far as the tour."

"I don't think she stole it!"

Sam looked thoughtful. "Do you want it back?"

"Not particularly. I didn't want it much in the first place. It has that fertility-goddess look. I don't really want any of that mojo around here. Let's leave the babies to James . . ."

"Sorry business mixing up sex and fertility."

"Very." She looked at Sam speculatively. "If you didn't look so tired," she said, "perhaps we could sort them out." She waited a moment, thinking he looked old as much as tired, and when he didn't respond with alacrity, she added, "But perhaps it would be better if I sorted them alone."

"Simpler," Sam quipped, having the last word at least.

Asur spread the cushions James had left for him on the veranda so
that they fit flush against the iron railing. When he lay down, he
turned his face to the rail, so he could look out over the river below
to Carrera del Darro. James was walking with Cy down there. They
had been up and back several times, often stopping to lean on the
stone wall over the river and look down, into running water. Sometimes they looked up as well, and once James had waved, and Asur
had waved back, his hand showing white in the streetlight against
the darkened veranda. He'd pulled the blanket up to his neck. He
felt homesick; the soft cushions, the clean blanket, reminded him
of his old bed. And he felt safe. He looked forward to a good dream,
something summery; maybe he would fly, as he often did in dreams.
He loved to watch flying birds, the swallows that worked the river in
the evening, even the bats that came out later. They seemed happy in
their wings. He felt air must be a very different thing to them than
it was to him.

He wondered idly what James and Cy were talking about down
there, what they could have to say so much about. He thought them
strange, but like him they were people who had left home and come
here. He didn't know why. He didn't ask. They liked him and let him
be. He thought he should do the same for them.

Asur looked straight down. He had seen movement down there.
Watching carefully, he could see a shape floating over the river rocks
toward a tree just downstream. The mother cat, something in her
mouth, was returning to her kittens, hidden in a tangle of roots. A
gray tabby, the cat was hard to see, seemed to disappear only to reap-
pear farther on, though she was walking in the open the whole time.
Now he heard the frantic mewing of the kittens. Suddenly, the tabby

leapt at the base of the tree and the mewing stopped. The catch must have been satisfactory. A rat, perhaps. Asur had seen them often in the vines along the Darro.

James and Cy walked on down toward the plaza, James with her arm linked with Cy's, Cy with his stick flashing in the streetlight. Asur could hear the stick tapping on the cobblestones; it was late and there was little traffic to cover the sound. He heard James laugh, a musical, weightless sound. He remembered having heard such a laugh only a few times in his life. Most of the laughter he'd heard in the village had been cruel. The child tried to laugh now, to laugh like James, a floating, approving sound. He could not. He sensed but could not understand that her kind of laughter could not be forced, that it required abandon. Then, for a moment, he felt jealous, and he wished Cy would go back to his house on Cruz Verde and stay there.

When he woke up it was still dark, not morning, not even close to morning. He realized he had been awakened by a sound, and then he knew it had been James. A match flared inside and she lit a candle. He could see her walking now, back and forth in front of the paintings she had been working on that morning, holding the candle up to them, one after the other. She took down one, then a second, and spread them on her worktable. Another she shook her head at and took down as well, setting it aside. That only left a single canvas on the wall, and she moved it down to the end, closest to the door onto Santa Ana. On the bare wall she pinned up two large sheets of paper side by side, then, shaking her head again, added a third, making a wide, white streak in the candlelit room.

She lit a second candle. She did not look toward the veranda, where Asur now lay watching her, entranced. She seemed, to the boy, possessed, and a little wild. She was sketching with charcoal, stepping in close suddenly and then stepping back, to stare fixedly at the wall. Her twin shadows leapt around the room while she drew, and stopped, abruptly, when she stepped back. Then her still shadows stood grotesquely elongated on the ceiling and back walls, across the twinkling mirrors.

She looked too big to Asur, monstrous. Her candlelit face revealed a hard, down-turned mouth that seemed, occasionally, to gasp for air; her forehead was knit, her eyes looked black and glittering. She wore black tights and a black smock, and except for her hands her body seemed more a phantom than flesh, more real in the shadows it cast than in itself.

James walked up to the sketch and leaned her forehead into the wall. She closed her eyes, just waiting. When she stepped back she saw it again, and she sketched quickly, with broad strokes, using the side of the charcoal now. Then she knew she was done. She walked toward the cupboard in the kitchen where she kept the Scotch, dropping her charcoal into a plastic tub as she passed the paint-laden tea cart. She poured out two fingers then walked back into the room, turning the chair from her worktable toward the new sketch. She drank. She felt drained, washed out. She was surprised by the sketch, by the size of it. She hadn't tried anything so big since art school. But she felt certain that the size was right. She slumped a little, her left eye compressed into a squint, considering. She knew a corner had been turned. It happened like that. She always painted within the strictures of an idea, not an idea exactly, a way of seeing. It seemed a world, and full of variations, thick with possibilities. She felt engaged, even immersed, in just this way of seeing. Then, quite suddenly, and without much warning, she would turn away from it, turn toward what for her was the next thing. Sometimes, the turn was proceeded by a staleness, a dry time, but sometimes, this time, the new way of seeing just swept aside what she had been doing. The change was heartless and absolute. She might tidy up, finish a painting or two in what was now the old manner, but she would never start another one. She would begin with the new, not looking back.

Time for a show, she thought. She'd e-mail the galleries that represented her, see when a slot for her work might be available. Looking around, she saw there were enough paintings for two, perhaps even three small exhibitions. She'd take some slides, decide which ones talked to each other, and arrange something. She'd probably need to make a short trip, perhaps even two, to attend openings. But there was no hurry. She'd ask for slots in the fall. Los Angeles, New York, perhaps Santa Fe.

James shook her head. Time enough to worry the business side of things later. She looked again at the big sketch. The owners of the galleries where she sold her work had been trying to get her to paint large canvases for years. She had resisted, just as she always resisted suggestions about her work. Paint big! As if the issue entailed nothing more than the size of the canvas. It didn't work that way. Things came in sizes. She didn't choose, she obeyed.

She liked the sketch. It was only a suggestion, but she knew already there was a painting in it. She had a feeling about the palette.

A strong sense of what was coming. Suddenly, she started, her head swiveling toward the door to the veranda, where Asur stood, arms down at his sides, just outside the glass. He was wearing only his underwear; his thin limbs shone dully in the candlelight, pale and waxy. His head was tilted to the side. A look of tremendous sadness suffused his beautiful face. His cheeks were wet; not so long ago he had been crying.

"Asur?" James said, opening the door. "Are you okay? ¿Estás bien? I," and she paused, "I thought you were sleeping. Did I wake you?"

She stood aside and the boy walked into the room. "Agua," he said.

James brought him a glass of water and he said he'd had a bad dream. He looked at James as if she were a stranger.

"I'm sorry," she said. She started to speak again but fell silent. She really had nothing to be sorry for, nothing to apologize for, so she didn't. Finally, she said, "You'll feel better tomorrow."

Asur took the glass of water back out onto the veranda and huddled under the blanket. He lay awake there for a long time, long after the candles had been blown out inside. He looked at the stars and was frightened.

James explained to the boy that she was going away, that she was going with Cy down into Morocco for a few days, ten at the most. The explanation took a long time; her Spanish made her slow, like being stupid or a child all over again. She said he could sleep on the veranda, that it would be better not to go into the Albayzín at night, at least not as Luz. He nodded, he understood. She showed him a jar that she had stuffed full of pesetas. She told him if he ran short of money, he should take some from the jar, that he should not steal. She hid the jar in a bushy, potted plant while he was watching, so he'd know where to look if he needed it. She asked him to water the plants on the veranda and gave him a thousand pesetas for doing it. He nodded.

"*Mañana*," she said. "I'm going tomorrow."

Then she went inside to pack a small bag and a knapsack. She took a sketchpad and a few pencils. With that, she could work on the big painting, prepare for it. When she came back down to the studio Asur was gone. She liked him, but she wouldn't worry about him if she could help it. She thought he needed to find a way to go home, for a few years, anyway. Perhaps then, if he was lucky, he'd be able to find a small world within the great world to welcome him. But he seemed quite sure his mother would not take him back. He seemed to think he could make it on the streets. James hoped he could, but she doubted it.

They took an early train out of Granada, changing at Bobadilla for Algeciras. They arrived in the heat of the day; the air hung like a gas flame over the town when they stepped out of the train station, but as they walked toward the water they felt a sea breeze streaming over the roadbeds and by the time they arrived at Plaza Palma they were comfortable enough to sit in the open at the Panadería-Café, to drink coffee and enjoy the daily carnival parading over the pavement. They liked the city's rough edge, the visible signs that it was still rife with street dealers, small-time moneychangers, and nighthawks, haggard in daylight as molting birds. They listened to the noise of chattering fruit sellers and housewives asking loudly for prices and watched skeptical backpackers eyeing baskets of sad, skinny loaves in the open storefront of a bakery.

Cy smiled, sniffed at his coffee and set it down. He nodded at the backpackers. "Stocking up for the crossing. Perhaps we should, too," he said, "but not bread. Apples, maybe. Didn't we see a bag of apples walk by a few minutes ago?"

"Over there," James said, pointing at a fruit-and-vegetable stand a couple of stalls down from the bread.

"But it's a short crossing, one apple will likely be enough."

James smiled, happy. "It does seem like it should take longer, be farther . . ."

"To Africa?"

"Exactly."

But even expecting it, when the ferry nosed out into the Straits of Gibraltar, James could hardly believe how close Morocco looked. A few short miles. In clear weather, boats here crossed never out of sight of land. And the day was fair. The water was littered with ferries going to and fro. And big ships, tankers and ships deep in containers were passing in and out at the Gates of Hercules, between the Mediterranean on the left and the Atlantic on the right. There were sailboats and powerboats. Tugs and barges. Windsurfers and jet skis. But it was the other boats, the ones she imagined, small boats with dark sails, ragged, that James found the most compelling. There must have always been a great traffic here, on the sea roads, she thought, where the two continents reached out for each other.

She touched Cy's hand where it gripped the rail. He pointed to Gibraltar falling swiftly behind, the great profile of the rock already getting blue with distance. Then they turned toward Africa, toward Tangier. The teeming hillsides over the bay, Morocco.

Inevitably, James was thinking of Matisse, his Tangier, as the ferry pulled toward the city. She knew not to expect to see Matisse's *View of the Bay* in the actual bay where they would tie up. No. That had been 1912. But she thought there would be echoes, in the bay and in the old city. She would be looking through his *Porte de la Casbah* at every gate. And his *Amido*, that boy, Matisse's *petit morocain*, that boy made her think of Asur. Asur, she thought, would have loved Amido's tangerine-trimmed turquoise vest and pink pantaloons. And Amido's hand blurred by motion, somehow that was Asur's hand, juggling.

"Are you ready?" Cy asked.

"Ready or not."

❖

14

The train clacked and rocked as only a slow train can. Outside it was dark, the few lights far away. Motion was reduced to a sound, the sound of wind. Inside it was dark, too, no more than a muted glow from the corridor finding its way into their "first-class" compartment. Cy slept, his unguarded expression now surprisingly serene. Perhaps it was the angle, his head on her shoulder, clear brow, lashes beautiful as a girl's, his lips caught in a half smile. He didn't seem to realize that they were uncomfortable! She wondered about his dreams. If he dreamed forward, toward his end, or back, back into the life that had brought him here?

In the seat across an old man sat upright, eyes closed, asleep maybe, she couldn't tell. He radiated an unassailable dignity, or at least not assailed by the petty troubles of traveling. A yellow beard fell from his wrinkled face. He wore a small hat, a kind of nightcap; the hat was part of his dignity.

Before Cy woke up she saw the pain that had come to occupy his face—a constriction around his right eye. While he was still sleeping she ran her fingers lightly over his forehead, a gesture meant to soothe him but, she understood, useless except as gesture; he was still sleeping. She did it, she knew, for herself. She had not often found a way, when Cy was awake, for such tenderness. She was waiting for a sign from him.

The old man stood up abruptly, his face turned to the pale light in the glass of the sliding door. He seemed to be reassembling himself; then he pulled the door open and for a moment the compartment was softly lit. Cy stirred. James saw a match strike in the corridor and the old man's face stark in the sulfur light, then orange in the cigarette's glow. It's a long ride to Marrakech.

"Where are we?" Cy asked, straightening up.

"It's very hard to tell."

"Still in the dark?"

"Yes, Cy, still in the dark."

He smiled weakly. "Then it's as I expected."

"Headache?"

"Most of the time."

"Do painkillers help?"

"Some. Sometimes. I have my little war chest of pills. Advil to codeine. But I don't like the ones that affect how I think. I'm not ready for stupor. I hope never to be ready for stupor."

"Ready for stupor," James echoed. "Sounds like a rock band."

"Please," Cy said, "no loud music. And I'd prefer no rocking, if you can arrange that." Cy caught himself, said, "In the morning we'll be in Marrakech, and the trip will have been worth it."

The last time Cy had been in Marrakech it had been winter, November, the trees full of small oranges. He remembered the face of a girl from New Zealand, when she'd caught a loose lamb in the markets, carrying it back to its pen in her arms.

They rode in silence. The old Berber returned from the corridor and sat down heavily. The peculiar smell of the carriage, the smell of vinyl and wood washed over and over in dirty water, the grime never cleaned up so much as rubbed around, that smell permeated everything. And there was a human smell in it, acrid.

James looked out the window, at the indistinct reflections in the window. They might as well have been in the underworld.

"Why are *you* here?" Cy asked, his voice pitched low.

"Why are you asking?"

"I'm not sure what I'm asking, what you asked me at the Tuareg, I guess. Why Spain, why here on this train?"

"It's hard to begin."

"We're on a long journey."

"Yes."

"So begin anywhere. There will be time."

"There's a tedious financial side to the story. I owned a house I couldn't afford. Not a grand house, don't imagine that, just a cottage, really, but in Santa Barbara. There was the house, a couple of bedrooms, that's all, a courtyard with a studio across, a garage apartment originally, with the garage underneath. The courtyard sat on a crest, and the studio was on a level with the courtyard; the ground fell away quite abruptly. The walk up from the garage was steep. The situation was wonderful. A big piece of property with a broken view of the sea from the house. A wonderful old olive tree stood in the courtyard. A eucalyptus towered over the studio and kept the whole place smelling clean. Dusty white walls, faded and mottled roof tiles. Small pines. Cacti. Flowers. I grew up in that house; then I inherited it.

"I had graduated from RISD only a few years before, and though I was getting some shows, and selling some paintings, I could hardly have managed the taxes on the house, much less the mortgage, though it was a small mortgage."

"*Mort*gage," Cy interjected under his breath.

"But I loved that house. I went home, moved in. The sea was there, and on clear days the islands floated offshore like a small flotilla. The sun descended into the sea. Later, the moon. I watched them go. Mockingbirds sang in the trees, all those other birdsongs. Scrub jays peered up from under their silver eyebrows."

"Flotilla," Cy said quietly, but the interruption didn't feel impertinent, and James resumed, smiling in the dark, thinking she understood.

Her warm voice moved nimbly through the syllables. "For all that, the place was run down. My mother had let it go. I spent a good part of every day in the yard under a plaited hat. My father had taught me how to trim out dead limbs, how to separate bulbs, how to hoe and rake, how to keep a garden. I was still using his tools; I could feel his hands in the worn handles. The work was half memory. I felt his hands on mine when I watered with the galvanized can he'd left when he died, remembering when I had been a girl too small to carry it and he'd held most of the weight, letting me tip the spout, send the bright water out in a shining stream."

Cy murmured, "Yes, beautiful."

"I loved the way the olive tree turned in the wind, now a dusty green, now a chalky silver. How gnarled it was! The halo of purple fruit it left in the courtyard, I didn't clean that up. I loved the stain, a durable shadow. The fogs over the water! The thick, honeyed light, like nowhere else in California. In the late afternoons, if there were clouds and the sun poured in under them, that light looked almost solid.

"Then I took everything out of the garage apartment, called it a studio, and started to paint. At first, I couldn't get the light right. Finally I had a carpenter open a window on the east side, toward the mountains, and I began to hang up mirrors."

"Ah."

"Some of the first were shards from a mirror that had hung in the house by the front door when I was a girl. I remembered my father lifting me up to have a look, to see my astonished face surrounded by the hats that hung on hooks all around the old oak frame. That was a treat! My face, grinning. Then the mirror came down in an earthquake and broke and was relegated to the garage. That's where I found it. In retrospect, the broken mirror does seem to have announced seven disastrous years in the house of James."

Cy raised his eyebrows quizzically but it was dark and James kept on.

"I'd inherited a little money with the house, and I'd sold my mother's old Mercedes for cash, but it was going. I couldn't quite look at the matter with an accountant's eye, but I felt the drift. A persistent anxiety about money, or about how the lack of money would sooner or later take the house.

"Then, something surprising happened. And almost all at once. I got known. One night, suffering through yet another small gallery opening, in Santa Barbara, I met the woman who would soon represent me. She swam in like a shark, looking nothing at all like Santa Barbara. She radiated a glittering, hard intelligence. Elegant, yes, she looked far more elegant than any of the Montecito or Hope Ranch women, but even so her elegance was obviously not the point. I saw the gallery owner freeze, not something someone owning a gallery should ever do. No. Then he started to fawn. But Gloria, I could see clearly from the other side of the room, was not the kind of woman who could successfully be fawned over. I couldn't hear what Alex said, but when Gloria responded he reddened and withdrew. Then Gloria, I didn't know her name, wouldn't have recognized it if I'd heard it I was so out of it, approached the paintings with a startling directness. Many people take Gloria's way with paintings as a kind of performance, but they're wrong. She is that serious, that direct. I can tell you I had started to sweat. She let me, she didn't hurry, which is not to say she looked long at every painting. A few she dismissed with a glance. When she'd been around she went back to the two I thought were my strongest work to date, and then she looked at a third, *Only Blue*. She nodded, not to me or to anyone else, but at the painting. And I saw at once that she was right. The painting had started wildly, almost impossibly, the composition terrifically lopsided and the palette very loud. I'd hardly begun when I found I was stuck. What I had didn't work, but it was—for me—unbelievably active. I put it aside. One day I pinned it back up and just solved it. It took some blues."

"The painting was abstract?"

"Not entirely, but more abstract than the stuff you've seen. Anyway," James sighed, "I warned you the story was long. Gloria didn't wait for an introduction; she looked around the room and walked right up to me. 'You the painter?' That's what she said. You know, Cy, perhaps I only became a painter at that moment, when I said, 'Yes.' I claimed my work in a way I hadn't before. And it claimed me."

Cy nodded in the dark.

"Gloria, maybe, claimed my work, too, unfortunately. But at first her claim seemed very fortunate. I signed on and she began to promote me. She arranged things, reviews, articles in magazines, notice in prestigious publications I hadn't even been dreaming about. A 'bicoastal buzz,'" James said sardonically. "Suddenly, my paintings were in demand. Well, not my work, exactly, but the work of Mad James. Gloria, you see, gave me the name. I'd been signing Madeleine James for years, and my friends had been calling me James since prep school. Never Mad James. But the name stuck. Critics, buyers, saw something 'mad' in the paintings. I couldn't paint fast enough—Gloria pushed the prices up, way up, saying she'd know the right price when I could just meet demand. As it happened, that proved a princely sum."

James smiled ruefully.

"And then?"

"Then it seemed I could afford my little house with a view."

"Ah, good."

"It only seemed that way for a little while, while my shining bubble of fame was rising into the sun."

"Then?"

"I finished with the work that had started with *Only Blue*."

"Finished it?"

"It played out. A year's work, done, just like that. I entered a period of floundering. A painter needs the character to be able to flounder well, have the patience to admit that this won't do, doesn't have it, isn't the real thing.

"I quit calling Gloria, so, of course, she started calling me, not often, but regularly. She began to talk more about timing, less about painting. She began to talk about making a visit.

"I raked the eucalyptus leaves that were deep in the drive. Took to sleeping odd nights in a hammock outside. I wasn't blocked. By the time Gloria arrived I'd been painting again for weeks. The new work was less abstract, and darker. No more Bonnard candy; I was working a lot closer to the somber palette of Vuillard. And something like sobriety, even serenity, had crept in."

"Not very mad?" Cy asked.

"Exactly, not very mad."

The train skirted the edge of a small city, at first a broken ghetto of mud compounds and tumbledown houses, then a drearier patch of electrically lit concrete with shops on the ground floor, but all shuttered up so late. The train passed through the station without stopping; for a second the name of the place, blue letters on a station placard, winked in at the window, but James missed it. Then the train was pulling away from the lights. The illumination in the compartment dimmed.

"You were about to describe Gloria's visit."

"She drove a restored black Citroën touring sedan up my humble drive."

"I guess that means she could afford more than one car." Cy laughed quietly. The old man had lain down on his bench, knees in the air, but managed, even reclining, to seem upright. His disinterest, Cy thought, made their conversation seem, if anything, more private than if he hadn't been there.

"Yes," James said at last, "she had cars plural, no doubt about it. She arrived, and I pointed out the view, the broken view of the sea with the islands floating near the horizon, and she said, 'Where's the studio?' She must have had an inkling. While she looked, I sprawled on the lumpy single bed I'd shoved against a wall, the same wicker bed I'd slept in as a little girl. I turned over the little jar of honey I kept for a toy, watching the gold bubble swim up again and again. And I felt lighthearted. Gloria said what I had already guessed—the new work had limited appeal. She thought a few collectors would stick with me, a few others might weigh in, but that this wasn't the work to sustain the Mad James buzz.

"'But do you like it?' I asked her. She did. Cy, she bought one for the bedroom of her New York co-op. She agreed to push the work in venues where she thought it might be appreciated. Gloria still represents me. But what she predicted, it came to pass.

"She suggested, for my career's sake, I might want to work a little longer in the Mad James idiom, to build a reputation. A big enough reputation might carry the market, make commercial what otherwise was not."

"Significant *might*," Cy said somberly.

"Yes. When everyone was paid, my Mad James year hadn't made me nearly what I expected. The value of those paintings kept going up, still is going up, but I didn't own them anymore. I hired an accountant. I found out that unless I wanted to counterfeit my own work, keep painting the same pictures, I still couldn't afford the house. But if I sold it, and went to live in one of the world's cheaper places, I could be independent, and I could paint as I pleased. So I accepted my parents' gift another way. I sold it."

"A good gift."

"But not the only gift. Cy, from Santa Barbara to Granada, it was a short move, from Spanish style to Spain, though it took years! And in making the move I slowly came to understand that in Spain what I liked best was Al-Andalus, the Islamic strain in the architecture. Quite mute in Santa Barbara, but some of the real singing in Granada. Now I'm here." James gestured toward the darkness, beyond the windows.

"Not just the architecture," Cy observed.

James slept a little and while she slept Cy looked at her, let her shape sink into him. Her small hands, beautiful for all the rough treatment they'd received. They were the hands of a woman who did not shrink from work, from handling the world, touching it. Like the old man on the bench opposite, Cy thought, she looked dignified even sleeping.

When James woke up, Cy was still looking and she saw him and smiled. After a minute, Cy said, "What other gifts?"

"Excuse me?"

"What other gifts did your parents give you?" When James didn't respond, he added, "Besides the house?"

When he saw James was crying, Cy put his arm around her shoulders, pulled her close. He was only a little surprised. He'd guessed that somewhere in her dignity she hid a great grief. He patted at her back awkwardly, stupidly. He let her cry. He kissed her hair.

"It never ends," James said.

"No." But Cy thought maybe it did, that there would be a final forgetfulness. A glance back that was the last. He imagined Charon's little boat, a skiff, he thought, just big enough for two, and one the boatman. He thought that skiff was poled across the river Lethe but he couldn't remember, not for sure. Rowing was possible, even sails.

"I don't want it to end."

"I know."

"If I have to suffer to remember, I still want to remember."

Cy nodded, his nose in her hair. She was going to tell him.

"I thought we were happy, a family. What did I know? I think now my parents were ambitious for a grander life, for Hope Ranch or maybe even Montecito, at least my mother. My father had fallen from the fast track before I was born. He'd failed, unexpectedly, to make partner at a big law firm in L.A. and had moved up to Santa Barbara to hang out his own small, private shingle. He had an office off State Street in the old part of town where he went daily to write wills, I liked to imagine, but most of his work was as a divorce lawyer. Thankless, acrimonious. He must have thought his gaudy credentials would have gotten him better in this world. But he never brought his disappointment home, at least that a child could see. To me he was Papa, always ready to indulge a girl's whims.

"He called himself the mockingbird, probably with irony, but at the time I thought it was because he was a wonderful mimic of bird calls. This was deep magic to me. I might've been on the floor in the living room, making a new dress for a paper doll, and from behind his newspaper the oddball trumpeting of a Canada goose would suddenly sound. It was so real I'd look up, expecting to see a V of geese on the ceiling. Or a sparrow hawk. Or chickadees perched on his reading lamp singing. He denied absolutely that the calls were his.

"His bird impressions weren't limited to calls and songs, he had the strangest way of mimicking their gestures, carriage, ways of walking. He habitually turned his head like a robin when he listened to me, and he could stand in a way that suggested a night heron, an undertaker's look if there ever was one, professionally mournful. He did his night heron in grocery lines, to make me laugh and shorten the wait. Or he'd walk jerkily, back and forth, like a crow, or waddle like a coot. How I loved him! But just occasionally, when I saw him sad, I'd think daddy's going to fly away, and it seemed terribly possible."

Cy stroked her hair, his heart foreboding.

"He was the best papa for me. He let me go free. When he saw I wanted to work with Play-Doh for hours and hours, or crayon the walls of my room, he didn't try to stop me, and he didn't suggest art lessons. He bought me the biggest box of crayons and pounds of modeling clay. He didn't try to tell me what was good. He took me to art museums and stood back; he filled a whole bookcase with art books. I never heard him brag on me or lament my oddities. He just said yes."

"And your mother?"

"Celia."

"Celia?" Cy asked.

"She didn't want to be called *Mom*. She taught me to say *Celia* when I was still having trouble standing up. She thought of mother-hood as a list of things to be done, and she did them without fail. Beyond that, Celia lived for Celia."

"Ouch."

"Celia's indifference wasn't all bad, Cy. She, too, left me alone long hours with my box of Crayolas or my set of Prang watercolors. She didn't mind the mess. But she must have rued the lost life in L.A., the glittering prizes so close somehow slipped away.

"She insisted on the Mercedes. A new one every third year. And ex-pensive clothes. The only thing close to discord I heard in our house was sighs, my father paying charge-card bills. My mother saying, 'I need the clothes.' She worked a little as a 'decorator' for the new rich in Hope Ranch; she lived the expected life vicariously, spending other people's money.

"I don't know when, or if, she fell out of love with my father. Per-haps she didn't; he was charming, a beautiful, harmless man. But his kind of lawyering counted for nothing in her eyes. She didn't see ours as a small good life, but as a failed life. Probably my father's odd but winning ways counted with her only as buffoonery. Mocking-bird. I didn't realize any of this until years later.

"Celia took a lover. She must have known my father would find out, must have wanted him to; a divorce lawyer would recognize the signs. He went north on a case, to Santa Maria. In the afternoon he called to say he wouldn't be home for dinner. The police found his car abandoned at a turnout on Highway 1 in Big Sur." Cy took James's hand and held on. He shuddered or she did, he wasn't sure which.

"The police said he'd probably wandered off the road to 'relieve himself' and lost his footing on the loose shales. Treacherous footing. In the dark he might not have realized that the ground broke away to a dead fall. At the inquest, his death counted as an accident. But I think not."

"Very hard for a girl." Cy tried to comfort her with his hands, but still, she cried.

"I'm sorry, Cy. I haven't cried about this for a long time. I don't blame him, I miss him. He went when I was fourteen, so many years ago. We weren't beggared. The insurance paid. My aunt, my father's sister, agreed to take me, and I was sent to Albuquerque and enrolled at the Academy there. I had a good life. My aunt Carol taught me the value of living well, what can't so easily be taken away. Ambition had passed her by. She was a doctor, but preferred family practice and worked more for free in clinics than for pay. She must have been a great mystery to my mother. But Carol had precious little to say about Celia, though Celia wouldn't have been much of a mystery to her. I had to ask several times to find out what Carol knew about my mother. She's the one who told me about the lover and that Celia had renounced him after my father's death.

"Celia lived on alone, and withered, for fifteen years. She was dying every one of them. For my papa, to go was probably an act of good manners, to step aside. I'm sure he never foresaw that his death would kill her slowly. She became a closet drinker, wan and brittle. I believe she played a good deal of bridge with her own kind. But she was broken, and, at last, she died."

15

In the plaza, Asur sat talking to one of the wild boys, the runaways, who sometimes laid claim to one or another of the shaded benches under the small trees. Even in the village, Asur had been a solitary child, as solitary as it was possible to be in a village where everyone was known. He'd been lonely, but not as lonely as another boy would have been. Still, he liked to talk to kids his own age and play the games children play.

But the runaways alarmed him, too. Jorge liked to talk about the big crimes he hoped to commit when he was just a little older and about what he'd do to any lost girl, any girl alone he might catch in an out-of-the-way corner. Asur said nothing. The other boy's bravado dumbfounded him. That he was expected to brag too never occurred to him. The two boys shared their lunch, Asur's *bocadillo* and milk and Jorge's cheap, sugar-dusted donuts. Jorge could be generous, and his caricatures of tourists in the plaza never failed to make Asur laugh. But when he talked big, a mean streak showed that Asur could not understand. Who would want to hurt a lost girl?

Asur said nothing about James, about the veranda where he slept at night, and nothing about why he'd been locked out of his house by his own mother.

Jorge liked to remember the beatings his father had given him, his bullying bigger brother. He said he'd go back when he was grown and kill both of them. He looked forward to the day.

If Asur said nothing about James or Luz, he did talk about his ambition to be a juggler, about how he hoped to get good enough to make big money as a street performer. Jorge didn't believe that was much of an ambition, and especially he didn't believe Asur saying, when he refused to join in a purse-snatching scheme, that he made plenty begging and didn't need to steal. *Plenty* was a lie, after all, but one that he, Asur, liked to believe was true.

On the bench, he practiced his juggling, and he had begun to be good at it, good enough to amaze Jorge, anyway, who would drop an orange in his hand if he took his eye off of it. But soon enough Jorge would grow bored with the show and wander off. Then Asur too would slip away. To skip rocks on the Darro, to feed scraps to the band of wild cats that lived in the riverbed, to try to make friends of them. Or he shaded up on James's veranda, watched the clouds sail overhead or the sure progress of their shadows down below. He watered the plants daily and wiped dust from the shiny-leaved ones with a wet sock when he thought he should.

In the evening, Asur begged as before, but he kept out of dark alleys, and out of the Albayzín altogether. He was learning to read the tourists and the shopkeepers, the churchgoers and the pale night dwellers of the demimonde. He studied those who said yes. Not the woman who stopped at five paces to open her purse, who decided in Asur's favor before he ever got close, but those who hesitated, whose eyes swung round to look at him, at Luz, or appeared stricken when they looked away. Those who needed encouragement he was learning to encourage. Begging was a skill and Asur meant to be good at it. His looks were in his favor, wet black eyes and an innocent expression. He'd spent cold nights before James had offered him the blankets, but he'd never gone hungry. He'd never been desperate, and he didn't want to be.

The juggler's appearances on the plaza were no longer mysterious to Asur, though even to regulars, to waiters and shopkeepers, Marcela seemed to obey no law; she did not appear like the phases of the moon, on a schedule, but like starfall, a fiery surprise.

Luz she met by appointment. Asur knew she had a black van, he'd seen the flaming advertisement she'd had painted on the side. He knew when she was away from Granada she was performing in a plaza in some other Andalusian town. In the small villages the children loved her, the woman who made fire dance in the night. In the cities, too. Even adults respected her, a lowly street performer, for her strength and athletic stride, and for her proud toreador manner. Comedy did not figure in her performance, and she began without prelude, always.

"Luz," she said, her smoker's voice low and hoarse, striding by Asur where he leaned against a wall of the Lisboa café. The boy straightened up, pulled at his dress, and followed her, the child's stride also suddenly taut.

Again Marcela's flaming batons wheeled in the sky over Plaza Nueva, the black and oily smoke visible for a moment before it mixed with the general blackness of the night sky. Again Asur collected the money, going round, his face shining with admiration for the juggler's skill. Somehow his face convinced, and Marcela never made more money than when she worked with Luz. She liked the girl and asked to see her juggle and praised her. She had begun to think of Luz as an apprentice, and Asur imagined he might become a sorcerer's apprentice, learn the magic spells he thought the juggler must possess, because he had never seen Marcela drop a baton, never even seen her hesitate.

Where the Albayzín gives way to Sacromonte, in the long narrow plaza defined by the Darro on the Alhambra side, the juggler put down her satchel and began immediately to light the batons. Here, where the town lights ended, the juggler's brands showed brightly against the Alhambra hill. She threw them high, and they turned on an invisible and rising axis, before falling again into her hands. A crowd had assembled; the juggler knew that Luz was moving in it. She thought she should perform a little longer, to give the child time to approach everyone. Concentrating, she realized late that a commotion had broken out in the crowd, and that the high keening was Luz's voice thinned out by terror. She caught one last baton then stepped to the side, letting the others fall as they would on the black paving stones where she worked. She stood at attention, looking into the crowd, eyes a little dazzled from the fire of the brands.

Then she did see Luz on the ground; a dirty man with a creased face had one hand in her hair and the other raised in the air to strike her again, and his hand swooped down. No one in the crowd had moved an inch; they stood transfixed.

"Goddamn you," the man cursed. "Look at me. ¡Mira mi cara! You goddamn girlie-boy."

Marcela picked up her squirt bottle out of her satchel and started forward, even now erect and calm. She sprayed the man with a heavy stream of kerosene as she drew near, and when he looked up, she kicked him full in the throat, and he stumbled back. Still, Marcela sprayed him, sprayed his shirt and sprayed him in the face. He was dripping before he registered that the liquid was kerosene, and he bellowed.

Marcela turned the kerosene on the ground, describing a broad arc between Luz at her feet and the madman who was gathering himself. She pointed the baton in her hand at him, and then touched it to the kerosene on the ground, and the arc caught, and flames rose up out of the paving stones.

Marcela bent over the writhing child. His nose was bleeding, and even in the uneven light of the flames the left side of his face had the ruddy look of a bruise coming. Asur started to crawl, gathering up the scattered coins in a large piece of the juggler's broken bowl. Marcela touched Asur's shoulder.

"*Dejalos.* It's nothing."

"Why me?" Asur sobbed.

"I don't know."

"*Estoy inocente.* But two times he attacks me!"

The madman shouted, "Girlie-boy! *Huequito!* Fuck you!"

Marcela straightened up, looking over the flames.

"Come on," she said evenly. Again, beckoning with her brand.

The man readied himself to charge, but two boys in leather jackets stepped in, restrained him, then pushed him down and started to kick him.

"*¡Mierda! ¡Hueco!*" They shouted as they kicked him.

But the man surprised them and sprang up, grabbing a heavy café chair, which he swung wildly but effectively, catching one of the boys, who went down, on the side of the head. The other boy stepped back, and the *loco* dropped the chair and leapt forward, wading through the fire, face contorted in a mask of rage. He bellowed, but it was not words. His arms swam out in front of him, trying to push the juggler aside to get at Asur, who was still hunting for coins on the ground, who hadn't seen that the madman was coming again.

Marcela took a half step aside; the baton flashed down, then up again, between the man's churning legs.

He emitted a sudden, "Huh," and then dropped to his knees.

Flames began to lick at the crotch of his pants, and he clapped at them with his hands, to put them out or because in his pain it was all he could think to do. When he pulled his hands away, flames started from his fingers like ten lit candles. For a moment, he held his hands up in a supplicant's pose, as fire began to climb up his shirt toward his up-turned face.

Asur had seen him now, a figure out of nightmare, out of the promised and fiery hell, here and screaming. His monster. His man. Then Asur drew himself up and shouted, "*¡El río!* The river!" And he pointed to the low, stone wall, no more than twenty yards away, beyond which the cool Darro shimmered over the rocks of the riverbed. "*Loco*, run!"

The man hesitated, peered at the child with cocked head, as if puzzled, and groaned. A look of unendurable sadness crossed his face, only to sink under a look of sheer terror, as flames jumped from his shirt to his beard. Then he was running, hands out from his sides. He ran within fire for the river, tumbled over the low wall and disappeared into the channel of the Darro.

In the ensuing silence, Marcela methodically retrieved her batons and extinguished them, stowing them in her satchel.

"Get up," she said, and Asur struggled to his feet, not hurt so much as stunned. He was a child who had been hit before.

"Can you walk?"

"I'm okay." But Asur shook, wobbly.

Marcela considered. She bent down and picked up the pieces of the yellow bowl she'd been setting out since she'd started to juggle for money. These, she tossed into the satchel, leaving the money on the ground.

"*Vámonos*," she said, just as she would have if nothing had happened.

And they walked away from the arc still burning on the ground, back toward Plaza Nueva. They walked in silence, as far as the first footbridge across the Darro, Puente de Espinosa, which, to Asur's surprise, Marcela led him across. She pulled Asur to a stone curb in the deep, green shade of a tumbledown wall. She sat down and signaled for Asur to sit beside her.

Within a minute or two they heard sirens, and two police motorcycles roared down Carrera del Darro toward Passeo del Padre Monjón. When they were past, Asur started to get up but the juggler put her hand on his shoulder and pulled him back down, saying nothing.

An emergency vehicle followed, crowding unwary pedestrians up against the stucco walls. First the lights passed, then the echoing sirens drew away.

"What did he mean, 'girlie-boy'?"

"Oh," Asur cried, his arms resting on the skirt stretched between his splayed knees. "He meant I am a boy in a dress."

"*¿Es la verdad?*"

"*Sí, es la verdad.* Always, I wanted a dress."

Two more police motorcycles raced by.

"I am a woman, but . . ."

"A true woman," Asur interrupted, "*una verdadera mujer.* I am a girl, too, but with a mistake between my legs."

"God makes many such mistakes."

"Why?" Asur asked simply.

"Maybe for Him they are not mistakes."

"But . . ."

"I know what people say," Marcela murmured. "But what do they know? They know what other people say. That's all."

Marcela stood up. "On Friday?"

"Yes."

And she walked off, across the footbridge, not looking back, her step quick but unhurried.

❀

16

Sam knew making deals in Morocco almost always involved drinking too much mint tea, but he said no to the third small cup a little curtly, and the shopkeeper noticed, and Paula must have noticed, too, but she gave no sign of it. She had been bargaining for a long time. An array of tribal jewelry had been spread on the floor at her feet, spread artlessly on a fine Berber kilim the shopkeeper perhaps also hoped to sell. It had taken Paula almost an hour to get to see the best of the shopkeeper's collection, which had, finally, been produced from worn cloth bags pulled out of an inconspicuous carved cupboard.

He had been persuaded to produce them by the knowledgeable way Paula had rejected the half-good pieces, realizing rather late what it would take to make any sale at all to this woman he'd taken at first for a casual tourist. Slowly it had come to him that Paula knew as much if not more about what they were looking at than he did. She had corrected his tribal attributions three times, not making a show of it, but firmly. That Paula had the knowledge, and knew how to make use of it bargaining, Sam respected. What he didn't respect was the way she inflamed the old man with her body, meaning to take every advantage she could get.

She had let him, even encouraged him, to wrap old, handworked reins around her waist, to demonstrate how they could be used as a belt. Paula had no intention of buying them, at any price. They weren't good enough to interest her, Sam knew it, but she twirled around under the old man's hands, playing along. And when she tried on anything, she struck a pose, standing with her back to the shopkeeper to look in the mirror, and twisting her head around to smile, to make sure he noticed the way her skirt tightened across her hips, the way her blouse rode up to reveal her dark gold skin. She knew, Sam was sure of it. He half expected the old man's glasses to fog. Now she was leaning over the ornate necklaces to give him a chance to peer down the front of her blouse.

Sam doubted her suggestiveness shortened the negotiations, but it did manage to exclude him from their transactions. And when Sam felt excluded, he felt bored.

"Time to go, Paula. Remember, we're on a schedule."

Paula, it surprised him, agreed. She said, "You're probably right," and the old trader made a false move, showed how little he wanted Paula to go without buying.

"But you make no deal," Paula said to him. "You want to sell something, you've got to make a deal."

Sam saw immediately that Paula had cast him in a role, so he stood up.

"What's your best price for these three?" And Paula swept the three best necklaces into a heap of amber, old French coins, and rare beads. The pile was not small.

Sam shuffled his feet, "Please Paula, please, let's go."

The old man spread the three necklaces out again, "For you, five hundred fifty dollars American. Cash price."

A surprisingly modest price, Sam thought, but he shook his head. He said nothing to the dealer himself, was careful not to challenge the man's dignity. "Paula?" He said, noticing that she had three one-hundred-dollar bills in her hand, letting the old man see the money.

"No," the man said, "please, I cannot get these things again."

Paula picked up one of the necklaces, pointed to the best beads, the rarest coins, "These are good," she said, then she pointed again, "but these are not. This," she said, pointing at a particularly suspect bead, "isn't even silver."

She picked the necklace up and put it in the man's hand, touching him. "I'm just a poor student of your country's beautiful crafts; I can't afford rich-tourist prices."

She reached up and Sam took her hand, pulling her to her feet. The dealer sat motionless on the floor, looking at the money spread wide on the ground in front of him.

"For two?"

"No," Paula said gently, "for three."

Sam looked around, at the glass cases mounted on the dingy walls, full of cheap silver and sad, reproduction daggers, at the stacks of kilims and kilim cushions on the floor. This shop on the road south out of Ouarzazate wasn't a place he would have expected to find antique tribal jewelry of real quality, but there it was, Paula had ferreted it out.

She bent slowly from the waist, reaching for the money.

"Three hundred fifty?"

"Deal," she said, and shook his hand.

Outside the light was dazzling. The dusty road ran between dry hills. There were a few shops here, and beyond, palm trees, the palm garden that made this place an oasis. The Drâa Valley lay before them. In the car, Paula put her arms around Sam's neck and gave him an excited kiss.

"I'm in the mood," she said.

"You're in the mood most often when there's no bed available," he observed, laughing; he wasn't in the mood and therefore difficult to bait. He was hot, ready for the Ka's air-conditioning to kick in.

"The mood comes when it pleases and goes," she added, "when it pleases. Can I help it if that's inconvenient?" She leaned in close, "Oh, I still think I could get a reaction." She ran her soft hand up the inside of his leg.

But then she opened the sack on her lap and started looking at the necklaces. They held up in the harsh light. She tried one on, twisting the rearview mirror around to have a look.

"Not bad, but not for me. Still, I'm thinking they'll bring real money at Tribal Arts. Jocelyn will have a list of customers to call about these. I doubt she'll even show them in her shop."

"Those Bostonians," Sam said. "So tribal!"

"They have their fantasies. And they can afford to pay for them."

Sam reached over and fingered one of the necklaces, holding it up so he could keep an eye on the road. "Wouldn't this be for a real collector?"

"Real collectors have fantasies, too, however objective they might sound. Your Qur'an man, for instance. His probably involves dancing girls," she giggled.

"He's ours, don't you think?"

"Not my type," she smiled. "Fat, bald, and German," she said, "I don't like. That plump little pasha. But if you're interested . . ."

"I'm talking business."

"But these are business, too," she rattled the beads, "good business. Even after Jocelyn's 40 percent there's probably fifteen hundred profit here. Maybe more."

"Yes, and? How far will that get us?"

"Us?" Paula mocked, "You pay yourself well for standing up and looking impatient."

"Don't I? Perfect timing." But they hadn't come to squabbling about money. Sam said, "Hold them up again." When she did, he spoke seriously. "Very beautiful. Not final beauty, perhaps, but a necklace like that is far more beautiful than 99 percent of 'designer' jewelry in the States. Beauty is hard; good materials shouldn't be wasted on inspiration," he quipped.

"Aren't these inspired?"

"No. A little maybe, but mostly they are obedient. The credit goes to the tribe, who worked it out strand by strand over generations, so even an ignorant girl can make beauty. Perhaps one girl does it a little better than another, but even the one without a special gift . . ."

"But the materials here are beautiful," Paula interrupted what was threatening to become a harangue. She touched the silver-clad amber and old, old trade beads; the thick, worn coins and glowing corals.

"And who decided these things were beautiful and worked together? Who said, 'Value these'? And the way that necklace is put together, the balance, the interlocking structure of the strands? And that's not even considering that the piece speaks, actually means something. Just compare the average here to what you get in a jewelry design class at one of our better colleges back home! The unfettered imagination is a terrible thing."

Paula shot him an exasperated glance.

"The horror." He smiled. "The horror."

She laughed at that. "You're impossible."

"But I'm serious!"

"Oh, no doubt. I'm just not sure why."

"Because it's an affront! Not just in arts, but in crafts, we're asked to call beautiful really dreadful things. If you have even a little taste, well, you just have to lie all the time about how beautiful it all is. You're asked to lie; you're expected to lie."

"I never found it all that difficult."

"Does that make it any better? When there was restraint, there was beauty in the arts. The individual participated in a tradition, was guided by it. Oh, there was innovation, but it was limited, hardly an individual prerogative at all. It was as if the tradition evolved a little under an individual hand; the tensions that were already there in the tradition worked themselves out. The old ways ramified into the new. The new." Sam paused. "Now everything has to be new, and therefore," Sam paused again, "grotesque and finally ugly. It's really that simple: the individual can't answer the charge to make it new. He can try, but . . ."

"Or she . . ."

"Okay, she, she faints under the enormity of it. Makes something, sure, something, and let the hucksters sell it if they can."

Paula pointed at a graveyard on a nearby hill, jagged stone slabs pounded pell-mell into a rocky slope. Nothing grew there to relieve the stark raggedness of the place.

"Now that," Sam said, "suggests final things," his head turning to look as they drove on by. But the sight had unstrung him a little and his voice sounded subdued.

"It doesn't suggest the possible consolations are of this world, no," Paula agreed. Then they were well by.

After Agdz, the bright sky softened a little under the influence of a cloud. They sat, silent for long stretches, seemingly floating over the pavement. Up ahead, a mud kasbah swam into view, rose out of the sand and rocks, impossible in its strange beauty. Abandoned, clearly abandoned, they could see that as their car pulled closer. A good deal of the structure had melted away, but what remained was imposing enough. It looked something like a castle, but not a stone wall anywhere in it. Mud and timbers, wattles. And not a great man's redoubt, either, but a compact village. Shade made where there was very little; shade and cool in summer, warmth in winter.

They stopped and got out into the sun, which though evening was coming, still bore down. The landscape seemed a little unhinged by the sun, by the heat waves lifting everywhere off the sand and exposed rocks. They picked their way across the hundred yards between the road and the kasbah, complaining, over what must once have been a field, though the soil now had blown away. Goats had done their part, still were. Sam noticed a couple moving away along the kasbah's front wall. The kasbah itself, they discovered, looked better at a distance. Making their way inside through an opening that had once been closed by a great door, they peeked down passageways with something like suspicion, Paula visibly whiffing the air. The mud-plastered walls were half down, the wattles showing. A good many timbers had been carried away, for firewood, Sam surmised, or to build again. Still, enough remained to give a feeling for the place, for the intense hive it must once have been, when the narrow passageways rang with footfalls and calling voices.

"I wonder where they went," Sam said, "and when, for that matter. Probably the call of the city, always a siren call."

"Some of the kasbahs were Jewish," Paula said. "Many of these places were abandoned when Israel got going. Whole communities of Sephardic Jews emigrated from Morocco when they got the chance."

When they reemerged, Sam saw a goatherd, a crone, sitting quietly in a small patch of shade cast by a single bush. She looked worn, in a blue dress and a black headscarf, a stick leaning against her shoulder, smoking a cigarette. She stared at them without compunction, as at yet another of the world's oddities. Then she twisted her head and spat.

Sam turned his back on the woman and took Paula's elbow, directing her away, toward the car, and to his surprise, she let him. The goatherd's look had been casual, and contemptuous, and Sam saw himself for a second as she saw him, a too-clean dandy come to exclaim over the picturesque poverty of Morocco. He felt to be complete he really ought to have had a camera, but his white ducks and melon-colored silk shirt, his fine Panama, were no doubt quite enough. And the beautiful girl. The goatherd would not have mistaken Paula, with her short blouse and loose skirt, for his wife. He felt tawdry, he realized with a start, and he wouldn't have thought that was possible.

The Ka had gotten hot in their absence, very hot. Sam sat down in it with a groan, his shirt sticking to him unpleasantly. The thick money belts he wore under it chaffed. Even in hundreds big money made a cumbersome stack of paper.

"You think that counts as the evil eye?" Paula asked, who had seen the old woman, too.

"Yes."

"Baleful, anyway. I wish I could muster a look like that."

"You have some looks."

"Not that one. Anyway, I'm protected." And she pulled from between her breasts a small, silver hand of Fatima, which she wore on a slender, black leather cord.

"Do you get a lot of comfort from that?"

"Well, here I am smiling, and there you are, looking like she spit on you."

"She did, didn't she?"

"I think she spit on the ground."

They drove by a road sign, Zagora, 70 kilometers.

"Not far, even at this speed," Sam said. "We should make it before dark."

Paula didn't answer. Her face wore one of her mischievous looks, and after a minute, she brought it out. "What you were saying before, about art, about the fakers and the hucksters, I mean. Shouldn't our sympathy be with them? We are, after all, fakers and hucksters, too."

"At least we know it," Sam said quietly.

"And Mad James, she doesn't know it?"

"Maybe she does. It's hard to imagine that painters, 'artists,' believe what they say about their own work, much less what gets said about it. But maybe they do."

"James says precious little."

"Maybe she's chagrined, after her big year, to have been reduced to a 'painter's' painter.' I've never known anyone content with a *succès d'estime*."

"Perhaps that speaks to the quality of your friends."

"Perhaps. But she's so serious. As if her work really matters."

"And our work?"

"Isn't it traditional? Don't we submit like the artists, the craftsmen who covered the walls of the Alhambra to begin with? Who glazed the tiles, who worked out the designs and carved the stucco? Aren't your forged pots informed by, if not actually part of, the tradition of Nasrid pottery in Al-Andalus?"

Paula was laughing.

"Isn't that why your work is so much more beautiful than any of the contemporary pottery we've seen in Granada?"

"Why thank you," Paula said, with mock solemnity.

"And my faïence work, isn't it as beautiful as what you see in the Alhambra?"

"Yes," Paula said quite simply, seriously, "just as beautiful."

Dusty Zagora was in view when Sam said, as an afterthought, "Among contemporary painters, I prefer the children of Dubuffet, who make it quite clear their work means nothing, is no more than a witty play of paint on canvas, surfaces."

"Play?"

"Play, literally and explicitly superficial. They know, anyhow, that they're living at the end of the world."

Paula looked out the window, at the first of the tourist shops, and with more interest at the market stalls across the street, empty now except for a pen of sheep and goats. Tomorrow, she thought, she would satisfy her sweet tooth there with a fistful of dates.

"The problem . . ." Sam started in again.

"Problem?"

"Yes. The problem is that they think it's always been the end of the world. They think the truth of their time has always been true."

"I think we should find our hotel. I think the truth of a shower would be good."

"Very funny. And then?"

"Dinner, Sam, then dinner."

❀

17

They met, as agreed, in the late afternoon, after a long nap in their rooms at the Hotel Ali in Marrakech. Cy had awakened to the buzz of his alarm, surprisingly clearheaded after the long night on the train that had ended in an extended bout of morning sickness in the vile WC, the railroad ties passing dizzyingly under the hole in the floor as he bent over it. He'd been close to blacking out, his head full of slowly revolving, pulsing lights. But he hadn't, and he'd stood out on the platform with the smokers until he'd felt good enough to go back to his seat, back to James. He'd prayed there would be no lower moment on the trip. When they'd gotten to the hotel in the medina, cheap and an old favorite, he'd insisted on two big rooms, for privacy, and to spare James his mornings.

Now she sat down next to him in the hotel's enclosed courtyard, looking freshly showered, dressed for a walk in loose jeans, red Converse, and a modest, brown shirt.

"Ready for the touts?" Cy asked.

"Forewarned."

They had agreed on a walk in the medina. When they stood up, Cy took her hand. They passed out under the arcades on Rue Moulay

Ismail and turned right, toward Djemaa el-Fna, the Assembly of the Dead, the wild, beating heart of Marrakech. The *calèche* drivers immediately began to call from the line of parked carriages across the street, and ahead of them, Cy could see touts and beggars pushing off from pillars and walls to approach them. Cy put on his stony face, saying no firmly to the first faux guide who offered to lead them through the medina. Cy insisted as they walked across the great, irregular square, the Djemaa el-Fna, that really it was quite deserted, however swarmed it might seem to James now. "A little later," he said, "after dark, it will come fully alive."

They wandered in the souqs, by haggling and hawkers, by jewelry shops and antique shops, by a butcher's stall, advertised by the head of a camel hung on a hook over the chopping block. Everywhere Moroccan women in robes walked in twos and threes. Their flowing forms, simple and vivid, appealed to James, and the way these simple shapes were repeated, again and again, felt like composition to her. And repetition and variation were everywhere, in the reds of the walls, in the elements of the architecture, the arches and the great studded doors, even in the irregularity of the passages. The constant turning and branching soon came to be expected, more familiar than not.

Of course they were lost, almost instantly, but if they were lost all they had to do was keep walking to be found, to find they had returned to where they started or emerged from the medina at one of the great gates in the old city wall, Bab Debbagh or Bab Agnaou, and from there they could plunge in again or take a petit taxi back to the Assembly of the Dead.

The shadows had thickened and the shop lights had come on when they began to tire. Cy stopped outside a shop, looking in at the tribal rings and bracelets on display there. He pointed out a heavy Berber bracelet, like a great silver gear, but with a half twist in the construction, so even still, it looked as if it were in motion, turning forward.

"Wonderful design," James said, nodding.

They went in, turned the bracelet in their hands.

"Important to touch such things," she said. "That's the problem with museums; it's all looking, too visual." She closed her eyes. "I like it," she pronounced, in the emphatic tones of a girl. She handed it back to Cy, whispering, "Show me how to bargain for it."

He asked to see a small, palm-sized mirror, clad in silver hammered into an extraordinary, geometric design. He looked closely at the small scratches and the pattern of the wear to be sure it was old, but he didn't ask if it was antique. He pretended to be bothered by a small blind spot in the silvering, rubbing it with his thumb. When he saw James's eye on the mirror, he smiled.

"How much?" He asked.

Twenty minutes later, they emerged from the shop empty handed, but when the shopkeeper followed them out, Cy closed the deal in the alley.

"So that's how," James said.

Cy laughed.

They wandered back toward the Assembly of the Dead. Evening had given way to night. Cy pulled the bracelet out of the little sack in his hand and gave it to James.

"How much was it?" James asked, amused, since Cy had bought the bracelet and the mirror for "one price."

When Cy tried to wave off her money she stuck a fifty in his shirt pocket, and he acquiesced, said, "Then dinner's on me."

He gave her the mirror.

To his surprise, she slipped the bracelet back into his hand. "I bought it for you, a paperweight, to keep your scandalous poems from flying away."

Cy said, "No, really."

When she insisted, he explained, "You know, one of the compensations of, of being sick, is that I've stopped wanting things. You should keep it."

"It's not a thing, Cy, it's a gift. Take it that way, that I want to give it to you," and she pressed his hand, with the bracelet in it, between hers. When she glanced up at him she saw that there were tears in his eyes, and she stopped, getting up close, to hold him. They stood there in the alley, leaning on each other, not speaking.

When they walked back into the Assembly of the Dead the human circus was in full cry.

"I see," James laughed.

She pointed over Place Foucauld to the great minaret of the Koutoubia Mosque, where it hung, lit, over the smoke of cook fires and the flaring light of the many lanterns and torches in Djemaa el-Fna.

"Look at that!" James said. "Almohad, isn't it? It does look like the tower in Seville, the Giralda."

Cy agreed. "Back then, the influence was from Al-Andalus back to Africa. The center was there, in Spain."

Drums pounded out in the plaza, which seemed to make audible the throb, the pulse, that visibly animated the crowd. Cy pointed to the balcony restaurants, to where the tourists sat, keeping their distance.

He squeezed James's hand, nodding toward the crush of the plaza, and said, "Let's risk it."

And James stepped forward, leading the way. As random as it looked from the edge of the plaza, out in it they found the crowd was honeycombed, performers surrounded by rings of gawkers. There were dancers, boxers, storytellers, acrobats and jugglers. Around the margins, those offering services plied their trades: tailors; shoeshine boys (one offered to shine James's canvas All Stars); a dentist with a pair of rusty pliers; herbalists; magicians, ready to concoct a potion for love or death from the makings spread on a blanket around them. Everyone seemed to have his own light, a lantern or a flashlight, and the chiaroscuro faces in the crowd were avid, even wild, and reminded James of Goya's famous black paintings. Cy looped his arm around James's waist as they watched the inevitable snake charmers, the hooded cobras standing at attention in lantern light to hear the piped songs.

When they walked by the palm readers, four or five wizened women, each with a stool to sit on and another for the person with questions, James stopped abruptly. Business didn't look good for the scrying arts, and perhaps it was that as much as curiosity that convinced her to take a seat on one of the little stools. James agreed to the price and bent her head together with the palm reader's, the two of them ducked half under a black umbrella.

James's palm looked very pale in the fortune-teller's hand while the old woman pointed and traced with a dirty finger there. Cy couldn't make out much of what the woman said, but he could hear her voice, thin and cracked. A man in a suit jacket squatted down beside them, translating what the fortune-teller said into broken French.

When James stood up, she seemed a little disconcerted. She said, "I was hoping for better."

The old woman looked up at them, one eye clouded with cataract, the other piercing, the tattoo on her chin like a blue zipper. "You," she said in clear English, pointing at Cy.

"No," Cy said, not unkindly, "I think I know my fortune."

She shook her head, said, "You," again, gesturing for him to take his turn on the stool.

"No, thank you," Cy said, a shade more emphatically.

"Go ahead, Cy," James murmured, and she gave him a light push. "It's cheap, a charity."

So Cy sat down. The woman's hands were hot and dry. She stroked the backs of Cy's hands, looking into his face, before she pulled him abruptly close, holding his palm to the lantern light under the umbrella.

When she touched his palm, she cried out, "Ai!" Cy tried to pull his hand free, but she held on. She cocked her head and put her good eye close. She said something to the man who had translated before, and he picked up the lantern. A bright light flooded Cy's open palm.

Cy felt James's hand on his shoulder, and he looked up into her encouraging face; he wanted to warn her, to tell her to stop her ears, but she looked ready for anything.

The old woman began to rock on her stool, back and forth, speaking by fits and starts. Cy could barely hear her, but the man with the lantern, his face alert, seemed to understand. As suddenly as she had begun to speak, she stopped, and she gestured to the man with the lantern, that he should translate.

"Water," the man said, trying to find the words in English, "*une grande fleuve, noire.*"

"A big river, yes, black."

The old woman nodded.

"*Les bateaux,* many boats, all crossing one way, going back. It's dark, green, golden prows. *Flambeaux.* Torches, in the boats. Great suffering."

"Ai!" the woman howled again, and Cy glanced warily into his palm. Then the woman spoke, in English. "You have suffered," she said. "That is in your face. But the river is in your hand. Crossing."

"And?" Cy asked.

"Great happiness."

"Happiness?"

"*Bonheur,* suffering and happiness together," the man said.

"At once?"

"Together. She sees the river. What's the word? Busy?"

"And?"

"That's all she sees."

Cy staggered up. He backed away, shaking his head.

James, starting after him, stopped midstride, turned back to the old woman on her stool, put her fingertips together and nodded over them, the smallest bow.

The old woman nodded back, then gestured after Cy.

When James caught up to him, Cy had gotten as far as a row of shoe-blacks at the edge of the plaza, spit and polish and a little lighter fluid burnt on the toe caps before the last buff.

"Well," she said, "you did promise another world, and I guess you delivered."

"She did, certainly. Quite a show."

James laughed, "Really good."

James took Cy's hand and they started walking. The black pavement gleamed in the night light, and they floated over it, not talking. Then they crossed out of the plaza, their hotel in sight.

"It's odd," James said, "but that business about the boats reminded me of the Muslims who would not give up their faith at the *Reconquista,* crossing over at the Straits of Hercules, from Costa del Sol back to Africa. They must have crossed in waves."

Cy said nothing.

They were walking under the arcade, along Rue de Moulay Ismail again, almost back to the Ali.

"I don't suppose that happened all at once, of course not," she said. "But I imagine it as a night journey, a tremendous sense of the lost homeland at their backs. If they were looking forward, that is, toward Africa, and not at Spain in their wake."

They agreed to eat in the hotel restaurant, a buffet in two large, yellow rooms. They sat on cushions at a low, round table, Cy hardly eating, but willing to try. He tasted the chicken tajine out of a clay pot, ochre, with olives and cured lemon halves stewed soft in it. Cy ate with pieces of barley bread torn from a flat, hand-sized loaf. He felt the real archaic bread in its shape, tasted, he thought, bread itself in its rough texture. A good bread in the beginning and still good. The very opposite of refined.

James wanted to taste everything, and her plate looked like a painter's palette when she set it down on the table. For all that, she ate lightly, too, perhaps not wanting to show a big appetite in the face of Cy's limited interest in food, though he encouraged her.

They were drinking small coffees and sharing a glass of red wine when a waiter led the musician in, a blind woman, slight, and oddly pale. She sat on a low stool, arranging the folds of her reddish robe and deep-blue headscarf by feel. When she was settled, a second waiter placed her instrument in her hands, an oud, long-necked with a gourd-shaped body.

Cy watched her, impressed by her passive but absolute self-possession. She plucked at her instrument, tuning it, as if she were alone in the room, as if the rattle of earthenware pots and plates and the low murmur of conversation weren't audible to her ears at all. Cy and James exchanged a glance, a look of shared confidence that the music would be worth hearing.

Satisfied with the oud, the woman raised her face, played a single note, and waited. Then, when the room had quieted down, she began. She sang. It wasn't a music to command every traveler's attention. It was high and thin and strange to Western ears, but those who listened could hardly resist it. She sang joy and the heart's grievances. Perhaps because she sang in an unfamiliar tongue, emotion was everything. Her voice carried it directly into the air. Her heart streamed from her mouth, unchecked. Yearning, elation, sadness and regret, and a keening note that was the very sound of lamentation. James heard this note and wished that Cy weren't hearing it, but it did not touch Cy the way James feared. What James felt was the loss of her father, and the looming loss of Cy, who she knew was going soon. The note Cy heard most distinctly, in everything the woman sang, was acceptance, that the constraints on her heart were in her singing untied. What he felt, she acknowledged, let fly over the tabletops and the silverware.

Then she was done. Most of the travelers had gone and a waiter was helping her get her oud back in its cloth case. The owner had come over to gather up the coins and bills that the diners had left when they'd gone out, and Cy and James each added a bill to the pile as they walked by. It seemed inadequate, almost irrelevant.

James said, "*Merci,*" and something like acknowledgment perhaps passed over the singer's face, but James noticed, they both did, that when she wasn't singing the singer had a peculiarly inexpressive face, passive and unlit.

"So that's Morocco," James said as they climbed the tiled stairs up to their rooms.

"Just another day in Marrakech."

"A woman doesn't need a faux guide when she's got you."

"That's right. You already have a faux guy."

"Oh notorious man . . ."

They had stopped in front of Cy's door. "Let me in," James said quietly.

Cy hesitated, "Not a mercy?"

James put a hand up and covered his mouth. She shook her head slowly. "Don't," was all she said.

Cy trembled as he leaned in close, tasted the dampness on James's neck under her hair. She smelled good to him. Not good or bad but good to him, as she should. Like the bread at dinner, warm and wholesome, nothing fancy or perfumed.

"Cy?"

He pulled back so he could see her face, to really look at her. He hadn't wanted to before, hadn't wanted her to look too directly into his face. But he let her look now; for better or worse he couldn't protect her. She wouldn't be protected.

"Cy?"

And he kissed her lightly on the corner of her mouth, running his fingers over her clear forehead, an eyebrow, down her cheek to her mouth, where he traced her lips.

"Yes?"

"Now is when I'm expected to say something terrible?"

"Yes," Cy said. "I'm ready."

"I don't believe it."

"Believe what?"

"Don't believe you heard all those things in bed."

"Did I say I did?"

James looked down Cy's gaunt body, at the revealed anatomy. She loved the odd angles, the unusual perspectives of making love, but she'd kept away from it a long time, had decided against the complications.

"You made it all up."

"I made a little up, maybe."

James laughed softly. "I knew it." And she ducked her head in close, rested her head on his shoulder, her cheek on his chest. "You don't make much of a pillow," she said, at last.

"That's it? Your best shot?"

"Do I get a poem?"

"I don't think so."

They laughed together.

"*Bonheur*," Cy whispered.

"Great happiness."

A few minutes later, Cy asked, "What was your fortune? You never said." But James was already sleeping.

When Cy woke up it was still dark. He got up anyway, quietly, to pull the shutters inward, open; then he pushed the windows out, and fresh, night air poured over the sill. He stood naked at the window, taking deep, slow breaths. He knew he was going to be sick, not for a while, but by dawn. His head throbbed dully and somewhere in that small sparks of light had begun to flare. Warning lights. He got back into bed, waiting, feeling James's warmth against him. How unlikely. How lucky. He thought all his life he'd never been thankful enough. And what if it was a mercy? What if James had taken pity on him? Was he fool enough to say no to last chances? A fool to the end?

James stirred. A few strands of hair fell from her neck, her shoulder began to turn his way, and she rolled on to her back, eyes open. "Here we are," she said.

Before Cy could speak he heard an amplifier switch on, and the darkness hummed, and he knew for the first time in the new day a muezzin in Marrakech drew breath to praise God.

"*Allah akbar!*" The voice loud, laden with desire, the words drawn out but clipped. Percussive. "God is great!" Again, the same muezzin, from a minaret close at hand, "*Allah akbar!*" Then a second, muted, in the distance. Then another, closer, and another not too distant. James and Cy, side by side, were lost in the midst of it. The call to prayer. The dark sky resonating with voices. Then the voices started to drop away, then there were only two still singing, then one, far away, in the Ville Nouvelle, perhaps. Then none. A few dogs howled sympathetically, a few roosters crowed, taking up their own business.

"What you came for?" James asked.

"What I thought I came for, yes. The dawn call. When the city is awake the voices get lost in the noise. You can't hear that the plea is passionate, that it's the voice of love electric in the air over our beds."

❀

18

Asur had not dared to put a dress on again. He kept his hair in a rubber band at all times, whether or not he was wearing the Sox cap. He had taken to juggling in the plaza, with his cap on the ground in front of him, and the homeless kids jeered because, although he was good, sometimes he dropped things. Usually it was oranges. He juggled mandarins until he got thirsty, then he picked up his hat and ate the little oranges.

The college kids on the plaza often tossed a few coins in his cap; they were friendly, encouraging. One day, the strange one with the Chinese face and weird hair set a small sack of oranges on the ground next to where Asur sat. But what mattered most to Asur was that, when he juggled, he made a little carnival of the world, charmed it, and he felt safe. That was the attraction. So he juggled most of the day and hid on James's veranda at night.

On the day he had promised to meet the juggler he showered under the garden hose on the veranda, put on a new pair of jeans James had bought him, long enough in the leg that he had to turn four inches at the cuff, and a clean shirt, the best he had. His only concession to Luz was a red belt, the shoulder strap off her purse. In the plaza he sat on a bench and waited as night came on, the sunset glow on the hills passing away into the black and blue of night. Asur never doubted Marcela would show. She had said she would come. So he waited patiently, looking across the plaza toward Elvira, looking for her determined stride, a figure with a satchel in one hand.

So he didn't recognize the young woman in the short, green dress, the yellow sweater and practical shoes, who wore her hair loose around her shoulders, until she said, "Asur?" She didn't quite recognize him either out of a dress. Asur stood up, and, face to face, they laughed. Marcela pointed to a restaurant table set out in the plaza and for the first time since he'd run from the village Asur sat down as a customer, under a green umbrella, the life of the plaza now a spectacle for him. He saw Jorge and a few other of the scruffy street kids, looking dirty and sad, sitting on steps, on a bench under a tree. In them he saw himself. His place. Tears glistened in his eyes.

Marcela looked at him, her eyes dark, impassive. When he had composed himself, she asked if he would like to eat dinner, and he said he would. Handing him a menu, she said, "Anything, *cualquier cosa.*" The starchy waiter set out the plates, bread and butter, soup, a salad, a Coke and wine. Before the entrées even arrived, the table had begun to get crowded. Asur had forgotten what it was like to sit down to plenty. Nor had he had many chances to do so in his short life, only at rare, family gatherings, at festival. Here, they just ordered and the waiter carried it out over the flags, plenty, excess even.

Asur started in, but he felt clumsy, the silverware itself strange in his fingers. He had grown used to eating with his hands, out of a sack. A bowl of soup was a novelty, and so was the spoon, but he was careful not to spill any on the white tablecloth or his clean clothes. He thought Marcela looked more like a young and beautiful mother now, less like a toreador. He stared at her painted face, the clever use of lipstick and rouge and how big and dark her eyes shone with mascara and a touch of eye shadow. For all the changes, Asur thought one thing remained the same: she still seemed surer of herself than other people ever did. And this was the very thing Asur loved best about her. He believed in her.

Even after eating his fill, Asur admitted he wanted ice cream when she asked. As they walked to the shop on Gran Vía de Colón, Marcela told Asur that she had been to the police, that she would not be charged. The man who had attacked him had been in custody many times. The police said he was a crazy man, *un loco*, often in fights and given to fits of shouting. An addict. A thief. Witnesses said he had attacked unprovoked, that the juggler had only tried to protect the child.

For all that, the police said they could not allow a juggler to set fire to anybody on the streets of Granada. She was forbidden to juggle fire in Granada again without permission. In six months or a year, perhaps, it would again be permitted. Until then, she must use no fire.

Asur started to object. He said, "But," and no more; Marcela had put her hand on his lips.

"But I might have been arrested, Asur. They have banished my fire, but I am free. I will light my batons in the villages or in Seville or Cordoba."

"And me?"

"Asur? Asur goes free, too. But the police are looking for a run-away girl, for Luz. They asked me, 'Who was that girl,' and I said, 'No sé, some street girl called Luz.' 'Where can we find her?' 'No sé.' I told them nothing, only the name, Luz."

"And the *loco*?"

"He's in a hospital. He does not talk, he screams."

"Luz is banished, too."

"*Sí.*"

"But Luz would be free in the villages, in Seville or Cordoba."

"Yes."

"With you?"

"Maybe. Will you tell me where I can find your mother?"

Asur frowned.

"I will ask her."

"You won't tell her I am in Granada?"

"No."

"I have an aunt, in another village on the *vega*. Maybe she would take me, if you don't want to, but I doubt it. She is the sister of my father."

Then they had ice cream, Asur three flavors and Marcela just one, *arroz con leche*.

Alone, Asur crossed Gran Vía de Colón, running in front of the cars that waited on the light. At the cathedral, he turned in. He wanted to pray, he thought, but when he sat down and tried he found he could not. He watched the faithful, who mostly were old, and women. He envied them, their lit candles and their prayers for intercession. In the village, there was a church but no great cathedral, and the arching vaults made the boy feel very small. His eyes strayed from the tiers of votive candles to the Crucified on his cross and back to the candles, thin tapers burning quickly into the sand. The cathedral was very cool, the candles the only promise of living heat. He shut his eyes, listened to the murmured prayers, to the shuffling feet and scraped chairs. He prayed for a home but not the home he had run from.

When he opened his eyes he saw a priest walking toward the pulpit. Arrayed. Asur thought the robes very becoming. The priest carried himself with a refined dignity, but Asur thought he saw a little twitch in the hips, something that made the robes swish around his ankles. They flowed, were nothing like the stiff legs of Asur's new jeans. And the boy had an inkling.

❧

19

In the garden, the wind in the palm trees made a dry sound, like a great fan slowly opened or wooden swords rattled. The hotel had been built abutting a palm garden, and the date palms still stood just beyond the bedroom window, their shaggy heads showing over a mud wall. In the night, they rose up a hooded darkness against the starry sky.

Standing on the balcony, Paula listened to the sound of the wind and less distinctly, to the sound of water running in channels in the palm garden.

Sam slept. He'd been nervous the night before, worried by a note from Alan saying he was delayed, would meet them in the morning, this morning, after a night ride out from Marrakech on his motorcycle. Sam thought he'd be lucky to make it alive. But the crazy were lucky, Paula had noticed it many times: no luck without chances.

A cock crowed but it was still night. Paula thought roosters were overrated as harbingers of dawn. All night long in chicken country you heard them come out with an occasional, tentative squawk, hoping to be first, maybe, but managing no better than eccentric. They were guys, after all. They crowed when they could.

The hotel had surprised her. She hadn't been expecting swank, nor to find two nights paid in advance. Sam had wondered out loud who had paid for them. He'd guessed the Algerians because he didn't think Alan's cut would be big enough to justify the expenditure. Paula had asked if terrorists would likely be so free with their money. Sam had shrugged, unsure himself.

"I mean, they're selling the Qur'ans because, because they need money?"

"One would think," Sam had said, hooking his thumbs into the waistband of his pants.

"And the German doesn't know where we're staying?"

"No. Alan said here. Herr Schmidt, he doesn't know Alan. And shouldn't, ever. Part of what we're getting paid for is knowing Alan."

Thinking about it now, standing on the balcony off the bedroom, Paula thought Alan had to have paid for the room. Alan wouldn't have told the Algerians where they were staying for the same reason Sam wouldn't tell the German about Alan, for fear the Algerians might cut him out of the deal. Still, it was an odd generosity. If by chance the Algerians had paid, it was likely the beginning of bargaining, something to split their allegiances, since they would ostensibly be bargaining for their client. Which didn't take into account that their allegiances were already split, their own interests more closely considered than Herr Schmidt's. Paula smiled, playfully, as if the money weren't real or the swindles in earnest.

She respected art, the real thing, and her ability to know it when she saw it. This had nothing to do with the smug judgment, *I know what I like*, the favorite slogan of those who know very little except what they like, if they can be believed even in that, since so many of them just happen to like the same few things. No, she meant the ability to know what a thing actually is, to know who made it, and when. In old things, such judgments are never final; there is always a degree of ambiguity. But they are objective, based on the things and not on self-referential standards.

When she spoke for the authenticity of the Algerians' Qur'ans, she would be all seriousness, but the deals swirling around that judgment, the players and the money, that she couldn't take entirely seriously. She had to remember the straight face, to make it. The effort was a strain, an occupational hazard. In the end, she hadn't been able to stand the museum world, because the public face was so reverent. Nor had she, finally, been able to subscribe to the notion that there was a compelling reason that the best should be in a museum. She thought collectors had as good a claim, even scoundrels. Sam thought he'd seduced her away from the museum, from restorations, but she'd been ready for a new life, for less solemnity. And Sam had delivered, if not the grand life he wanted for himself, then, certainly, capers. A little solemn theater on occasion, too, of course, but they never pretended between themselves that the deals were anything but theater.

Even the sex was theater. Her last performance as the innocent, that's how it had begun. Sam had wanted that, wanted it to have been his finger to defile her. His cock to crow over her staggering limbs as she made as if to crawl away. Her *oh*, as if in surprise at the size of it, when he penetrated her for the first time. As if she hadn't been first among friends at thirteen. She'd bullied a college boy living at home next door into showing her how to do it. Afterward, he'd cried, ashamed and frightened too because she knew his kid sister. She had laughed in his face. And when he got over his fear and his shame and wanted to show her again, she had taunted him until he'd spit on her. "Oh Jimmy"; then she'd let him do it again.

Her performance of the innocent for Sam, she thought, had been such a good one because she'd had so much practice at it. Of course, he must have known better, but he'd liked the fiction and as a story he liked it even better. The ogre with innocence smeared on his hands. She'd heard him, overheard him telling it more than once, and she'd let him, never objected, not even in private.

But she had taxed him in other ways. Like Jimmy, Sam had been made to spit on her, to piss on her, too, if he wanted to fuck her. He'd said, "No," but he'd come round. She thought for her too there should be the kind of pleasure she liked in it. At first, she just hadn't cared whether he wanted to, whether his sense of propriety was offended or not, but perhaps it wasn't propriety so much as aesthetics. In Sam, she thought, the two things seriously overlapped. But after a while forcing him had become part of the pleasure. To drive him out of the roles he chose for himself, to see him naked as he swung his nozzle over her, over beauty, his beloved beauty.

Surely the Sam he pretended to be might have found a way to like it; hadn't he wanted to defile her? But he was only ogre enough to finger innocence, to diddle a girl. A small, dime-a-dozen kind of ogre, the kind a woman with a mind to could keep on a leash as a pet. And hadn't she?

Paula looked over her shoulder, through the open door, at Sam in bed. *Mon petit ogre*, she cooed. To her surprise, Sam answered; she hadn't thought he was awake.

"Isn't that the ogre's robe you've got on there?"

"Come and get it. Come on, don't miss your chance to swagger out naked under the giant, phallic palms."

"Allah akbar," the muezzin's dawn call broke over the palm garden. Before it had died away they heard, as if in response, another voice in the village, answering, *"Allah akbar!"*

Sam pulled a pillow up round his ears and groaned. "Great, maybe, but not very civil. If that was a party now'd be the time to call the police."

Paula laughed. "You call," she said. "I like it. It's quite beautiful."

"Always aestheticizing."

"Me? Sam, you hypocrite, you . . ."

"Maybe, without the amplifier."

"Maybe what?"

"Maybe it would be beautiful. Our only hope is an outage."

Then Sam remembered what day it was, a money day, and he climbed out of bed, wound a sheet around his waist and walked toward the balcony door.

Paula watched him coming, her head cocked appreciatively. "Men in skirts," she said.

Sam stayed in the shower a good long time, comfortably smug about how well he'd acquitted himself with Paula, even on the second go. He stroked himself affectionately. His body. He liked to think he took care of it. He washed with fine, milled soaps, spent small fortunes on shampoos and conditioners. Probably about average, for a woman, he thought. But it had worked; his hair was shiny and his skin smooth and remarkably unlined. He dressed well, everything the best. Excellent material carefully tailored to fit his frame. Even the Panama hat he wore habitually in warm climes to keep the sun off his face had cost him seven hundred dollars and a good deal of trouble. After he'd found a make of serious quality, he'd rejected a half dozen as lacking sufficient character. Sometimes, shopping, he'd noticed a bit of exasperation on the part of the staff, even in exclusive shops. He stepped out of the shower; when he touched the rough towel, he sighed.

By the time he was ready to face breakfast it was time to meet Alan in the dining room. Sam stopped at the door and looked at Paula critically. He asked if she had anything less likely to offend the Algerians.

"Complete *purdah*, do you think? Perhaps we could poke a few holes in a sheet and throw it over my head?"

"Seriously."

"Seriously what?"

"They're likely to have an exaggerated sense of propriety. They're strict Muslims, I believe. Sharia and all that jazz."

"They're men. More *purdah*, more pornography. That's the real law."

"Perhaps."

"Sam, these clothes are modest; Western yes, but modest." She put her arms down, palms forward, a gesture that said *behold*. "My shoulders are covered. The skirt almost drags in the dirt."

Sam considered. "True enough," he said, "you look good, a proper lady," but it wasn't so. The clothes were modest enough, but Paula looked provocative in them. She always did.

They found Alan in the dining room, smoking and drinking white coffee. He looked not to have slept or showered, red-eyed and dusty, his heavy black beard bristling. Like many a big, shambling man, he displayed an easy, if sloppy, friendliness, struggling up with a loopy grin to offer his hand to Paula, and, as an afterthought, to Sam.

A waiter brought around menus and Sam looked at his critically, hoping they wouldn't have to watch Alan eat. He feared it might be gruesome. But Alan said he'd be sticking with caffeine and nicotine, afraid a single egg might send him to sleep.

Sam and Paula ate while Alan talked. He'd arranged two meetings, he said. The Algerians had insisted. One in the morning and one in the evening. As he understood it, they wanted to get half the money well away from Zagora before they handed over the second Qur'an.

"Cautious for bandits," Alan said.

Sam looked up from his marmalade, thinking.

"They're sending a man at eleven. He'll direct us to the first meeting," Alan added.

"Will there be blindfolds?" Paula asked.

"I don't think so."

"That was a joke."

"Oh." Alan managed to suggest mirth, twisting his face into grotesque jollity. "I'm sorry," he said, his gaze taking in both Paula and

Sam. "I believe I suggested from the beginning that these are rough guys, the kind who settle things with guns and knives. Don't forget that. But they've got the goods, rare and wonderful Qur'ans they are willing to sell."

"Making a speech?" Sam inquired dryly.

"Look," Alan said, suddenly hot, "this is maybe a one-time shot for you, but I've been cultivating this connection for years, and I'll be seeing them again. So can the attitude. I've dealt with them before—this isn't a business they want to be in, and just because of that they want an extra measure of respect. We just do it their way, okay? No questions."

"Finished?"

"No. It's not too late to back out, but it's going to be soon. You need to be sure you've got the guts, the stomach for this kind of business. Do you?"

"For what?" Paula said.

"The guts to face down a challenge or accept a rebuke, to suggest trust when you find a man with a gun a little frightening. And stomach enough to realize where your money's going, for more guns, more night raids on villages . . ."

"Enough," Sam said quietly. "You sound like you want the high ground, which is ridiculous. We know. We've been around."

"Moral high ground? That is funny," and Alan laughed, his mirth unforced this time. "No. Just business, okay? No mistakes."

The Algerians' "man" turned out to be a fresh-faced boy of about twelve, a boy in a ragged sweater vest, slippers peeking out from under his robe. He climbed nimbly into the small backseat of the Ford

Ka and directed them from there. Down around the back side of the palm garden, across a bridge over an irrigation ditch, and right, on into a part of town that was not mentioned in their guidebook, working class, the buildings plain and the streets dusty. Sam drove slowly, negotiating the uneven ground as best he could. He looked at the boy in the mirror, plainly excited; at Paula, strangely impassive; and at Alan trailing behind on his motorcycle in the cloud of dust the Ka put up even at slow speeds. The last observation was satisfying. Sam felt a familiar calm, the calm of the event. His confidence returned: they would at least have the advantage of knowledge. They would know more, he felt sure of that.

The boy pointed to a massive door in a brown wall, blue handprints around the frame. The Ka had not come fully to a stop when the door was pushed open from inside and an elderly man, wearing a full white beard and a burnoose, stepped out to welcome them. The boy went in ahead of them. Alan went next, with Paula and Sam behind. They saw two or three robed and veiled shapes going away, the women, as they walked into a central courtyard. The Algerians were there, sitting cross-legged on cushions.

The old man beckoned toward the cushions across from the Algerians, who did not stand. They stared at Paula, at her freckled face and sloping eyes and at the habitual sultriness of the way she moved. Then they looked away, faces stern behind their black beards. They put their heads together, their words buzzing between them, clearly displeased.

The old Moroccan whispered something to the Algerians, and they quieted down. Alan introduced them, Ahmed and Moustafa, and then Sam and Paula, first names only. The old man offered tea and sweets, and they said, "Yes." He turned his head and spoke softly and the boy, who must have been waiting in the next room, entered with the refreshments on an old tinned, copper tray.

Alan explained in French, with a fluency that surprised them, that Sam and Paula represented another man, a German national, who was a collector of Islamic art.

"And who," Sam interrupted, "had not only an expert's appreciation for Islamic antiquities but a warm sympathy for contemporary Muslim causes." This was solid fiction, but, Sam thought, the appropriate lie.

Ahmed looked at Sam curiously, suggesting by the slightest sneer that he was not to imagine that the German's sympathies were welcome.

The old man nodded—they were all guests in his house—saying, "May he have many sons."

"*Inshallah*," Ahmed said, dryly, as if he doubted Allah's goodwill in the matter.

Alan resumed. He explained Sam and Paula's expertise, dwelling on their work restoring a *cármene* in Spain, in Granada.

"In Andalusia?" Ahmed asked rhetorically. "Is our mark in Al-Andalus indelible, or do the Catholics there sell our heritage to the tourists, as the safe Islam, Islam without Muslims? Do you think in the hundreds of years of Islam there we Muslims imagined a '*Reconquista*'? How surprised would the 'Andalusians' be if we came back?"

Alan and Sam exchanged a startled glance. Sam felt the Algerian was waiting for an answer, so he said, primly, "Very," and to his relief Ahmed laughed, his face wrinkling up around his eyes.

"Yes, very," he said, and they all laughed, the tension eased somehow.

Paula raised a hand and covered her lips, as if modestly to veil her laughing mouth, but in reality to hide the fact that she wasn't actually laughing.

She thought the Algerians were likely demented, but they were ardent; a warmth suffused their faces, which made them attractive in a rough way. Even across the tea tray and sweets she could feel their body heat, smell that they were rank. They were men. Next to them, Sam looked very pale and a little bewildered.

As if by prior agreement, Alan stood up, shook hands with the old Moroccan, and nodded to Moustafa and Ahmed, who nodded back, if curtly.

"I'll leave you to business then," he said. "Sam, Paula, I'll be waiting back at the hotel." When the door had closed behind him Moustafa called to the boy, who carried in a worn, leather satchel. When Moustafa reached up to take it, Sam saw the checked handle of a pistol protruding from under his robes, where it had been hidden between his leg and the floor cushion he was sitting on.

The boy picked up the tinned tray and the old man set Alan's abandoned cushion where the tray had been, the Algerians on one side, Sam and Paula on the other. Moustafa slipped the Qur'an, wrapped in a yellow, and not entirely clean, silk scarf, out of the satchel. Then, as if it were terribly fragile, or explosive, he placed the book gingerly on the cushion and plucked the corners of the scarf back, leaving the Qur'an revealed.

Sam wanted to compliment the Algerian on the drama of this little routine, high marks for showmanship, but he presumed the comment would not be well received.

"Almost a thousand years old," Moustafa said simply, turning the pages one at a time, his manner insisting that they admire the calligraphy and the illuminations. Sam did so, his language measured but his tone warm with enthusiasm. He did not hold with those who thought it wise to denigrate anything you meant to buy, as if any expression of admiration was a bargaining weakness. There would be time to register reservations later. Better, he thought, to delay the adversarial note as long as possible. And he found nothing more natural than to praise the Qur'an. Even setting aside the illuminations, anyone with an eye for Arabic calligraphy would have been struck by the beauty of the scribe's hand. Sam lamented the advent of the printed book, the loss of the distinctive mark that was the calligrapher's style, the rush away from beauty to sheer numbers, to accuracy, at best. And this Qur'an had been illuminated by a master.

"I'll need a little more light," Paula said, and Sam said, "She'll need a little more light," as if he were translating. To Paula's surprise, her request seemed to have been anticipated, and soon she was looking at the book under the precise light of a halogen bulb.

She pulled on a pair of white gauze gloves to keep the oils of her skin off the pages; she realized no one else would ever have treated the book with such elaborate caution in all its long history, but she had seen how fingers can blacken a page. And it made her seem professional, which would no doubt carry them further with the Algerians than actual expertise.

The binding had been replaced, not surprisingly, but the present binding, tooled leather, was old enough to have developed a pleasant patina of its own. Not offensive. More importantly, however many bindings the Qur'an might have worn in seven or eight hundred years—Moustafa's thousand exaggerated—the pages had not been significantly encroached upon. The calligraphy and illuminations were centered on the pages, and the binding loose enough to allow the book to lie fully open. Paula leaned forward, paging quickly but carefully clear through, making sure the Qur'an was complete, every *sura* there.

Sam watched her, he loved to watch her at work, the way concentration stripped away her habitual irony, all her posing, and left her nothing more than a beautiful young woman, the look of an innocent, freckles, eyes set obliquely over a mouth slightly pursed.

She took out her loupe, looking at the condition of the finely polished paper, at the calligraphy: the broad nib of the scribe's reed pen had been used to remarkable effect. The calligrapher, clearly a master, had written in a wonderfully open yet delicately balanced *maghribi* script in sepia ink. It never failed to astound Paula that this ink, literally colored by soot, could be so beautiful; the variation in the density of the sepia tones itself was exquisite. The vocalization had been marked in red, the *tashdid* and *sukkun* in blue, and the *hamza* in yellow. The colors showed little fading, were quite bright, and stood out wonderfully. Gold trefoils separated the verses, and blue and gold medallions shone in the margins. The Qur'an was clearly Andalusian—the use of paper rather than vellum for Qur'ans in the Magreb had been a much later development—and Nasrid, very likely from the vicinity of Granada itself.

And not signed, although many old Qur'ans bore a signature, not surprisingly, perhaps, given the exalted esteem accorded to calligraphy in Islam. In spite of Sam's celebrating the anonymity of old, Islamic work in general, it was only anonymous with respect to the name of the artist; it was always executed in the manner of a school, a place and a time. Paula didn't think the absence of a signature made the work anonymous; the individual was in the work, in every stroke. The artist might not be named, and there was an advantage in that, Paula thought, but the advantage wasn't in the artist's relation to the work, in the suppression of the self, so much as in the work's relation to audience. Not knowing the artist's name, you couldn't prefer the artist to the work; all you had was the work, so you saw it more clearly.

Paula turned her attention to the illuminations, to the illuminated panels and carpet pages. She found the conception of each one, their interrelations, the execution, all wonderful. Some colors, she knew, had faded a bit, the paint had flaked a little in places or worn thin enough that it had begun to disappear. Here and there the burnished gold had sloughed away. The condition of the whole, however, was very good if not excellent. The aridity of North Africa was a fortunate chance, a great good for preservation. Here, the danger was desiccation; things didn't mold.

Paula wondered if this Qur'an had come across the Straits of Hercules at the time of the *Reconquista*, in the great return, or before. Certainly, taking a last look at the lost garden, at Andalusia, reduced to what you could carry away, you would have taken this Qur'an, no doubt about that.

She closed the book, carefully refolding the yellow silk over it. Slowly, she pulled off the gloves; then she leaned her head close to Sam's to make a whispered report, the Algerians watching her curiously.

With so little to bargain about, and with the Algerians' asking price more than fair, they soon agreed on a figure. If they had been buying it for themselves, for keeps, they would have been happy, but they weren't, and paying so nearly the full price left little to skim. They weren't there to settle for the German's fees.

Sam had counted out and banded hundred-dollar bills in bundles of ten at the hotel, and it took him only a few seconds to produce the money.

Paula smiled brightly at the Algerians, which elicited no more than deeper frowns. She thought they were at that place where attraction flips into hatred, perhaps even before it registers as attraction. She'd known men in America of a similar stripe. The dangerous, the righteous. Men who tried to resolve the tension between the world and their God by hating the world, by hating women especially. Just for attracting them. It was their own desire they struck out against when they clarified the world with violence. She did not smile again. Having recognized the edge beyond which was abyss, she stepped back.

The Algerians counted the money carefully, examining the bills for watermarks—they made use of the halogen light, too—making sure none of the hundreds was too soiled to pass muster when they were buying rather than selling.

Then they were done. Moustafa said in unaccented English, "The boy will come for you again, at seven. This," he pulled a sealed envelope from the folds of his robes, "is for Alan. The other half tonight.

Tell him not to come again. We don't need to advertise our business with a parade."

Sam and Paula stood up, the Algerians did not. They left it to the old Moroccan to show the Americans out, to observe the civilities.

They found Alan asleep in a deck chair on the terrace of the hotel, mouth open, in the shade of a palm tree, the top button loosened on his jeans.

"Like the guy in Brueghel's *Harvesters*."

"Perhaps not quite that undone," Sam said, "but close."

Sam bent down and shook Alan's shoulder gently, until his eyes opened and he blinked and was awake.

"Go okay?"

Sam handed him the envelope. "They said the other half tonight, but your attendance is not required."

"Not required?"

"As in not wanted."

"I see."

"As a party, not all of that jolly, anyway."

"No."

"I'm taking a walk," Paula announced abruptly. She'd remembered she wanted to sample the dates from the local palms.

They'd expected to be directed back to where they'd met before, but the boy shook his head, waving them out to the highway and left, where the road ran toward Algeria before finally petering out at M'Hamid. When they passed a road sign with distances on it, the boy pointed, said, "Tamegroute." It was miles in the dark.

Sam laughed. "Wonderful, right into the Sahara. You don't suppose the Algerians crossed the border around here, in the desert?"

"They don't seem like camel-riding guys to me," Paula replied, "but I imagine it's possible."

The boy said, in French, that Tamegroute was a religious center. "There's a Qur'anic library, famous." He looked back and forth between them, sitting in the front seats, and added, "*Un peu fameux, ici, au moins.* Many old Qur'ans."

Sam drove on, wondering why he'd been so sure they'd know more than the Algerians.

"Are you a student?" Paula asked.

"*Oui.*"

"*Ici?*"

"In Algeria, at a madrasa."

Sam said, "You're not from Zagora?"

"No."

"How did you get here?"

The boy shook his head, looking suddenly wary. He pointed toward a few town lights glittering in the desert ahead, "Tamegroute," he said.

But before they reached the town he pointed again, to a dirt track leading over a low hill, away from the Drâa. Sam took it very slowly in the Ka, not a car made for off-road travel. They were going ahead on faith alone now, he reflected grimly. If this was a trap, they were beyond help already.

When they cleared the ridge a single light came into view, a stone hut, perhaps a goatherd's shelter, with a lantern hanging in the door. When Sam pulled to a stop he glimpsed a robed figure in the glow of his brake lights, a man in a burnoose with an automatic rifle slung over his shoulder. The boy jumped from the car and ran into the lit doorway of the hut.

Sam turned his head toward Paula. She cast him a rigid smile.

"And you," she said, "cautious Sam."

He started to speak, but she cut him off.

"Nothing to say, Sam, nothing at all."

They climbed out of the Ka. A man-shape filled the hut's small door, Moustafa, who said, "Welcome."

"*Bon soir.*" Sam's voice sounded a little pinched to Paula's ear.

She nodded gravely.

"*Bon soir.* A long way to bring you in the dark; I am sorry. We have enemies, maybe. We are careful."

"Yes."

"All will be well."

"*Inshallah,*" Sam said, in spite of himself.

Inside, the hut was surprisingly comfortable. A carpet had been spread and there were cushions to sit on. There were hot coals in the hearth with a tea kettle set right in among them. Mint tea, in small glasses, and, oddly enough, Oreos.

The second Qur'an wasn't as fine as the first. It was as old, perhaps older than the other one, and it had weathered the years as well, but the calligraphy was uninspired. The illuminations, Paula thought, were likely by more than one hand, perhaps by as many as three. Some were eye-catching, boldly conceived and skillfully executed; others seemed half-hearted, perfunctory.

Still, workmanlike illuminations sometimes showed well, were borne by the larger conception of the volume. But here, the illuminations played alone, even suffered by the company they kept, from the discoordination of the whole. For all that, the Qur'an was authentic, old and well preserved, and Herr Schmidt would no doubt be proud to have it.

Sam nodded when Paula had finished whispering her report. There was no need to say that this Qur'an presented a better opportunity for them, if they could bargain with the Algerians. Again, Sam regretted how helpless they were, how exposed, even endangered. How much bad cop would be possible in the circumstances?

But none was required. Moustafa himself suggested that this Qur'an was less valuable. He said he'd asked for an opinion in Tamegroute. Of course, he understood that with a well-documented provenance the Qur'an might still command their original asking price on the open market, but on the black market . . . He spread his hands. He offered to discount the price 40 percent, better than Sam and Paula had hoped for. They left the hut exulting, Sam's money belt still fat with unspent hundreds.

They drove through the dark on the narrow, paved road, Zagora in front of them, the stars hot and close overhead. Fingers of the Sahara glittered here and there under the crescent moon. The desert was not far. Paula looked at Sam's face in the dash lights, and she found him handsome all over again; the worry that had disfigured his features had withdrawn. He looked light enough to levitate, happy, and a little richer than before.

At the hotel, they looked for Alan in the lobby, but he wasn't there. Sam rapped on his door, the envelope of money in his off hand, but the door did not open. He walked back down the tiled hall frowning, and when he got to the lobby, he saw Paula with the key to their room in her hand, looking blank, stricken.

"He checked out, not long after we left."

"That bastard."

Their room had clearly been searched, and the Qur'an was missing from Sam's leather valise. He hadn't hidden it, just put it away. There was a letter where the Qur'an had been, scrawled in a large, childish hand:

Sam—

Magic starts in misdirection, but you know that. Look, I enjoyed this. And may I make a suggestion? Mali is beautiful this time of year. The Dogon. Vernacular architecture. A place to die for. And the music! It's a pleasant country to hide in, if you should find you need one.

—Alan

P.S. My best to the little lady. A bit scrappy, but a looker. Don't forget her when you count your blessings.

20

Cy filled the watering can at the spigot and lifted it to his hip, resting it there. It had rained at least once, he thought, while they'd been in Morocco. He'd felt the dirt in a couple of pots and deep down there was still a little moisture in the soil. But the water would be welcome. The hibiscus looked stressed, its leaves hung limp from their stems, and the open blooms had fallen.

Cy decided to water it first, and he let the water stream in around the flower's roots. He felt certain it would soon recover its starchiness. Then he watered the geraniums and the herbs, a small oleander potted in an old olive-oil can. Cy went slowly. He felt ill and tired and not disposed to hurry. The evening was coming on but things were quiet down in Cruz Verde.

When he'd finished with the flowers, he sat down, looking into the end-of-the-day life of the *placeta*. A few old *grenadinos* passed, strolling, keeping alive the old ways, the *paseo*, in the Albayzín. The men very upright, the women bent forward a little under their black headscarves. A familiar dog trotted into the square, looked around, then hotfooted it back out the way it had come. Some kind of terrier mutt, disappointed, perhaps, to find the *placeta* empty.

Cy leaned back and closed his eyes. They'd crossed back from Tangier on a night ferry, the waves of the Straits of Hercules black but flaring with the ferry lights. He could still hear the hiss of the bow wake, as if the water were a great bolt of black silk cut by shears. They'd stood with Africa at their backs, returning, the shore lights of Spain and Gibraltar rising out of the sea, getting brighter, as the ferry crossed over. Now Cy sat in his own dark, thinking again about the palm reader's fortune, and how James had responded to it, imagining the Muslim return to North Africa to escape the swords of the Catholic kings at the time of the *Reconquista*. Those Muslims who wouldn't convert. Cy wondered if it had been like that, a great crowd fleeing all at once in boats. The *Reconquista* had taken lifetimes. And almost the last Muslims to go had been the Nasrids of Granada. That year the Catholics made the same deal with Iberian Jews; most of those not renouncing their faith were scattered in diaspora around the Mediterranean, the Sephardim. Many had followed the Muslims down into the Magreb and made a life there. Who, Cy wondered, had been the less tolerant then, in 1492, that year Columbus sailed?

Even the Gods came and went, believers carrying them away in the light of consciousness. Peoples come and gone, the faithful and the apostate. And individuals. No one did better than make a sojourn. Cy leaned back, looking into the sky where the stars had come out. He did not feel singled out by his disease. His lot was common. But the common lot was exacting. He remembered a gravestone he'd seen back in Pittsburgh, in a cemetery not far from his carriage house. Just a name and the inscription, "Lived 12 minutes." He remembered the Cy who had stood over those words, the sudden grief. He'd tried to understand why the parents had chosen to specify the number of minutes their son had lived. The parents had wanted to claim, he thought, that even the shortest life was a life.

He fell asleep. And it took him a moment to realize that the rapping was not in a dream, but at the door to his house down on the *placeta*. He stood up quietly and leaned over the rail to see who was there.

"Paula?"

Her face came up unguarded, looking scared.

"Are you okay?"

Paula nodded but did not look okay. "Where have you been?"

"Marrakech."

"With Mad James?"

Cy nodded. "Weren't you in Morocco, too? With Sam?" he added.

"Yes, with Sam, but we've been back a couple of days. Are you going to let me in?"

Cy switched on the bare bulb in the stairway down and shielded his eyes with one hand, holding onto the rail with the other. He stopped in front of the door, hesitating, but then he threw the bolt and pulled the doors in. Paula stepped inside, up against Cy, and banged her forehead on his chest. When she looked up there were tears in her eyes, and Cy frowned. Paula glanced around at the rubbish, and Cy said, "The livable rooms are upstairs. These were workrooms or storerooms, I don't know. I try to ignore them."

Paula started up the stairs toward the unshaded bulb and Cy tried not to notice the way the light fell through her dress. Then he did look, and she turned and said, "I got a copy of your book, the one

Mad James wasn't ever going to let me see. Got it all the way from the States. It came while we were in Morocco."

"Keep going," Cy said, as she turned at the top of the stairs. "There should be a breeze up on the roof."

Paula left her sandals on the landing before climbing on up. Cy glanced at them before going into the kitchen for glasses and something to drink.

"Looks more like your bedroom than the roof," Paula sang down the stairwell. "What's a girl to think?"

"Outside," Cy said quietly. Then more loudly, "There are chairs outside!"

"I'm afraid I haven't been shopping," Cy apologized, handing Paula a bottle of sparkling water and a glass. "And my hospitality is not that famous to begin with."

"No? I thought it was; your book, I mean . . ."

"No. And just recently I haven't had many visitors. I'm wondering why you're here, as a matter of fact. Not to talk poetry, surely?"

Paula said nothing.

"Some trouble, I'm thinking."

"Yes, trouble. It's Sam."

Cy looked at Paula doubtfully. "If it's jealousy I don't think your coming here will calm him down. He made me a visit, too, you know, before Morocco. He issued a kind of warning about you. Made you sound quite dangerous."

"Sam?"

Cy nodded.

Paula got up and leaned on the rail, looking across toward the lit ramparts of the Alhambra. "It's not jealousy," she said. "He is the jealous kind, but that's not the trouble this time." She turned her head and her shoulders a little and her spine bent in a sinuous line. "It's money trouble."

"Ah."

"It's just that I don't know what he might do. When he's pushed, he pushes. That's his nature. But he's never been pushed like this, not that I know of. I'm afraid. He seems ready for anything. I'm afraid the time might come when I will need to run. I might need a place to hide. Just for a few hours or maybe a day."

"Here?"

"I'd like to know I have a place to go."

Cy thought he should say no but he looked at her and he didn't.

He said, "I hope it doesn't come to that. It probably won't. I don't think he'd want to lose you."

"That's what frightens me. He thinks he has a right to whatever he wants."

At the door going out Paula pressed up against him again and growled, "I'll be back for that poetry lesson another time." Then she was gone.

Cy watched her cross the *placeta*, watched her until she disappeared into the alley up. He doubted if she should be walking alone so late in the Albayzín, but it was her choice. He shut the door, thinking that the stairs back up and the climb into bed would be quite enough for him.

Cy slipped out of his shoes and tried to get comfortable on the bed. Lately, his joints had been hurting, as if the bones of his skeleton had begun to grate together whenever he moved. On his side, with one pillow under his head and another between his tucked-up knees, he could rest, forget his body for a few minutes at a time. He was worse. Or maybe just tired from traveling. That was possible. But he thought it more likely that he was worse, that down in Morocco he had passed another marker that he'd never see the other side of again.

He found he couldn't sleep, not immediately. His eyes ached. When he closed them they seemed to glow. A memory from his life in Lahore plagued him; the memory wasn't painful, wasn't attended by shame or guilt, but it wouldn't let go. He had been at a party in a distant part of the city. Happy, he'd been happy. The world beautiful under a mulberry tree inside walled grounds, under a thick canopy of leaves.

He was in every way the outsider there, a forbidden man to the woman he found suddenly smiling on him. So, of course, the sparks had blown in the dark thick as from a fire at night. Just that. The night shade full of flowing sparks. Then he'd sat alone in the back of his car on the way home, his driver negotiating the traffic, terrible, even at that hour. They had come up on a trailer, two trailers, loaded heavily with steel I-beams. In the surge of traffic they had pulled even with hypnotic slowness, like the slow motion of dream, and when they got up to where the tractor should have been Cy had seen that the trailers were moving under power of four camels in harness, a man standing on a platform with the reins in his hands. It hadn't seemed possible, those camels pulling in the heavy traffic.

Cy couldn't explain it, but the image, the way they had floated up on the right of the straining camels, it had stayed with him. And haunted him now.

❖

21

Asur sat down on a bench in the Plaza Nueva, a small white sack of mandarin oranges clutched in his hand. The shadows seemed pressed back in the noon sun, dense and green under the small trees planted in a row on the Alhambra side of the plaza. Asur was wondering if their roots reached down to the Darro, here, where it ran underground. Looking to his right he could see where the Darro disappeared under the city in Plaza Santa Ana, and he thought the river, if it ran straight, must pass just under his feet. He considered putting his ear to the ground to listen for it, and might have, if he hadn't been so clean. James had brought him a t-shirt from Morocco the color, she said, of the Marrakech walls, with a small blue hand printed on the front where the logo goes. This morning he'd put the shirt on over his jeans. Today, he thought, he looked like a boy with a mother.

He'd left as soon as James was up; she painted in the morning and when she worked she would not be interrupted. She was a different person when she was painting, utterly remote. He knew not to speak to her, that if she heard him at all she would be startled. Later, she would be friendly, maybe tell him about her trip or ask about the juggler. But he wouldn't tell her what had happened, about the burning man. That man, he was gone now, and Marcela had said he was going to stay gone. Asur imagined the *loco* in a cell with bars and a big padlock. He imagined him asleep or drugged, his arms bound in the long sleeves of a straightjacket. The child knew there was no reason to fear him now. But Luz, Asur thought, Luz was banished, too. The police were looking for her, if not for him. Even now, he didn't want to let her go.

Asur took out five of the little oranges and started to juggle, his hands moving lightly as he tossed the oranges into the bright air over his head. He smiled. Suddenly it felt easy, his hands, the mandarins, obeying a pattern passed down from juggler to juggler almost forever. Now passed down from Marcela to him.

First one, then another of the oranges disappeared overhead, and he twisted around, expecting to see the grinning face of Jorge. But it was not Jorge. It was Sam, who said quietly, "Don't run." Asur stood up, to be ready, if running should suddenly seem the better choice.

Sam stepped back, held his hands up to his chest, palms out. "It's okay. Yes?"

Asur nodded.

"You remember when you worked up at the villa? *¿Recuerda?*"

"Yes."

"You took something, something valuable. I know you did."

Asur said nothing.

"You gave it to James. She showed me. She doesn't know you stole it. She doesn't know that you are a thief. And I'm not going to tell her if . . ."

The boy shook his head. "I didn't steal it."

"Oh, you did. But don't worry. I'm not going to tell her. Okay?"
Sam smiled, looking at ease, his Panama tilted to one side. He tossed
the little oranges back to Asur one at a time. "You're getting good."
Sam mimed the motions of juggling. "Much better. I've been watching. What do you say?"

Asur said, "Okay."

"But I need *un favor*. You do me a favor and I'll forget about the
little figure. She'll never know."

"What?" Asur said.

"That you're a thief."

"What favor?"

Sam walked slowly around the bench, peered at it critically, and
finally sat down next to Asur's sack of mandarins. "I need someone
to crawl under a room in the villa. I want to hide something down
there. But where you get in it is very small, and under there, it would
be very dirty." Sam brushed at his white ducks. "Not for me. You'd
want to put on some old clothes," he said.

"That's all? Go under a house?"

"Yes."

"When?"

Sam looked at his watch, which read 12:00. "In two hours? You
remember where I live?"

Asur nodded. "In two hours," he said; then he darted in and
grabbed the bag of oranges and leapt aside, looking back over his
shoulder at Sam as he walked away.

Sam pulled a small leather-covered notepad out of a pocket and
flipped it open. Most of the items on his list he had already checked

off; now he pulled the silver pencil from its sleeve, adjusted the lead, and drew a line through the words *the kid*. He wondered how much the kid was worth, really. Not as much as the stolen Qur'an, not to him, anyway. But he thought he'd find out how much. You couldn't really tell how juicy an orange was until you squeezed it. He stood up, shoved his hands into the loose pockets of his white ducks, and started to stroll.

Asur looked down on the Darro, watching the swallows as they skimmed along the stone walls of the channel. The street was narrow, the sidewalks narrower yet, especially on the river side. Still, he liked looking at the river, so he risked it. He looked up at James's veranda when he came even with it and she was there, sitting in a chair behind the potted plants. He waved but she did not see him. When he called her name her head came around and she smiled and beckoned for him to come over. He crossed the Puente de Cabrera and turned into Santa Ana. Although he ran he found the door was already ajar when he got there.

James was washing her hands at the sink in the kitchen when he walked through the door, quietly closing it behind him. She smiled at him, asked if he was hungry. He said a little and she stood at the counter, making sandwiches. Three, he noticed. She spread a purple olive butter across slices of bread from Nujaila, and carefully cut several paper-thin slices off a block of hard cheese. Then she washed and sliced a cucumber and three small tomatoes. She dabbed at the half-assembled sandwich with a knife dipped in soft butter. He had tasted this sandwich once before and found it heavy, dry, and somehow raw, but he'd eaten it. He didn't expect James to eat like a Spaniard.

When James saw Asur eyeing the third sandwich, she said she was expecting Cy.

"Oh," he said as she covered it with a piece of plastic wrap.

"But I'm not sure when," James said and smiled. "We can eat outside." She handed him a Coke out of the fridge, taking a bottle of sparkling water for herself.

When Cy unwrapped his sandwich at the table on the veranda, he noticed Asur's plate and raised his eyebrows in a question.

"He said he had to meet someone, I think," James said.

Cy nodded. "Well, I guess that's good."

"It must be. He passed up paid work here for it—I was going to do a few sketches of him. Pay him for modeling."

"Perhaps he's shy."

"Not that shy, I think. But there is always pride to be considered."

"I know it," Cy said. He was trying to decide if he should say anything about the huge canvas James had gessoed and hung on the wall, or mention the stack of crayon studies that now occupied her worktable. He had seen a few of these in Morocco, but only in glimpses. Finally, he said, "Something new cooking?"

And she said, "Yes," and that was the end of it. But he was glad she was working. That she wasn't going to flounder but start right in again.

He watched her sprinkle coarse salt over the leftover cucumbers and tomatoes. "You can have this," he said, pointing to the half of sandwich still on his plate. "It's good, but half is enough. I'm diet-ing," he added impishly.

She smiled, said, "Very funny," and meant it, but added that she'd stick with the vegetables. When she finished them, her fingers dart-ed between her mouth and the table as she ate the coarse salt off the black glaze of the plate. The salt, Cy thought, looked like stars, small constellations shook out in a sign of new beginnings. James's new beginnings.

"So can I sketch you?" James asked suddenly.

Cy looked up and found she was looking at him intently. "Would I get paid or is that deal only for the kid?"

"It would be strictly for art."

"A chance to participate in the creative process?" Then Cy really was laughing, and James joined in, her laughter clear and musical. Cy laughed so hard he began to feel woozy but still he couldn't quit. "God," he said at last, trying to suppress the impulse to giggle, "I haven't gotten that hysterical in years."

"So can I?"

"Do I get to keep my clothes on?"

"No, I don't think so. You could recline. On my bed."

"On your bed? An odalisque?"

"Exactly. I have seen; I won't be shocked."

"But James, I'm shocked every time I look in the mirror."

"It's the only way I've known you."

"And nothing would happen except you'd sketch me?"

"That's right."

"I'm thinking you might get a poem yet."

When she had him arranged the way she wanted on the bed he was uncomfortable and cold. So she wrapped his feet in the bedspread to take the chill away and sketched quietly. After a half an hour, Cy said he was sleepy. She told him that was okay, that he should relax. He woke to find she had folded the bed spread over him from both sides, and that he lay on the bed trussed up like a corpse on a funeral barge, or, he thought, in sudden recognition, just like the dead he'd seen in Lahore, carried on their beds through the streets over flowing crowds of mourners.

He looked at the red shutters of the door over the veranda, trying to judge the time by the intensity of the light. Still bright. He had begun to shy from the light even when his head didn't ache. Even on good days now, if he spent much time in the sun, his eyes felt heavy in his head and seemed to glow deep into his optic nerve; the effect was unpleasant and difficult to ignore. He felt that way now. He pushed free of the white spread and put his feet down on the cool terra-cotta tiles. Finally, he looked at the dial of the travel clock on the stand next to James's bed. He hadn't been sleeping more than an hour. But he felt refreshed, awake again.

Downstairs, he could hear the soft clatter of James's cleaning up, the rustle of dishes and silverware being washed. A very pleasant sound, it seemed to him. He felt a what-if taking shape in his mind, what if he had met James before or if he were not sick, but that kind of imagining no longer possessed him as it once had. It felt vain. He dressed slowly, pulling his loose linen shorts up over his skinny shanks. He ran his fingers over his ribs, tested his sternum, the keel bone, with his thumb, and thought ruefully that soon he'd be able to play his rib cage with a spoon. Then he pulled a gray t-shirt over his head and slipped into his sandals.

Sitting on the edge of the bed, Cy noticed a blue bowl full of dried pomegranates on the shelf of the nightstand, and he lifted it up and set it down on the bedspread. They were small, fit easily into his hands, and he rubbed at the leathery red skin of one of them, admired the little leather crown where the flower had been. Maybe more like a clown's hat than a crown, he thought idly. Because Granada means *pomegranate*, tourist shops sometimes carried them as a cheap souvenir, but James had seen them differently, their beauty in a blue bowl.

Walking Granada, Cy had often noticed how a pomegranate figured in the design of a grate or on a downspout, on the blue-and-white tile plaques that served as street signs in the city. He liked them, they seemed a small grace. The dry pomegranate so light in his hand. And he sat remembering, how Persephone's return to the underworld had been confirmed because she had eaten two or three pomegranate seeds from the hand of Hades. And he thought, he wasn't sure, that the same might be true of Eurydice. In some versions of the Orpheus myth, hadn't she too tasted the ruby seeds? He thought she had. Maybe that was it, maybe that was the answer to James's question, Why Granada? Maybe it was the pomegranate's association with the underworld that had brought him here.

He put the pomegranate back in the bowl, the bowl back on the stand, thinking, maybe not. Just now, James was in the kitchen downstairs, and he thought what he wanted most was just to go down and see her. She was there, that was the happy fact.

Sam had carried Paula's worktable into the courtyard with considerable difficulty and dirtied his clothes in the process. His mood was bad. The few stairs down were narrow and there was an iron rail to deal with, but he had managed it in the end. Then he'd dragged it into a newly restored room in the main building. He'd retrieved her chair and shelves, carried her bisqued and glazed pots two at a time, carefully putting them back on their shelves. Then he'd carried down the leather-hard and bone-dry pieces; the clays in plastic buckets; and a great number of test glazes in containers, seemingly in anything that would hold a liquid; and the notebooks in which she'd scrawled glaze formulas like the recipes of an alchemist. He noticed the potting wheel in a shed in the courtyard and was glad, very glad, he hadn't had to wrestle it down the stairs.

Still, working steadily, he had Paula's studio reassembled, except for the bed, which he had not moved, before she got back from the errands he'd sent her on.

"What's going on?" she said, dropping the sacks of groceries on the ground.

"Just rearranging the furniture a bit."

She walked up the stairs and glanced into what had been her workroom.

"This is my room," she hissed, coming back down.

"Was your room," Sam said. "I need it for a few days."

"I sleep there!"

"Well, you did. Besides, I changed the locks, and if you couldn't lock me out, I'm sure half the fun would be lost."

Paula glared.

"Maybe more than half. It's just for a while, don't worry. I'll give you the new keys, all of them—"

"I'm not sleeping with you!"

"Well, don't, but you'll have to find another bed. We're going to have a guest."

"I wouldn't sleep with you if—"

"Oh, I know. You're going in for Cy. But haven't you noticed how he looks? He's dying, his flesh is coming off in tatters. First James and now you chasing after a dead man. All the appeal of Lazarus."

"Fuck you."

"You can have him, but by now he must stink."

"Enough?"

Sam shrugged, looking at his watch. "We have ten minutes, if you're enjoying yourself."

"What guest?"

"James's little friend."

Startled, Paula shook her head from side to side, her eyes flaring. "The little thief?" she said at last, incredulous. "Herr Schmidt? He'll be pleased you're planning to pay him back by opening a hostel for street kids! How long do we have before the thugs show up, Sam? Maybe you wouldn't mind having your legs broken? So what are you doing? Starting up a charity! Sam, oh Sam . . ."

"He'll be a paying guest."

"What?"

"James will pay."

"She will?"

"She'll pay to get him back."

Then Paula understood.

"She has the money," Sam continued, quietly. "She'll pay. She's the kind that won't be able to say no. Count on it."

"Don't you think, Sam, she'll have other options? Like the police?"

"*She* won't think so," Sam said decisively, looking at his watch again. "I'm going to tell her I've locked the kid in a Gypsy cave. A nice Gothic touch, no?" He laughed. "Take the groceries inside," he said abruptly. "Do something useful. Make lunch. You do know how to make lunch?"

She turned and ran inside, up the tiled stairs to the second floor where she stood back from an open door, looking down into the courtyard. She hid in the shadows, letting things happen. She felt excited, a little aroused even. She didn't have a long wait. The knocker rattled the heavy door and Sam opened it and let the child in. The boy looked little different than any other runaway. Perhaps his features were a little finer, his eyes a little brighter, as if rimmed in kohl. But even his pretty face the boy shaded as far as possible under a worn baseball cap. He was looking intimidated, at a disadvantage, and when Sam pointed to the stairs to her workroom he climbed them, Sam close behind. Somehow, Sam had mastered him. Then they stepped through the door, and she saw Sam pulling it closed. There was a small shout, stifled, then quiet.

Paula stood transfixed, hardly breathing. A few minutes later Sam reappeared at the door, looking relaxed, even a little slouchy, his habitual starchiness eased. He worked the key in the lock and tried the door. Satisfied the door was secure, he came down the stairs and crossed toward the main building, the boy's cap tucked under his arm. When he was inside she heard him whistling.

In the afternoon, a wind came up, cooling the plaza and the cobbled alleys of the Albayzín. Thin clouds in horsetails streamed high over the city, and the light yellowed and thickened in the late afternoon. The sun went down. Evening brought a light chill in the air, a refreshment, like sherbet, after the sun at midday. James ate a little cold rice she had cooked in the morning and a can of American soup, tomato. Cy drank a small coffee and glass after glass of sparkling water. He wasn't hungry. James only offered once.

After dinner, he surprised her by announcing he thought he might be able to eat a little ice cream, and they went out, walking toward a favorite shop on Gran Vía de Colón. Cy walked awkwardly. He leaned heavily on the silver bulb of his walking stick, with James holding his off arm lightly to keep him from stumbling. He felt as if the world tipped with every step, and he wondered if his balance was now impaired, if he was becoming vertiginous. Already he couldn't imagine attempting a walk like the one they'd taken only two weeks ago, out through Sacromonte and on up the Darro. Already that day seemed suspended in amber, remembered as if from a century hence. And those walks in the medina at Marrakech! Never again. He was quite certain there would be no days that good again.

After the plaza they kept to the alleys, which were quiet in the evening. A few couples deciding on a restaurant for dinner, some boys eyeing a shop full of video games, a lone walker. They emerged onto Gran Vía de Colón just as a city bus roared past, and Cy turned his head from the sound and the fumes. Even on Gran Vía, the buses seemed enormous and loud, the sound echoing back and forth between the stone façades of the buildings that fronted the street. When he looked at James he saw she was parodying his own consternation, and he laughed as best he could.

They went inside and Cy sat down in a wiry café chair while James ordered for both of them. Mango for Cy and something almost black in bittersweet chocolate for herself.

Cy watched James licking at her cone, a worried look on her face, as if the ice cream might get away from her. Her hair was coming undone, too, and a few coppery strands threatened to stray into her mouth. Cy reached across with a finger and pulled them back up onto her shoulder. He found James's fumbling with the ice cream terribly endearing, so sweet and young it hurt. The girl in the woman, peeking out, a bookend for the skeleton in the man showing through in him.

"In Lahore," he said, "in mango season, many streets are lined with great pyramids of mangos, a man or a woman with a hand scale standing by each pile selling them for just a few rupees apiece. When they are in season, everybody has them, and I suppose then they are hard to sell. But everybody is buying them, too, and has a favorite kind, or thinks the best ones are only available from a single man on a particular street corner, and of course in a distant quarter of the city. But James, at the height of the season, they are all wonderful, and the sight of those yellow pyramids along the streets, the sight of them alone was enough to make me happy then, in Lahore. Ever since, when I get a taste of mango, like this," he indicated his cone, "that all comes back, the heat and the humidity and the great green domes of the big trees and dust caught up in little khaki whirlwinds or blowing away like a sheet of diaphanous yellow silk. I was in love with all of that." Cy looked over at James, his eyes sparkling. "So," he said, "would you like a taste of this?"

"No," she said, giggling, but then nodded and leaned across the table to lick at his cone. She seemed to consider the flavor carefully. "Good, very good," she said gravely. "But I can't taste any dust in it."

"And I thought ashes got into everything."

They rested often on the walk back up to Cy's place on Cruz Verde. Again, the *placeta* was quiet. The *borrachos* seemed to have abandoned it, or perhaps had been pushed from it by the police.

Cy twisted new tapers into his two candelabras and lit them, leaving them both at the far end of the room from the bed, one on his desk and the other on a chair in front of his sacred shelf.

When he turned his back on the candles his own jumping shadows darkened the room down where James sat waiting on the bed. He reached his arms up over his head and danced stiffly toward her; he managed, even, an awkward spin. And his shadows, a whole tribe, danced on the far wall, shade dancing in front of shade.

"Now that's a *danse macabre*," he said, sitting down next to her. But to her he had looked a single tall shade rimmed in fire, like the sun in eclipse. His body fell into elongated, interesting poses. She felt guilty to notice, but she knew she couldn't help it, and she thought Cy wouldn't mind. She wasn't sure. But he wasn't shy. He said he had been, but that the shyness had already died. At first, James hadn't been able to credit that he'd ever been shy, that shyness and the impulse toward exposure in the poems could have lived together, but she had finally come to see how shyness might have fed the poems. But all that was over now.

She lifted a hand and began to unbutton his shirt. Her fingers brushing the hair on his chest, the infamous pelt of his poems.

"No one ever liked this?"

"Some said they did," he smiled wanly. "Mostly they were men in bars."

"You didn't believe them, even the men?" she said, pulling his open shirt off his shoulders, uncovering the pale and thin statue of ribs that was his torso. In the candlelight, he glowed, yellow but not sallow.

"Stand up," she said. When he did, she turned him around toward her and pulled at his belt, threading the extra inches through the buckle slowly. She let the pants drop, then tugged the loose shorts down.

James stood up and pulled the dark sheets down to the bottom of the bed, helping Cy lie back down, pulling his pants off his ankles and swinging his feet around on the bed.

"Are you getting in," Cy asked, "or just putting me to bed?"

"I thought I'd stay a while."

Cy watched as she took off her clothes. He loved to look at her. He noticed her skin looked a little drawn, lined. But it was the body James had lived in, and that living had shaped it, given it its own kind of story and polish. The scars spoke, but so did her carriage, her strong shoulders and sinewy, used hands. The hands made by years of handling the world, knowing it. She had not shied from touching, from taking hold of things, and did not shy from touching Cy now.

She curled behind him, massaging his shoulders and neck, his head through a thatch of black hair that was not well kempt. She thought that even since the first time she had touched him, in only a few days, he had grown gaunter. The bones around his shoulders, in his neck, seemed to be rising out of his skin. She reached around him, felt how his chest pulled in under his sternum.

"The keel," he said. "Deep for sailing rough waters, for sailing in winds." He pulled his head back, said, "I am my own figurehead. Maybe you should paint a name on my side, The Cyrus."

"I could do that."

"I'll need implants, though, to carry it off."

She ran her fingertips over his nipples, tight against his ribs. "You might," she said, "but I think I prefer that other thing, the old boats that just had an eye painted out by the prow, one on each side."

Cy rolled over, nodding. He looked at James, running his fingers lightly over her face, her neck. "Yours can be the face to launch this ship," he said quietly. He leaned in and kissed her on the collarbone, on her cheekbone. Cy nudged her and she rolled onto her back and he put his ear beneath her breasts and listened to the pulse of her heart.

He thought he could hear where her blood streamed underground. He thought he could hear the wind where it sounded in the hollows of her chest. In the candlelight, he trailed his fingers down. His own fingers like a breeze passing over landscape, like a whispered regret. Far down, just above her knee, he touched a little scar. Something written, a small history he would never know if he didn't ask now. And he didn't ask. He turned away, pulling up his knees. James rolled back toward him, pressed herself against the whole length of him, drawing her knees up too.

"Do you want me to stay?"

"You should go before it gets too late. The Albayzín isn't safe late, as you know."

"Isn't it safe here?"

So she stayed. She heard Cy's teeth chatter, as if he were cold. "Oh Cyrus," she thought he said, followed by low and cheerless laughter. But perhaps it had been "Osiris," another joke. She held on. But she felt Cy floating out of her arms. It wouldn't be long now. She remembered wading in the Russian River as a girl, on a vacation in Northern California. Her family had been staying in a cabin in a row of cabins in a green meadow where the river ran smooth but swiftly. She remembered her dad with the yellow sun on him, joining the singing of a flock of meadowlarks. She'd met a girl from another cabin, and they'd waded into the river holding hands, the water cold around their knees. And a little farther out, the water swirling around their thighs, and the other girl had stepped in a hole behind a submerged boulder. James had held tight but the girl's hand had slipped free and she had turned in the tail of the pocket behind the boulder and then the current had taken her, floating away. She hadn't screamed, just gone. Like that, James thought, Cy would be going too. Still, the girl hadn't gotten far. James's father had been watching the whole while and stepped into the river downstream and fished her little friend out of the water with one hand and set her down on the bank. He hadn't made any speeches about being careful or the danger of the river. He'd smiled at the girl, patted her on the shoulder awkwardly, looked upstream a moment at James in the water, and walked away, pants dripping, back to his bird watching.

Asur woke up suddenly from a bad dream only to find himself still gagged and bound at the ankles and wrists. He was thirsty and needed to pee at the same time, and it was dark out still. In the dream he had seen the *loco* again, still burning, running in flames, like something out of the grim warnings he'd received on the *vega*, the promises of hell. But the *loco* wasn't dead. And he wasn't dead. So why was he here?

He burned in his armpits, in his groin; claustrophobia had gripped him in waves and he had struggled against the silver tape but he hadn't been able to rip free of it. In the end he'd gotten tired. His mind had gone elsewhere. Out on the *vega*. Far up the Darro. He had slept, then awakened, terrified again.

Sam, sitting just out of sight above his head, was whispering how boys like him brought good money in the brothels in Malaga, in Barcelona. "A good price, a very good price. They like them gamey, like you. With pretty eyes. In a little dress. I think you'll know how to please them. Maybe you already know."

He was made to use a chamber pot, his feet still bound, while Sam watched. How the man laughed at him as he quivered over the pot, trying to keep his balance! Then Sam re-taped his wrists before he could wipe himself clean and tossed him back on the bed.

22

James had left early, before dawn. It had been the hour when Cy most wanted to be alone, and she had honored his wishes. The walk through the Albayzín had been good, prepared her to paint. The alleys were wet with a light rain that had blown through in the night. The cobbles glistened, the white walls looked blue. Only a few taxis plied the lanes in Plaza Nueva. She came in through the kitchen and clicked on the light in the studio, glancing at the length of canvas she'd tacked to the wall, where she would begin today by drawing a few cartoons she had worked out in her sketchpad in Morocco. It was time to stand up and paint, to face the difficulties.

She looked out onto the veranda expecting to see Asur stretched out in his customary place by the railing, but he wasn't there; then she remembered the rain. There was a dry spot out of the weather up close by the windows but Asur wasn't there, either. She turned on the outside lights and was surprised to see the neat stack of his bedding looking sodden where he'd left it the morning before. This was unlike Asur and quite suddenly she began to worry. She went out and hung the sheet and blanket on the rail over the river, leaning the cushions where the sun would find them early. Then she went back inside, dripped a cup of coffee, and began. With charcoal she worked at the long reclining figure that was Cy. It filled and overfilled the unstretched canvas. Much bigger than life-size, she knew when she was done it would nevertheless be hard to see. She wanted it to provide a bounding line for other things, the lines of his body alive in the sinews of the painting. Much of what she wanted felt amorphous, not yet evident, but she had enough to begin.

James finished working early in the afternoon. She cleaned up carefully; organizing her tools still felt like painting to her. It was an attitude she'd adopted from an old teacher years before, an ungrudging respect for her brushes, for tools, the materials. Everything clean and organized, ready for the next day.

She carried a bag of peanuts and a couple of oranges out onto the veranda, where it had turned hot, in spite of the high haze that thickened the light over Granada. Before eating, she folded Asur's bedding and made a neat pile of it out of the weather. Then she stood at the railing, still expecting to see him, wading in the Darro or running up from Plaza Santa Ana. But he was not there. The feral cats, however, were out and about, the kittens now big enough, apparently, to be allowed out of the den. Asur's cats, but able to get by without his handouts. She favored a striped kitten, black and gray and already a wanderer, it seemed, walking well up the Darro toward Sacromonte.

While she was eating she heard the buzz of her doorbell. She walked through her studio and the kitchen to her door on Santa Ana, stopped, and peered through the peephole, at Sam, as it turned out. She opened up, and Sam smiled, cocking his head beguilingly.

"I have a present," he said, holding out a shopping bag bearing the logo of one of Granada's most expensive boutiques.

"Oh?"

"Can I come in?"

James followed Sam into her studio where he took a chair. "Something big, I see," he said, gesturing vaguely at the canvas hanging on James's work wall. "Something with the dying lover?"

She had sat down too and didn't answer. She lifted a sheet of purple tissue paper out of the bag and was now staring down into it at Asur's dirty Red Sox cap. She lifted it out.

"Not really your style, I suppose," Sam said quietly.

James lifted her eyes and looked hard at Sam. "What's this all about?" she asked at last.

"I need some money, a lot of money."

"So?"

"Well, I want yours."

"Mine?" James shook her head, disgust thickening her voice. "Where's the child, where's Asur?" James stood up abruptly, as if called to attention.

Sam didn't move, but he followed James with his eyes. "I don't guess that's a serious question," he said at last. I want a hundred thousand dollars. And soon. I have a bill to pay, and I don't want to pay it with a pound of flesh. Not mine, anyway. So I'm thinking I'll pay it with Asur's."

"I don't have it."

"Well, no, but you have a few days to get it. The boy is in a cave, one of the old abandoned Gypsy places, like the ones in Sacromonte. There are a great many of them roundabout. But I guess you know that. I'm not going back there, and I'm afraid the boy is tied up, and gagged, so you can imagine it might get unpleasant. No food, nothing to drink, in the dark. Spiders. But he should last a few days, I'd think."

"Why, why me?"

"Does anyone else care?" Sam sprang to his feet, gathered up the cap and bag and tissue paper and started for the door. "Oh," he said, stopping and swiveling around in front of James's mirrors. "Don't go to the police. I mean, you'd have a bad experience. I wouldn't know what you were talking about, if they came to me, and by the time all that got sorted out the boy would be dead. Very likely, don't you think? And really, who is this kid? Do you know? Is he really missing? Is there a missing-person's report signed by a responsible adult? His mother or his father? And if he is missing, why is some American painter looking for him? Or her?

"And you know, under pressure, I might have to admit to having two little obscene paintings by Mad James herself in my possession, paintings I'd say you asked me to sell to 'discreet' collectors. Signed work, and featuring the lost boy himself doing some pretty funky stuff with that famously naughty boyfriend of yours. Such a stink, and right when Cy's dying! The paintings make it quite clear why the boy would want to run away again; you can rest assured of that. I painted them last night, James. Some of your best work, if you don't mind my saying so, typical, but a little less fussy than most of your stuff. Just get the money, James. Clean American hundreds. Then hang a dress over the rail," he pointed out toward the veranda, "when you're ready to buy the boy back."

The nausea didn't ebb out of him until well after noon. Still in bed, Cy rubbed at his face and groaned. The skin around his left eye felt like clay. He sat up, struggled into his robe, and picked up the sloshing pan by the bedside to wash out in the bathroom. But when he tried to stand he had to set the pan back down and steady himself on the bed. The floor had rolled under his feet. Finally, he braced himself on the rickety side chair he kept by the headboard, and using it as a walker, negotiated his way across the bare floor to the bathroom, the sick pan riding on the seat of the chair. He dumped it into the toilet, rinsed the pan in the sink, poured that into the toilet too, and flushed. Then he set about washing his face, one hand clutching the back of the chair. Even the water felt wrong. Not as wet as it should have. He wanted to look in the mirror but was afraid. He patted at his lips, his eyes, with a clean bath towel. Then he did look up into the medicine cabinet mirror.

"So," he said quietly, staring. His left eyelid had drooped half shut during the night, and the white of his right eye had filled with blood. He reached up and pried open the sleepy eye and found it too was red with blood. He looked, he thought, demonic and stupid at once. He ran a little water into a cupped hand and carefully drank a swallow. It tasted rusty but good. He hoped it wouldn't start him heaving.

He lowered himself into the chair he'd pushed into the bathroom, resting his elbows on his knees, and gazed vacantly at the tiled floor. Soon, very soon, he'd need to be going, before he had no choice left but to wait. Every morning now was another chance to wake up paralyzed. He'd been ready before James, or closer to ready. And for a moment he hated her. He hated her sad eyes, her clear gaze, the way she did not look away. He hated the very things he loved about her most, all those things that made it harder to leave. He thought he understood now how death slipped up even on those who knew they were dying. He hadn't meant it to come to this. He'd meant to be gone before this.

He leaned over and turned on the tap to run a bath. When it was full he hung his Beacon robe over the back of the chair and slipped in, let the warm water come up around his chest in a rush. He filled his lungs and felt his body buoyed up. His hull, his hulk. Ragged and spectral.

And still death was a metaphor. The boats crossing in starlight. The seals surfacing left and right, their heads bent to listen to the hiss of the keel, soft eyes glistening, watching. What are the creatures of this place if not half seen, appearing and disappearing as the known world drops forever in the wake? The eyes on the ship's prow darkening, slowly going blind. The fog rising up thick and gray out of sea waves. The horizon lost.

Then he washed, ducking his head to wet his hair, lathering, rinsing, to get clean. After he dressed he donned a pair of sunglasses. Even inside and alone he wanted to hide the evidence of the small stroke or nerve damage, of just what he didn't know or much care. It was a sign, it meant more as a clear sign. Plainly legible. He would die disfigured and soon.

At his desk, he started a letter to James. He asked her to take for herself the Yomut *engsi* off the floor and the sacred shelf, books and all, if she wanted them. He said the money in the desk drawer should go to Asur. It wasn't much. He'd spent what he'd had, most of it, not expecting to have a use for it. Now, he wished there were more. He wrote out a phone number in Pittsburgh, which he asked her to call with the news. She shouldn't worry that the call might be painful. It was the number of a lawyer, who had a letter of her own.

Cy sat looking at what he'd written for a long time. Directions, that's all. He wanted to say more but couldn't, not now, not yet. Later, maybe, but he doubted it. So he wrote James's name on an envelope and stuffed the sheet inside, thinking as he did about how best to deliver it.

23

"If you did that, could you get by?"

James shifted uneasily, not liking the question. She leaned down and picked up a glass of whiskey from the floor, drank a little, and shook her head. She stared absently at *The Blue Newspaper* where it hung on the wall, then said at last, "Even if I can't, does it matter? I can't just . . ."

"Of course it matters," Cy snapped, angry in spite of himself. "No one is going to paint your paintings but you. And if you pay, what does the world get instead? A fat Sam." Cy fell silent. After a few seconds he said, "Forget I said that. I'm sorry."

"What Sam gets hardly matters. I'm thinking about Asur."

"Oh, I'd say it matters," Cy said grimly.

"I can't just let . . ."

"But would Sam actually let the boy die? Isn't that a wholly different thing than his kind of petty scam?"

"That's just it, I don't know. I wouldn't have expected any of this from Sam. I thought he was harmless, that he was all talk." James looked out into the *placeta*. "Sam has that on his side, doesn't he, our uncertainty? We don't know."

She took another drink. "Look Cy, I could get by. I might have to get a job, but something part-time would do it."

"Where?"

"It might mean going home. To teach, who knows? I haven't had time to think about it."

Cy pressed his thumbs to his cheekbones and massaged his forehead with his fingers, thinking. He laughed. "Pornographic paintings of the old poet and Asur, eh?" Cy shook his head. "That's a nice touch, shows style."

"Gall's more like it."

Cy stifled a yawn. In spite of the shock of the news, or maybe because of it, he could feel himself shutting down. He'd been finding it increasingly difficult to function when he was tired, and he was tired almost all of the time. He was thankful James had her back to him, hadn't noticed.

"Cy," she said loudly, "Paula's down—"

Before James could finish her sentence they heard a rap on the door down on the *placeta*.

"Paula?"

James nodded.

"Now what?" Cy cried. Then he said, "James, would you let her in?"

"Let her in? Are you sure?"

He sighed heavily. "I don't think there's anything to gain by keeping her out." Another knock echoed up the stairwell. "She stopped by the day we got back from Morocco. Late. She said she was afraid Sam was going to do something crazy. I guess she had reason." Then he turned his head to the door over the *placeta* and called out, "Coming!" To James, he said, "Please!"

James stood up and started down the stairs. When she opened the door, Cy heard Paula's frightened, "Oh!"

Then they were coming back up, their angry whispers audible above the sound of their feet on the treads. Cy turned in his chair as they crossed into the room. Paula looked startled but flirtatious too; the glance she cast at Cy pleaded for mercy. James walked in stiffly behind her, her face wintry.

"We were just talking about the company you keep," Cy said, looking up from behind his dark glasses, a feeble smile on his lips.

"And?"

"We don't like it."

"No. I wouldn't think so. Look, I came because, well because I'm scared. I thought . . . I never imagined Sam would do anything like this. He didn't tell me until he already had the boy. He just came home and said it was done. He was lighthearted. He thinks the whole thing is just funny. He doesn't seem to care about the kid at all. I'm afraid for the boy. I don't know if Sam will ever let him go. I—"

But Cy had raised his hand to silence her and she stopped short, out of breath.

"I can't get the money all at once," James said. "It's going to take a few days. Maybe longer. He has to feed the child. He has . . ."

Paula looked at James uncomprehendingly.

"Will you tell him?"

Paula nodded.

"I'm going to want some kind of proof he's all right . . ."

"Okay," Paula said numbly. "But what about me?"

"What about you?"

"It's the German. If Sam can't come up with the money, he's going to send someone to . . ."

"Who cares?" James said. "You're expecting sympathy? As if Sam isn't dangerous too? He's got to make sure Asur's going to be okay. He's got to."

"James!"

"What?"

"I'll pay."

The two women stared down at Cy, huddled in his chair, his face half hidden by sunglasses.

"I can get the money tomorrow."

Then he stopped short, said, "Well, I can get eighty-seven thousand dollars tomorrow. That'll have to do; it's all I've got. But look at me, what am I going to do with it now?" He gestured at his emaciated body. "My bills are paid."

Paula leaned down and hugged Cy, sobbing. But James stood back, silent, a doubtful look on her face.

"But I have a condition."

Paula straightened up, her features suddenly sharp. "What is it?"

"You, you Paula, have to set the boy free while Sam helps me get to the bank. You understand? Otherwise, what would stop Sam from keeping the boy? He might come after James again."

Paula nodded. "I'll tell him."

"I can trust you, can't I?"

"Yes."

"You'll be sure the boy isn't hurt?" Cy stood up, wobbling only a little.

When Paula said, "Yes," again, Cy took her head in his hands and kissed her hard in the middle of the forehead.

"Go tell Sam this is the best offer he's going to get. I'll expect you both here at one o'clock tomorrow. Now go."

Paula walked around James on the way out. At the top of the stairs, she turned back and said, "I'm sorry. I wanted something else."

"Tomorrow," Cy repeated, "one o'clock."

"Well," James said, a sad, quizzical smile on her face. "I guess there are things I don't know."

"I'm sorry. I had another idea about the money. But this is better."

"Are you sure?"

"Yes."

James stood close, putting her arms around Cy, who was quaking. "You okay?"

"Help me to the bed."

When they had him stretched out James sat down next to him and they talked. Cy wondered aloud if Paula had come on her own—fearing what Sam might do—or if she'd been sent to convince Cy, and through Cy, James, that Asur was in real danger. However they turned the question around, they couldn't come to a conclusion. It seemed impossible to know. But they agreed if she'd been sent, she likely couldn't be trusted.

When James asked to stay, Cy said no. He needed to think, and he wasn't finding thinking easy. He hurt and wanted to be left alone, didn't want to be seen, not by James most of all.

"Come back, tomorrow. Come about 2:30."

"You're sure?"

"I'll leave the door open. Let yourself in. It'll all be over by then."

She started to thank him but Cy reached out to cover her mouth.

"Okay," she said, pushing his hair back with her fingertips. "To-morrow."

24

Cy worked the extra material in the waistband of his pants around to the back, where the fall of his linen sport jacket would cover the evidence. He adjusted the suspenders he'd bought only a few weeks before. At the time, the purchase had seemed a good joke, a little fragment of an old age he'd never live to see. But he had lived to see a body that made sense of suspenders, though he hadn't tried them on before. He was trying to look like a man a bank would take seriously, for Sam's sake. That morning he'd shaved very carefully, tidying up his sideburns and cleaning off the hair that wanted to grow down the back of his neck. He thought now he hadn't looked so clean-cut since his mother had dressed him. Except for the dark glasses, which were required if he was going to look presentable at all. The blood had drained from the whites of his eyes but left them a bruised yellow, like egg yolk stirred in milk.

He leaned over to pull on his socks and felt the world whirl a bit. Vertigo attended any sudden movement of his head. So he went slowly, pulling on one sock at a time and then his shoes, still bright from the shoeblacks of Morocco. He stood up carefully, and, with his cane to balance him, made his way over to his desk.

He sat down and read over the letter he'd written for James one more time, then picked up his pen and wrote carefully, "I am sorry about the lie. There is no money. I spent it. All I have is in my desk, for Asur. But James, for a moment, listening to Paula, I felt rich. What a gift! So I agreed to pay the ransom. Don't forget, sweet James, how you chided me in Marrakech for not knowing how to accept a gift. You were right. And the old palm reader, she was right, too: great happiness. Even now, it buoys me up." Cy leaned back, a skeptical expression on his face, then signed his name. He folded the letter and put it back in the envelope, which he tucked into the back pocket of his trousers.

With a garbage can between his knees, he reread the poems he'd written since he'd arrived in Granada. A few of the very short pieces he thought good enough, and he made a small stack of them, anchoring them on his desk with the heavy bracelet from Morocco. The rest of the poems he crumbled one at a time and dropped into the can. With difficulty, he carried the can outside, set it on the terrace, and lit the contents with a match. He stood at a little distance while the poems burned, then stepped in when the flames disappeared under the lip of the can and stirred up what was left with the lip of his cane. He knew it wasn't a job you could leave to a friend with any confidence.

Back inside, he arranged his wallet, passport, and bankbook in a neat little stack on a side table and then sat down to wait. His watch said 12:55, almost time. Sam wouldn't be late, Cy felt quite sure of that. His eyes strayed to James's painting where it hung quietly on the wall. Living with it had proved an education. He hadn't gotten to the end of it. The painting did not assert. It waited for you to enter the field, to question it. Then its answers were never full, never unambiguous. And yet, the effect wasn't coy. The painting resisted analysis, not by tricks, but by simply making analysis feel irrelevant. The satisfactions of *The Blue Newspaper* were close to the paint.

At 1:00, Cy stood on his third-storey terrace, looking down on the empty *placeta*, his fingers wrapped around the rusty iron railing. He watched as Sam strolled into the little plaza, looking carefree, with Paula trailing behind, head down. Cy smiled grimly. Dapper Sam, a guy to give dandies a bad name. When Sam rapped, Paula looked up and Cy nodded to her.

Sam's head tilted back and he peered up at a foreshortened Cy, just a face behind dark glasses under a rim of hair. Then an arm floated out over the railing and beckoned.

"It's not locked. Come on up. I might need help with the stairs."

Cy heard the door hinges squeak and a rumble in the stairwell. He turned toward the room but stopped in the doorway. When Sam's hat appeared at the top of the stairs, Cy started forward. He picked up his bankbook and passport casually, but then made a little display of getting them into the inside pocket of his linen jacket.

"All packed?" Cy asked.

"No. Did you think we were leaving?"

"Just hoping, I guess."

"Not really going to matter to you."

"Not for long, no," Cy said simply.

Paula finally emerged out of the stairwell, looking hesitant. Cy wondered if he could trust her to follow through. He wondered how much of her concern for Asur had been show, how much of it real feeling. Even if it had all been real, he didn't think that meant he could trust her. But maybe it only mattered that he could pretend he trusted her.

"Are you okay?" Cy leaned his forehead against Paula's, turning his back on Sam, who sighed loudly.

"It would have been something beautiful, I'm sure," Sam said.

Cy swiveled around toward him. "Probably not, Sam. My record's not good."

He turned back to Paula. "But you're going to set Asur free?"

"Yes."

He kissed her on the forehead, like a girl or a daughter. "Will you help me down?"

And she did. Cy put his arm around her shoulders and leaned on her as they went down the stairs, Cy's cane clattering behind them. And moving so close to her, his hair tangled up with hers and his face rubbing against her smooth cheek, he did regret that he hadn't known her when he was able. There was something about the lithe yet slightly awkward way she moved, something about the way her eyes seemed a little out of focus and her lips a bit loose. So desirable. Then he thought of James and was ashamed. But still he murmured, "Oh, you," somewhere near Paula's pink ear. She heard him and smiled, tears springing to her eyes, and she brushed his mouth with hers. Then they were at the bottom of the stairs and Cy stood clear of her.

Outside the door, Sam said, "So are we ready? Have we finished with touching endearments?"

"The key?" Paula asked.

Sam glanced at her sharply but then pulled a key chain out of his pocket, separating out a squat but shiny key and handing it over.

Paula walked slowly out of Placeta de la Cruz Verde. She waved before disappearing behind the white wall of a corner house.

"Just let me lock up," Cy said, stepping back inside. But he didn't lock the door. He pulled the letter for James out of a back pocket and set it down on the stone floor where James couldn't miss it when she arrived later in the day.

Sam was waiting for him. "I'll still be fucking her when you're dead."

"Paula? I suppose so . . . Maybe. But I'd think after this she'd have had enough of you."

"She likes this, Cy, don't you get it? Just any kind of excitement makes her drip."

"You must really love her, talking like that."

"Did I say I loved her? I should hope not."

"Lucky girl," Cy said, turning away from Sam and starting to walk toward San Gregorio, the stepped alley that led down finally to Elvira and from there on to the commercial center of the city. His bank was on Calle Reyes Católicos, for him a long ways. He walked close to the wall on the right, ready to catch himself if he stumbled, and used the stick in his left hand at every step. He could hear Sam coming up on his right and when he pulled even Cy glanced at him. He wasn't surprised to see Sam looking cheerful, confident. Cy thought Sam was the kind of man who would be happy in hell if only he had someone else there to push around.

But when Cy stumbled Sam caught him by the arm and held him up. "None of that," he said.

In Plaza de San Gregorio, Cy sat down on a stone step to rest. Sam stood, meaning to keep his fresh clothes clean. There were buskers in the plaza, playing quietly and well. Cy pulled a banknote from his wallet and dropped it in the hat when it came round. Here, Little

Morocco started. Calderería Nueva had the feel of a real medina. Of carnival. For as long as Cy had known Granada he'd loved this place best. Here life was not so furtive but made a little display of desire. Long looks and shy glances, bread in open hands, drinking and the ritual of tea. Writers bent over their notebooks: he had been one of them. Nighthawks by day. Pickpockets. Vegetables in stacked boxes on street corners. A child begging, a child like Asur. Wanderers and businessmen. Drunks. Scholars making their kind of sense of it. Artists too. A black dog sniffing the signs, tail up. Housewives and husbands. Cy hunched over his cane and walked down Calderería Nueva, saying goodbye. Everything washed in light. Faces clear and innocent. The walls, the cobbles, alive.

They walked by a rack of postcards featuring Lorca's knowing little sketches. Then the tourist shops, the glittering abundance. Cy peered into the sweet shade of the *teterías*. A waiter smiled at him, familiar, welcoming. In Nujaila, even the severe wife nodded over a counter covered with Moroccan baked goods, for the first time acknowledging she knew him. Cy tipped his head to the side, felt his chin come down and the smile on his face. He heard laughter and he stopped to hear it better. The lilting rise and fall of laughter. He held his free hand out to the sound and felt the sun flutter in his palm.

"What are you grinning about?" Sam asked, trying to sound irked but not quite carrying it off. His confidence had failed him; looking at Cy he felt rattled. "Ready?" he asked.

"Yes," Cy said, "ready." And he started to walk again. But inside the thick shade of a broken building, Cy saw a column of sunlight alive with motes, and he stopped again. The light teeming.

"Cy?" Sam was back at his elbow.

"Yes," Cy said, gesturing at where the light fell through a hole in the roof, far back inside the building's broken hulk.

"What? What they're doing here won't qualify as restoration, Cy." Sam looked around and shook his head. "Gaudy and shoddy all at once," Sam said, "awful."

"Gaudí," Cy murmured, remembering the eccentric architect.

Sam heard him and said, "Another idiot."

Cy smiled. Even Sam, a little ahead of him now, moving slowly, glowed in the afternoon light.

"Are you alright?"

"I'm fine, Sam. Nothing to worry about now."

They crossed Elvira. Soon the sound of Gran Vía de Colón poured down the alley and they walked toward it, Cy leaning into the volume as if into a wave, Sam resisting the impulse to hurry ahead. They crossed at the light nearest the cathedral and Sam asked for the address of the bank.

"On down Reyes Católicos," Cy said mechanically, but he was thinking that Asur would probably be free by now, that at least it was too late for Sam to call Paula back. And he felt quite sure the child would not be easy to catch again. Anytime, anytime was a good time now. As they walked down Reyes Católicos, Cy looked at the stream of traffic in the roadbed, the asphalt and hot cars pitching up shimmering heat waves in the canyon between the low buildings.

"I can't see the attraction," Sam said abruptly.

"No?"

"Paula . . ."

"Paula again?"

"You're not her type."

"Am I a type?"

"I read your book. How's that one go, the one called 'Gherkin'?"

"Sam . . ."

"Yes?"

"This is my bus," Cy said, stepping into traffic. For a moment, it all seemed very distant, the rushing bus, Sam reaching desperately for the sleeve of his coat. Cy knelt, and he felt that everything he'd set going in his life had led him right here. A patch of pavement, his hand on the smooth knob of his cane. He looked up into the reflection in the windshield of the bus, a silver shining, blue sky rushing in to fill it up. Then he felt Sam pulling at his jacket, and he grabbed Sam's arm and held on.

The bus hardly shuddered. Twenty yards on it jerked to a stop and the stricken driver opened the doors and ran out onto the sidewalk, back, to where two bodies lay crumpled in the street. Quite suddenly the street was full of stopped cars. There was a momentary hush in which the driver called out to his God. Then, in the distance, horns started up, a great clamor of angry drivers with no idea why they were stopped.

25

James stood in the shower, rinsing in a stream of cold water. She gasped, but it was an old habit. Not a mortification, but an enlivening of the flesh. She didn't like the way warm water made her sleepy, forgetful. She liked to get out of the shower remembering. She let the water run, thinking about Cy. It struck her how much there was to remember already. When you're interested, she thought, you see more, remember more. Which was the problem with distance, with the kind of distance she'd cultivated for most of her adult life. For art. And yet she was painting very well now. Not even Sam had been able to stop her. This morning, she'd painted in a rush, hardly able to keep up. There had been far less going back and forth between problem and answer; she'd just seen her way through. For an hour, the years of discipline had seemed mere preparation, and this painting the real work.

James shut the tap and shook like a seal before stepping out of the shower. She looked across into her bedroom and saw that her alarm clock read 1:45. She'd promised Cy she would arrive at his place at 2:30. Time to dress and walk and not much else.

But she couldn't stop herself from sitting a minute before the big painting. The figure of Cy in the landscape was muted now, but still he was there, his torso and limbs the contortion in the shaped earth. Probably she would call it *View of Granada*, but its secret name, her name for it, would be *Going*. The fragmented cityscape taking shape in the hills did owe a little to Greco's ominous *View of Toledo*, but as much to the disjointed perspectives of landscape in the backgrounds of Byzantine icons and Buddhist frescoes. The landscape was plastic, formed out of felt importance rather than any adherence to classical notions of perspective. James had never painted anything remotely like it. There were continuities in the palette with her recent work, and some of her trademark confounding of figure and ground, but the painting was a clear departure. Something new. She hoped Cy would be able to come see it. If not, she'd roll it up and take it to him.

As she was picking up her purse, she noticed that the plastic sack with Asur's clothes, which had been on the veranda, was gone. When she stepped outside she saw wet footprints to and from the rail over the Darro. She walked slowly over to the railing. From there, she could see Asur, down below, bathing in the river. He was naked and scrubbing furiously between his legs with the bar of soap that James kept at a sink on the veranda to clean up with after painting. While she watched, he squatted down in the stream, splashing himself, rinsing the soap off. He had balanced his clean clothes and a towel on a rock on the far bank, but the clothes he'd stripped off lay scattered in the dry grass.

"Asur?" James spoke softly, trying not to startle the child.

But he was startled and his head came up with a frightened expression on his face. "No," he said.

"Are you okay? ¿Estas bien?"

"No!" he shouted.

"Come up."

"No, no, no!" the boy cried, wading out of the water and pulling on his clothes.

"Please!"

"No!" First the balled towel and then the bar of soap soared over the rail. "No!" Asur shouted again. "You're bad luck! Look at your eyes, you have the evil eye. El ojo malo. No!"

When he had his shoes on he started upstream at a run, but James wasn't going to chase him. If he wanted to run, he should run. She'd been trying to help him, trying, but maybe all she'd managed to do was to bring the boy more bad luck. Wasn't her gaze the very thing that had attracted Sam's attention to him? She took a deep, sudden breath. There was no doubt about it. And for a moment, she seemed to see the dark shadow that had clung to her good intentions. She put her hands over her face, not to see less, but to see the shadow more clearly. And she sobbed, her heart filling with dread.

Asur ran awkwardly, the untied laces of his shoes trailing him, his feet shifting in his loose sneakers painfully, but he didn't stop until he was under the second bridge over the Darro, the Puente de Espinosa. There, he tied his shoelaces, tucked in his shirt, and combed at his long wet hair with his thin fingers. He felt okay, scared but at least free. And clean. Sam had left him alone so long he'd sullied his pants, and that had been yesterday. His face flushed just thinking about it. He'd stuffed the pants in his plastic bag before he'd run, not wanting James or anyone else to find them. Not ever. He was going to throw them away. They might come clean but the memory would never wash out of them.

Asur walked a few steps farther upstream then leapt rock to rock in the Darro until he was across. He clambered out of the stream's channel and made his way up and left, into the trees on the lower slopes of the Alhambra hill. He just wanted to get out of sight, to hide. He hadn't gone far, a little beyond the ruined Puerta de los Tableros, when he found a low depression behind the crumbled foundations of what had once been a wall, perhaps a spur of the city wall. He thought the hollow was deep enough, if barely, to shield him from Carrera del Darro in case Sam should come looking.

The tree standing over his hiding place rustled; a wind wound down the valley of the Darro, coming from somewhere higher and cooler, the Sierras. Asur relaxed, letting his eyes droop. Through his slit lids he let the sunlight break again into a gold design. When he opened his eyes he saw a lizard eyeing him from the rocks above. The Alhambra hill hummed with insects, more than before. Real summer was coming. He tried to judge the hour. 2:30, he thought, or a few minutes after. He was a little less sure about the day of the week. He tried to count back, but in the room it had been dark most of the time and he'd slept; he didn't know how much. He'd been asleep when Paula came. She had already cut him free when he woke up and saw the door standing open, a heavy beam of yellow sun angling down to his prison floor. He'd sprung from the bed in a single motion, not sure if she would try to catch him. But she hadn't, and he hadn't waited, he'd just gone.

Still, he thought today was the day Marcela was coming back for him. She'd said 9:00 on the plaza and Asur would be there. He could check the newspapers at the kiosk a little earlier to be sure of the day. He'd have to show himself on the plaza, scared or not, or miss his chance. He was hungry, but he'd wait to eat. He could wait. He wouldn't show himself again until he had to. Even the plaza, full of people, frightened him now. Danger hid in the shadows, but it walked brazenly in sunlit streets too, sat drinking a coffee and eating pastries under an umbrella, drove a taxi maybe, or might appear abruptly bent over the handlebars of a racing scooter. The sudden way things happened in the city frightened him, crowds of people but a familiar face rare, and that face, he thought, maybe only looking friendly. On the *vega* it was the odd face you didn't know. But that was over. He couldn't go back there. Those faces, they knew his face, too. Luz. By now they would all know about Luz, about the dresses, and they would not forget. Not ever. To remember, that was the way on the *vega*. At his school, they'd still snickered about Lorca.

Paula didn't know why she'd snuck into Asur's cell so quietly, as if she were sixteen again and returning late from a date and hoping not to wake her sleeping brother. Feet bare, scissors in her hand. She'd cut the tape on Asur's ankles and wrists before he opened his eyes. When he ran, his mouth was still duct-taped shut. She hadn't wanted to talk to him. What could she say to explain? She didn't think words would undo anything, change anything for the boy. He was free to run, that would be the only thing that would matter to him.

She hadn't seen Asur confined in her room. Sam'd had the key; he'd visited Asur alone. He'd taken a straight-backed chair in with him and sat with the boy for an hour or two at a time. The chair stood at the head of the bed now. She wondered what stories Sam had told the boy, there, perched in the dark, his voice coming disembodied over the headboard. Stories to keep Asur from the police, from going back to James or Cy? Sam was good at stories, at telling the kind of stories that changed how the world looked.

Paula knew already she was going to remember forever how the boy had looked when he hit the sunlight standing in the door, how he'd lit up suddenly, as if running in flames. Wide-eyed, his mouth taped shut, his hair flying, his arms and legs churning the sunlit air, and then gone. A door slamming in the courtyard out into the winding alleys of the Albayzín.

She opened the shutters on the windows and turned on the primitive chandelier that hung in the middle of the ceiling. The room stank. The sheets on the bed were yellow where Asur had lain and, she thought, likely rife with lice and fleas. She wadded them up, took them outside and burnt them in the courtyard, first dousing them in paint thinner. She considered dragging the mattress outside as well but decided to leave that to Sam. And the rest of the cleaning up.

She began to worry around 2:30. By 2:45 she was out walking, heading down toward Plaza Nueva. She thought what if, what if Sam had decided that almost ninety thousand dollars was enough to make a new start somewhere else, but only enough for one? She'd failed to even consider the possibility that he might stiff the German and leave her to face him alone, or to run on her own. Probably he would turn up. Probably he was celebrating with a drink. Or things had not gone smoothly at the bank. Or he had been arrested. But wouldn't the police have come looking for her?

She slipped on a cobble and her heel caught and her ankle twisted, not badly, but enough that she came up limping. She swore. She was

sick of Granada. Sick of the smelly picturesque and the endless has-
sle of living abroad. Sick of Sam and poets sick unto death.

She rounded into Placeta de la Cruz Verde almost running and
charged right up to Cy's door, pounding at it with her fists.

"Cy!" she shouted. "Cy!"

When there was no answer, she backed away from the door, looking suspiciously at the upper floors of the house, but the blinds had
been pulled shut. The house felt abandoned, as if it had been shuttered for the season.

"Are you there?" Paula shouted one last time, and, not getting a response, she spun around and headed down toward the plaza. Cy had
said his bank was near the end of Calle Reyes Católicos, close to the
central post office on Puerta Real. She thought she could find it.

Inside, James stood back from the blinds, watching. When Paula
gave up she turned back to the room. She had been alarmed when
Paula first hammered on the door, before she'd called out. For a moment, she'd thought Cy had come back, for a moment she'd feared it
was the police. But it was only Paula. Pathetic Paula. Paula wanting
to be wanted. Always that. To stand in a circle of drooling men. Paula
had wanted that, James thought, and she'd gotten it. The world going stiff with lust all around her. She had the real thing, a power, if
a foreign power. James had to admit it. She looked again at the letter
in her hand, where Paula was not mentioned. But Cy less sick, she
knew, would not have been proof against her. And even sick, maybe
he hadn't been. James didn't know, not for sure.

She stuffed Cy's letter in a pocket and looked down at the Yomut
carpet on the floor. An *engsi*, Cy had called it, a door rug. Hers now.

She would take it, she wouldn't say no to his bequest, though the door it covered for her would always be Rilke's "hopelessly open" door between life and death. If she closed her eyes, she could still hear Cy reciting from Rilke's *Orpheus*, his guttural and passionate growl and then the catch in his voice.

James hadn't been surprised when she pushed open the door to Cy's house to see the letter bearing her name on the floor in front of her. She'd half expected it. She was trying now just to follow his instructions, not to wonder too much about what he'd done. She knew if she didn't act now she wouldn't be able to; she could feel the coming grief pressing up at her larynx and at the back of her eyes. She tried not to think. She carried the books from the sacred shelf over to the rug in two armloads, then wrapped them up in it, with the sheaf of new poems, tying off the ends like a sausage with a roll of duct tape. She hoisted it onto her shoulder, finding it heavy, cumbersome. Then she stuffed the envelope of money for Asur into the waistband of her pants and picked up the light shelf in one hand and *The Blue Newspaper* in the other and started down the stairwell, banging the walls as she went. At the bottom of the stairs she set the load down and lurched back up for the duct tape. She taped the two ends of the rolled rug together, making of the whole an ungainly hoop, which she slung over one shoulder and under the opposite arm. The result was still awkward, but she thought at least now she'd be able make it across the Albayzín to her studio without dropping anything. Standing in the *placeta*, she decided to lock the door before pulling it shut. She didn't want the option of coming back.

The commotion on Reyes Católicos was visible from Plaza Isabel Católica when Paula limped by the kitschy monument for Columbus without a glance. A bus had been pulled up on the sidewalk and a pair of police cars stood in the curb lane, lights flashing. Two lanes had been cordoned off with pylons and emergency tape. Uniformed police maneuvered the traffic through the two remaining lanes, but even so traffic was jammed up not only on Reyes Católicos but on Gran Vía de Colón as far as Paula could see. A tide of pedestrians washed around the scene, men and women arguing, gesturing, kibitzing on police interviews. But even at a distance, Paula could tell the carnival atmosphere was running down. People were turning away. The ebb was on. Paula didn't think of Sam until she was well into the crowd. She walked slowly on by the bus, then stopped, looking out at the street quizzically, feeling anxious and stupid at once.

"An accident," a man said in careful English.

Paula glanced into his face, a Spaniard. He looked at Paula appraisingly.

"What happened?" Paula said simply.

"That bus," he said after a short hesitation, "it ran over two *peatones*, walkers. Tourists. Americans, I think. Maybe that's why the big investigation. Even dead, they are Americans, important maybe." And he laughed.

"Men?"

"Yes, two men. They say one with a cane, crazy or drunk maybe, he walked right out into the traffic. The other one, he tried to save the crazy one. A big hero! But a dead hero. *Muy muerto*. Right there." The man pointed out onto the blacktop, at two bloody patches. "That one," he said, "he had the cane. He was knocked over there. That one," the man pointed again, "he fell under the wheel."

"Oh," Paula said mechanically. She was looking at one of Sam's shoes lying forlorn in the gutter.

"Are you okay? Can I buy you a coffee?"

"No." She registered that there were splinters of Cy's cane in the street as well.

"Wine, maybe?"

Paula turned on the man abruptly, took in his leering look, and said forcefully, "No, not now, not ever." She pushed her way out of the crowd, walking back the way she had come. She didn't speak to the police. She felt nothing. She was leaving already. There would be the police to avoid, and Herr Schmidt, but she was free to go. Everything was in Sam's name; she didn't think the police, much less Herr Schmidt, would be able to trace her. But she'd need to move fast.

She rented a room for a night at the Hostal Britz on Plaza Nueva, telling them she would be back later with her luggage. It was an odd room, on the fourth floor and shaped like a wedge of pie, and by chance the very room she'd slept in her first night in Granada, a little over a year before. If she was going to be hiding, she believed in hiding in plain view, and nothing could be more central than a hostel facing Plaza Nueva.

From there she hiked up the Albayzín hill, limping but determined. She stopped in the street in front of the *cármene*, taking a minute to be sure that the police weren't there. Then she packed swiftly, her clothes, the necklaces from Morocco, their few small

valuables, and Sam's stash of dollars. Everything fit in the tiny Ford
Ka without difficulty. She'd decided to keep the car for a couple of
days, just long enough to get her well out of town.

Paula opened the studded door out of the courtyard a last time.
She felt, suddenly, an impulse to linger. She had grown accustomed
to the scale of their life here, and to the fragmentary elegance, some
of which they had made. She went back inside the house, looked
curiously at her ceramic forgeries, then tossed them one after another into an open hearth. She was proud of them but couldn't claim
them as her own. And without Sam, she didn't have the contacts to
sell them, either. Nor did she feel like leaving them for the German,
whenever he turned up to claim what was his.

At the last moment, she thought of Sam's little pornographic
paintings in the manner of Mad James. Perhaps they would make an
appropriate parting gift. Sam had propped them on a small chest of
drawers in the bedroom. A little joke in the Sam manner. Not very
funny and with a barb in it. She shook her head angrily. She wasn't
going to get wistful about Sam, for God's sake.

She ate a light dinner on the plaza, sitting at a table by herself. A
strolling guitar player stood by her table making eyes for an entire
song, his singing a little strident, his guitar playing a little too flashy.
Perhaps he thought she'd swoon, a lady alone. She gave him a small
tip and nodded curtly. When the gitanas came to her table with flowers, she was quite brusque. If it's a stickup, she thought, they should
use a gun. She drank too much wine, a bottle of an overpriced red all
to herself. It was still early when she returned to her room for Sam's
paintings. She thought she owed James a visit. She had news. She

stood at the balcony in the Hostal Britz, listening to the night sounds rising up from Plaza Nueva; in fair weather, it seemed there was always a party on in the plaza, an echo of fiesta all year.

Her watch said 9:00. Down below, she saw the child, Asur, come walking out of the plaza toward her hotel. For a moment, she thought he'd seen her, but he was looking much lower down, at a black van idling in the taxi lane, flames painted on the side panels. Paula felt a pang for the boy; what must he have thought bound up on a bed in a dark room, Sam whispering lies from beyond the headboard? Claustrophobia, fear, for sure. Anger, despair? Perhaps even boredom, after a while. The boy surprised her by running the last few steps to the van, opening the door, and getting in; it immediately pulled into the traffic lane, going away.

James had thought maybe she could wear out her heartache, and she'd walked for hours on the Alhambra hill just to tire herself out. But when she opened the door to her house Cy was still dead, she felt sure of that, quite sure that he had found the resolve to carry through. She wondered how, but the question seemed morbid and finally beside the point. Asur was free, she had seen him. Cy had succeeded in that. She set about hanging Cy's sacred shelf on the wall by her bed, within arm's reach. She put the books back in place one at a time, finding them soft, well used but gently handled. She thought the way the books had been used said something about Cy, about how he loved. She had felt it herself. And she wondered how he'd made it through life without marrying. But there were a lot of books on the shelf, she thought wryly, each one of them as carefully handled as the next. Perhaps that was it, all the explanation she should need.

She removed the duct tape from the back of the Yomut *engsi* and
was relieved to find it came off clean, left no stickiness. Someone—
maybe Cy—had sewn satin loops on the back of the rug to hang it.
But her house was small, and she saw no place to hang it on a wall.
Still, surely it was too good for the floor of a painter's house? She
never knew what she might be tracking around on her shoes. In the
end, she decided to take down her curtain of mirrors, to hang the
rug in their place, where she could see it while she painted. Perhaps
it was time to be done with reflections, to let the mirrors go. She'd
keep the silver-clad mirror with the blind spot that Cy had given her
in Morocco, let that be enough. But she wasn't up to taking the mirrors down now, her heart frozen in her chest. She rolled out the rug,
sat down where the design crossed at the center of the field, running
her hands over the low pile, tracing one of the *guls* with a finger. She
liked the way the carpet invited you to look through the crossing
frame to the four-paneled field with its repeating design of floating
guls. The *guls* had a going-on-forever feel, as if it was only on the field
of the rug that the diagonal rows of *guls* ended so abruptly.

She raised her eyes. Her big painting loomed ominously over
the room. It had the raw strength of unfinished work; it radiated a
dark light. Maybe the oddly illumined darkness owed something to
Theodore Roethke's "In a Dark Time," which Cy had quoted to her
approvingly in a voice muffled by emotion, "All natural shapes blaz-
ing unnatural light." He'd said the poem alluded to St. John of the
Cross's *Dark Night of the Soul*. She thought now that Roethke's lines
had somehow gotten into her painting, the way things did when she
was working, without her intending it or knowing it. Every painting
had its own gravitational field and called to itself what it needed.

Looking now, with Cy gone, James realized she had buried him in the landscape of Granada while he was still living. Buried him bodily in the hills, his shape in their shape. The hills were more Cy than Granada. She didn't know how to think about that. She hadn't intended that the painting should honor him or anything as sentimental as that; she had seen him, that was all, and she wanted to witness what she had seen. And there it was, a painting strange even to her. All she wanted now was to finish it, to do well by the promise of it.

She got up to take a closer look, feeling, all at once, a little spooked. When the doorbell buzzed she jumped. She walked to the door on shaky legs; she couldn't bear to look, just called out, "Who's there?" her jaw twitching and her voice cracked. Then she jerked the door open without waiting for an answer, not able to stand even a moment's suspense. She was expecting the police but somewhere a hope had kindled that it might be Cy. But it was Paula, Paula again. Not looking ashamed enough.

"What?" she snapped. "What do you want now?"

Paula bowed her head.

"What?"

"I thought you'd want to know. I . . . Can I come in?"

"Know what?"

"About Cy and . . ."

"I know."

"What do you know? Can't I come in?"

James stood aside and Paula walked in carrying a shopping bag from Corte Inglés. She stopped dead when she saw Cy's rug on the floor, glancing at James in confusion. She started to ask a question but then thought better of it.

James came up beside her, pointed to the rattan chair by her work-table, and said, "Sit down."

"There was an accident," Paula said hesitantly, not sitting.

"Yes. Cy's dead?" James said flatly.

"Cy, yes, and Sam, too. How did you know?"

"Sam?"

"They're saying he's a hero."

"Sam? Are you crazy? Who's saying that?"

"On the street. On the TV news, too.

"What happened?"

"You don't know?"

"Not exactly."

Paula explained. "It happened on the way to the bank," she said finally.

James kept her head down as Paula talked, just letting the news rain over her. When Paula had finished, she said, "It was a sacrifice."

"What?"

"Cy's death. There wasn't any money. Cy lied about the money. He never intended to get to the bank."

Paula shook her head. "Oh," she said quietly, "poor Sam."

"Poor Sam?"

"I guess he died a fool."

"If Cy'd had the money, would Sam have been less a fool?"

Paula took the two small canvases Sam had painted in Mad James style out of the Corte Inglés sack and set them on James's worktable.

"I thought you'd want to see these destroyed yourself," she said. "I wish I could explain them. He had talent . . ."

"Yes," James said, "he did, and what did he do with it?" James's hand trembled as she pointed at the paintings. In the one on top, Cy held a spread-eagle Asur by the ankles, the boy naked, upside down. Man and boy faced forward, the boy's face wild, his hair radiating in spokes around his head, while Cy's face recalled the grim pleasure of Goya's *Chronos Devouring His Children*. "A hero?" James sobbed. "So that's what, the good news?"

"I didn't say the news was good," Paula trembled. "I didn't even say it was true. It's what people are saying. It's what I heard them saying."

Looking at her, James realized Paula had begun to shake, and she relented. She didn't mean to. She stepped up close, saw, for the first time, someone else behind Paula's beautiful face. She leaned in close enough to wrap her arms around Paula's shoulders, to press her own head against Paula's head, and she held her like that, listening. "'A time for weeping,'" she whispered, finally, her lips close to Paula's ear.

Later, James made the call to Cy's lawyer in Pittsburgh. There wasn't going to be anything further for James to do; there were plans in waiting. In death, Cy's Pittsburgh life would reclaim him. He'd be going back at last; he'd planned to all along. It didn't matter, she could see that. And it wouldn't matter if his life in Granada remained unknown there. A life was always bigger than the stories that got told about it; "something brighter, and yet more full of shadows," wasn't that what Cy had said?

The next morning, James painted. She'd gotten up wanting to, but had been surprised neveretheless that she could. She ranged, back and forth, in front of the big canvas, stepping back occasionally to consider it, the whole of it. Even as she worked a bit of viridian into the blackened palette of her *View of Granada*, she was thinking of Cy, of his phrase for springtime, "the coming green." Spring had come, its green veined the foothills of the Sierra Nevada visible from her veranda right now, but she didn't go out to look; she was seeing another painting, her next, with cypresses greener than they ever look in nature. Something emphatically lit, more day than day. A companion piece to the *View of Granada*, perhaps, connected as if by roots underground.

Suddenly, she was tired. Exhaustion claimed her. She cleaned up mechanically, hardly able. She went up to her bedroom, pulled the shutters in, and flopped back down on the unmade bed, where she slept fitfully for an hour, maybe two. She woke up remembering Cy on his back in the middle of the bed that last time when she'd sketched him, how he'd looked after she'd tucked the sheet around him, his head on a pillow. Laid out, that's how, James sobbed. It was as if, all unknowing, she'd prepared him then for the crossing. The whole time she'd known him, Cy had been looking over his shoulder. She understood that. But he had looked back, she thought, he had wanted to.

ACKNOWLEDGMENTS

For attending to this story while I was writing it, I am grateful to Keith Oderman, David James Duncan, Winston Fuller, Louise Lamar-Fuller, Parveen Seehra, Jessie Harriman, Tom Condon, Mark Brazaitis, and Sara Pritchard.

I would like to thank the Fulbright Program for an appointment to Pakistan, and my students and friends at Punjab University and at the National College of Art in Lahore; and the Eberly College of Arts and Sciences, West Virginia University, for a sabbatical grant, which first took me to Morocco and Andalusian Spain.

I am indebted to the West Virginia University Press: Pat Conner, Than Saffel, Sherry McGraw, Stacey Elza, and Andrea Ware.

— *Kevin Oderman, Spring 2006*

Kevin Oderman, professor of English and creative writing at West Virginia University, is the author of the prize-winning collection of literary essays How Things Fit Together *and a critical book on Ezra Pound. He has twice taught abroad as a Senior Fulbright Lecturer, first in Thessaloniki, Greece, and subsequently in Lahore, Pakistan.* Going *is his first novel.*

CPSIA information can be obtained at www.ICGtesting.com
Printed in the USA
BVOW06s1909131015

422304BV00017B/61/P